Silent Marionette
침묵의꼭두각시

A Story of a Comfort Lady
어느 위안부의 이야기

Nily Naiman

chipmunkapublishing
the mental health publisher

Published by
Chipmunkapublishing
PO Box 6872
Brentwood
Essex CM13 1ZT
United Kingdom

http://www.chipmunkapublishing.com

Chipmunkapublishing gratefully acknowledge the support of Arts Council England.

Consultant and co-writer- Brian SW Kim
Illustrations- Park Eun Kyung

About the Author

Nily Naiman was born in Israel in 1953 and grew up in that country. On the background of the many conflicts within the Jewish community, the horrors of the Holocaust, and the Arab-Israeli conflict, she has been seeking to portray the common. fundamental elements of humanity, good and evil, war and peace, love and hate, and trauma.

Her novels are fascinating journeys of women and their families searching for identity while enduring desperate and painful times. The women in her books are larger than life, and their stories are all based on true events and on the life of the author. Naiman deals with emotional problems which have scarred these women very deeply.

A common theme in her books is the phenomenon of post-traumatic silence, a condition from which she herself suffered for a long time after being molested at the age of twelve by a relative.

Culture and personal history aside, these are women who have the ability to cope and the strength that makes it possible to face their problems and their pain. Naiman intertwines tragedy with irony and romance in an impressive way. All the women in her books are on the verge of destruction and disaster. The situations of despair, embarrassment, and pain that she creates have a deep emotional quality. The heroines of her novels seem to bear the weight of the entire world on their shoulders as they struggle to preserve whatever human dignity they have.

The book *Silent Marionette* has been the project of greatest import to the author. Most of her family, aunts and uncles, perished in the Holocaust. All that is known of two of her aunts is that they were pretty young girls who were taken to service the

Nazis. This tragedy, together with her own experience and the story of the Asian comfort women forced to serve the Japanese, all came together for her in a very personal way.

In addition to *Silent Marionette*, Naiman has published four other books: *Ahuva (Beloved)* is a powerful story of the tragic love between an Arab boy and a Jewish girl in Israel. *Mongolia* is a sweeping family saga covering two generations and four continents. *Tambourine* is a novel of the "Parrajmos", the Gypsy Holocaust, in France. *Songs and Poems for Andres* is a book of poems related to *Tambourine*.

About the Co-Writer

Brian SW Kim , born in Seoul, R.O.K in1954 worked as the General Manager of ifpi (International Federation of the Phonographic Industry) Korea Office from 1989 through 2002. While there he was responsible for managing enforcement teams which provide professional raids against music piracy.

He was involved in the administration of ifpi Korea Office with duties including scheduling staff, technical training, recruiting and projecting, and monitoring results of anti-piracy operations. He also attended various international meetings around the world on behalf of Korea Music Industry.

He has experienced in the music business as license manager of Warner Music as well as Popular Music Journalist contributing his articles on weekly and monthly magazines in Korea for many years. He has also experienced in teaching English in both high schools and language academies.

As an enthusiastic scholar and disciple of English Literature, he is currently working as a co-author for Nily Naiman and trying to seek a newly established career in his life. He has two lovely daughters Ji-hyun and Jina whom he loves more than anything in the world, though Ji-hyun, the first one is unfortunately suffering from autism.

This story is based on true events

Silent Marionette
침묵의꼭두각시

New York –USA -2008

My sister is crying, "I have no place in this world."

The despicable, contemptible law lives,

Tortured her and made her a barren woman,

She will never be loved and she will never be a mother.

In front of my sister, I bow; I kneel to the ground,

Touching the dust of her feet.

You have a place in this world my sister,

A very special place,

You are the heart and soul of my nation,

You are beautiful, the prettiest of all,

The purest of all, you are the holiest of all holy.

Here is your home; here is your crown,

You are a queen, the queen of all mothers.

You are my sister you are my mentor,

You are my pride!

Seoul Korea - 2007

You asked me for a testimony of my life as a comfort lady. I have refused to do so for many years. Those memories were buried very deep somewhere in my shattered heart. How can I ever talk of things I cannot even think about? How could I describe things that are beyond words to any human being? I would not find the right way ever to describe those times. It was beyond the strongest words in the dictionary. What will I tell you, that it was unbelievable? Evil, Crazy, Wicked?

I was not raised to be a comfort lady. I was a simple girl from an honest, hard-working village. I lived a simple but nice life in my simple home, with my brothers and sisters. I had dreams like any other girl, I had collections of shiny stones and shells, I knew how to make paper butterflies and birds. I was the best runner in the village and I could climb trees higher than any boy could in my village. I had fantasies that I would be able to go one day to school like my brothers and shine like a star on the track.

I was matched to be married a few days after I was born to my father's friend's son. He was a good boy; he became my best friend at a very young age and it always made me feel safe knowing that he would become my husband. There was no fear of the future; everything was crystal clear, my husband, my work in the field, the food we would eat, and my love for my family. Until the day the Chokppari (short devils) came.

I know I have a short time left in my life, I can feel Death's presence, and I hear him calling to me softly, comfortingly, to come join my dead family. I am ready to die now, I no longer feel sullied, or dishonored. I am not a sinner. I am not a traitor. At this point, at the end of my life, I feel as pure and innocent as I was before I was kidnapped at the age of fourteen.

Dear authors, I put into your hands now a true account of what I went through at the time of the War. This is my painful story of my time as comfort woman. Let it be a testimony and a memorial

Silent Marionette
침묵의꼭두각시

for all the comfort women who suffered under the Japanese occupation.

Though the unforgivable, unforgettable history will never heal easily, we should record what was forced upon us for the future peace of the world and the history of all humankind. That is why I have decided to tell you my painful personal history after more than fifty years' of silence.

This story is based on true events. It was written in memory of the "comfort ladies" who were kidnapped by the Japanese from their homes across the nations of the Pacific. I am calling on the Japanese government to come out and admit their heinous crimes and ask for forgiveness from the families of all those 200,000 women who were used as sex slaves, tortured and killed in the most humiliating circumstances. The morality of the Japanese will forever be in question until they admit to their crimes.

Manchuria 1943

Before long, I know, there will be footsteps in the hallway. A guard will stand and unlock the door to my chamber. "Maikko-san your first guest is here." I close my eyes to face away from the light; the familiar cramps are starting in my guts. As if on a signal, the heavy footsteps stop above me, a belt opens up, a zipper opens, and then I can barely breathe.

Someone is pushing me to a kneeling position. My arms are pulled back hard and tightly bound together behind me. I am painfully aware of the sounds of my own breathing; the fluttering of the fear shakes my bones. He does not speak; I can hear his heavy breathing. "Omani" (Mom), I whisper. He will kill me; this is the end. This time the pain will drive me to death. I bite my lips so hard that I feel the gush of blood coming into my throat. "*Hanul isiyo! Nere zom salnyo zusirayo*!" (Help me god! Please help me!)

My thoughts focus on a familiar memory. I run in the wheat field; I can feel the warm wind on my face. I untie my braid, and my hair flies in the fresh air. I am happy, so happy. Yong-soo (龍洙) is chasing me, laughing. He will be my husband when we grow up; he is my best friend.

I am glad that the matter of marriage was settled when I was born. My father and Yong-soo's father were best friends, and arranged for the two of us to be married. I do not have to worry about a mean, nasty, ugly husband because Yong-soo is funny, pleasant looking, and he likes me the best of all the girls in the village.

I am then forced back into cruel reality, and this soldier does not say a word. The sound of his breathing says more than million words. The quiet ones are the worst. He will hurt me; he will enter my body like a thousand swords. He spreads my bottom;

he has a cold, heartless pair of hands. The sharp pain tears me apart. He is raping me wildly. I can feel the blood gushing out and I bite my lips.

"*Yong-soo yai!*" I scream in my mind Come, take me far from here! My Yong-soo is standing on the hill laughing; his hair is flying with the wind. "Don't cry, Pil-nyo (畢女); it will be over soon. I am waiting for you!"
Now I run into his arms; his warm lips are on my lips, his arms around me. I am loved, I am safe.

This sweaty pig can tear me apart, beat my lights out, stab me to death, but I am in my village and I am safe with my Yong-soo. He is off me at last; I am quiet, he zips up his trousers and coughs as if he is uncomfortable. I pull my dress down. My head is still lowered. I hardly ever see the faces of my rapists; they all look the same to me anyway.

He stops for a second at the door, and I know he is looking back at me, as if he wants to say something. However, there is a long line by my door, a long line of hungry beasts. There is no time for personal conversations. Did he want to tell me about his wife, or maybe he had something to say about his daughter who might be my age?

It does not really matter. The next one is already zipping down his pants. My head is down; I have no interest in looking up. "*Yoko nishinasai!*" (Lie down!) He commands me.

This one sounds young and eager. With luck, he will skip the torture and leave me fast. He drops on my body and, as I thought, he is inside me in an instant, breathing into my face. "*Anatano me wo hirake nasai, baishunfu!*" (Open your eyes whore!) He yells, and I open my eyes. He is as young as I thought, and his sweat is dripping on my breast.

His teeth are stained with tobacco, and he has thin lips. I know that those with thin lips are usually the most dangerous ones. With time, I learn how to define the rapists' nature by their facial features. I do not feel him inside me; he cannot even get a full erection. The red flags are rising in my mind, but then the cycle turns from bad luck to good luck.

Somebody knocks on the door. "Get out, soldier, we are under attack!" The young man stops his aimless digging in my body and gets up. I sigh in relief; there will not be any work for a while.

We are simple people, we are. We live simple lives in a simple village among very simple-minded neighbors. Our birthright and destiny is work, hard work. We are each born with a strong pair of hands, a strong pair of shoulders and a strong will to survive. We inherit a tradition of persistence and resiliency; it takes an awful lot to break us. We live by the cycle of the seasons. We know when to plow the earth, how to nourish it and renew it. In return, it gives us food to put on the table.

For centuries, my village has survived hard times, tragedies of man and nature: floods, droughts, famine, plagues, and earthquakes. There have also been enemies, crazy, evil emperors, foreign devils, misery, hunger, wars and desperation.

However, we went on repeatedly in the best, proud Korean tradition, to repair the damage, to work the land, to plant the rice and grain, to mend our homes, fix the roads and build new life over and over again. The babies kept being born in spite of any hardship, and new generations were brought into being again and again.

We Korean villagers believe in nature, we believe in its cycles. It is our way of life. The seasons, good and bad fortune, and our fate all have their cycles. That is the basis of our survival. When it is bad, we fix the damage and plant the rice again. We survive thanks to our basic believe that life is built on cycles. After bad times there will come good times, after every rain there is a calming sun.

Our elders taught us to trust and respect our ancestors who struggled and suffered to give us this land. Korea was built on sweat and blood, and we were supposed to be inspired by that and love our country and our land no matter what happened.

My village is surrounded by beautiful mountains high and low. It sits by a stream that is as clear as a mirror. The village is traditionally well known as one of the places where many beauties have been born throughout Korean history. I was frequently told ever since my birth that Korea had a famous proverb saying, "*Nam nam, Buk nyo*" (南男北女), which means that "the best male comes from South but the best female comes from North."

At night, we would light the candles and lantern lamps and sit together. Mother would plan the chores for us girls for the next day, and father would light his pipe. The little house would be the warmest, safest place on earth for me.

For the most part, the Japanese left us alone. The Japanese army established an office building in the village. They hired some Koreans to work for them, and put them in charge of our education and our lives. The soldiers hardly ever passed through our village. We heard stories of burning farms, raping of girls, kidnaps, murder, and torture; but the elders always told us that we were safe as long as we minded our own business and stayed out of trouble.

Stay away from freedom fighters and act as if you are not interested in anything but your work and your survival. Never engage in political discussions, never state your opinions about the Japanese, and remember that among your best friends and neighbors there could be hidden collaborators who will sell your names to the enemy for one lousy sack of rice.

Mother would sometimes go to the town political gatherings that the Japanese imposed just because she would get a bag of flour or a little millet. Mother would do anything for some free food. She would sing Japanese slogans, bow to the Japanese flag, and even salute the Emperor's photo. After all, free is free and free is always good. Since my brothers were always hungry as wolves, and my sisters and I were always craving this and that, Mother had to have the kitchen always full and functioning.

When the boys would come back from school and we all gathered around the table, no matter how many dishes mother would prepare and spread all over in front of us it was never enough. There was always fighting over the dishes and who took more and the noise would be horrendous. Abazi would have enough after awhile. He would knock his fist on the table as hard as he could until the whole meal would jump up and down, and yell "Quiet!" The entire household would freeze; even the cat would arch his lower body up and spread the hair on his tail wide open from fear.

Nobody would want to get on Abazi's bad side. If one of the kids deserved a beating, Abazi did not take it lightly. He had his theory about raising children. If they got the present of being born, they had better deserve the life that they had been given.

Those who spoil their kids to grow up a bratty burden on society should be lined up and shot. If you do not discipline your child, you hate him, end of story. Abazi had a thick leather belt, and when it was time to put his theory to work he would take it off his pants and use it to the fullest. Those who got a beating from him could not sit on their bottoms for a whole week.

Silent Marionette
침묵의꼭두각시

Korea- 1942

The year 1942 was a good year for father's sweet potatoes. Even if he had to give most of his profits to the "Japanese war effort", we still managed to get along just fine. There were always several dishes on the table and enough rice for everyone. However, in the beginning of 1943 very little food was available. We were always hungry. At mealtime mother would put a bland soup on the table.

We would all feel the pinch in our stomachs. Mother would scoop for father first, then my older brother Pil-ku, then my twin brothers Pil-nam and Pil-sok. Those two were always starved; they spent their lives looking for food and swallowing it. They would sit by the stream, and if they got lucky with the fish, they would devour it raw.

I could be on my knees begging for a bite, and those two would not even leave me the bones. My stomach was always rumbling. I would look jealously at the full scoops my brothers were getting, knowing that mother would leave us girls only a bit of liquid. Pil-sun (筆舜) would look at me and make an angry face. She was never shy about speaking her mind; that is why she got beat up the most by father.

To our horror, she once blew up at mealtime and stated that there is no justification for mother giving bigger portions of food to the boys. What did they do to deserve it? They hardly ever worked, they got to go to school and get an education, and they never even lifted a finger to help mother or to bring some money or food to the house.

We girls worked all day to our bones in the fields. In the home we cleaned and cooked and we had to work the gilssam (loom), weaving our backs off to dress those boys. It was not fair, she said, just not fair! There was no justice in the world!

Mother and I looked at her in shock; father's face got all red. He got up heavily from the chair and came very near to her face. He looked straight in her eyes for a second and then slapped her across her face with all his might. I think the whole village heard the ring of the strike. Then he said very quietly, "*Ode ebi ape mal dekku ziriga.* (Do not offer your opinions again in front of me!) *Min han eminai* (stupid girl). I will not be as generous next time!"

Pil-sun was older than I was; she was seventeen. She too had been matched by father at birth -- to the son of the head of the village, a fat obnoxious brat whose entire world was focused on food and cruel games involving the torturing of alley cats. He would catch the poor creatures by their tails and turn them round and round until they died in agony. I hated that boy; I always wished I could take him on. As fat as he was, I was sure I was so much stronger than he, and I swore that if he laid his hands on our cat or any of our animals I would kill him, mayor's son or not.

Pil-nam and Pil-sok used to drive Pil-sun crazy, making fun of her, telling her that on her wedding night her fat groom would crush the life out of her under his weight and then eat her for dinner. Pil-sun was terrified of the prospect of marrying that boy. She used to cry to mother and beg her to change her fate. Whenever that fat boy would pass by, she would mumble, "I'd rather die!" "If they will not cancel the wedding," she would say to me "*Sonmok galnasri zukko malteya!*" (I will slash my wrists!).

She was a good artist, Pil-sun. She would sit for hours drawing views of the mountains and forests around the village. She would also draw pictures of our family members. She had an incredible memory for details. We did not need to pose for her because she remembered every feature of our faces. However, most of all she liked drawing herself and her secret love. She had pages and pages of sketches stuffed under her blankets of a boy she liked who was my older brother's friend.

At night, Pil-sun would stretch under her blanket and call the boy's name into her pillow. Sometimes she would teach me how to use the pencil to create shades and lights, how to catch special features in a person's face. I never thought I could be as good as she was, but I would take the pencil since she insisted, and would practice every day with her.

I would work in the field looking impatiently toward the schoolhouse. I could hear the boys echoing the master, memorizing the Japanese amendment. This would be their last session of the day, and Yong-soo would run to me in the fields to tell me that he loved me. I would drop everything, shake my braid loose, and run with him aimlessly. Like two young horses, we would roll on the ground and tickle each other.

"*Nare zal hal kkini dugo bora*!" (I will be good to you) he says. "You are the prettiest of all!" His breath is getting heavy and his hand is under my blouse. I feel my body tightening up. He is rubbing against me, his lips on my lips, and I push him away. "*Wa irane!*" (Stop!) I say. "My father will kill me!"

Yong-soo lets go reluctantly and strokes my hair. "*Oke dunzi, Mengse ko nere sarang hani kkane!*" (I will always love you, I swear!) he says. The sun is warming our hungry bellies and I feel guilty for my good fortune. I have gotten the best boy in the village and Pil-sun is stuck with her bad luck. Yong-soo takes out a sweet rice cake from his pocket and cuts me half of it. We hold hands lying on our backs gazing at the sky, and I pray that time will freeze forever.

I hear mother calling me, "Yaya, where did you go? Yaya!" Yong-soo giggles and I get loose of his tight hold and run to mother, my hair all wild and loose. My shirt is open and I am covered with mud. She gives me her tired look and says "*Emina iga son mosm gachi gogi moiga!*" (You behave like a wild animal) "*Nere oke hamun zokan nanzi?*" (What am I to do with you?) "Look at yourself! Were you with that boy again?"

I hug my mother. I am her favorite and I know it. She used to tell me that I was a copy of her when she was a little girl. She would brush my hair taking her time with me, more than with my sisters, sighing quietly and then braiding my hair slowly. I do not have to turn around to see the tear coming down her check. "Omani, don't cry," I say, my heart crying for her.

Mother told me she was once just like me when she was young: pretty, untamed, and joyful. She was the oldest in her family. "Our sort," she said to me once, "have the hardest time living in this man's world. Defiant women suffer the most; they are never happy. A woman is nothing but a tool. We are supposed to cook, clean and raise the children quietly."

Mother and father were fighting most of the time. Mother could not stand father; it was obvious. Her parents forced her to marry him and were grateful to get rid of her. One less mouth to feed was all they cared about. Father himself was never raised with tender love. His family was very poor and every day was a new war of survival.

There was not too much time for emotions when you raised your children in times of struggle. What was important was to pass another day, and the focus was always on "where is the next meal coming from." Father took my mother as a wife because he was forced to. Now his duty was to feed her and make children. That was not easy on a young man. He had never known love and did not know how to give it.

Mother was always unhappy and he did not understand why. He did his duty. He brought food to the table somehow every day, he made her children; he truly did not understand what was making her so unhappy.

There was a war out there, the money was tight, and not too many people came for the sweet potatoes. Who had the money for that these days? Father gave up on explaining that to mother. He had no time for conversations, no time for regrets and deep philosophical discussions.

 Father was sure that he was always doing his best and doing the right things. Only at night when he went drinking would he allow himself some luxury of feelings.

I would hear him at mother's bed, weeping, "What in the name of Buddha do you want from me? *Dowa zugure, nere nimza bakke do ikkaso!*" (Help me, please help me Myung-za, you are the only one I have got!).

It was clear to me that my father was the authority in the house, but I knew since I was a little girl that without my mother he would never be able to survive. He was very dependent on her physically and emotionally. I learned at very early age that men need to feel they are in control and in charge, but inside they are just frightened little boys who need their mothers all the time.

I also understood that there is always an enemy out there to watch for. It was women against men, children against fathers, and Koreans against Japanese. In my world somebody was always against somebody; this was only natural.

We were basically living peacefully even though we were under occupation. We heard the rumors and nodded our heads sadly as if the stories were about some distant land. There was a Japanese police office in our village, but Koreans who were paid by the Japanese government usually ran it. Japanese officials would come every once in awhile to check the station. They let us be as long as we did what they said and avoided trouble. As a way of demeaning us, they made us take Japanese names. Mine was Maikko.

Poverty was rampant because of the Japanese colonial policy of exploiting every resource available. There were rumors that Japan had no difficulty in recruiting young girls from farming villages to work for them as many desperately wanted money.

One day I happened to hear Uncle Joong-gu (重九) and my father talking about new rumors. Uncle Joong-gu said that many girls in their teens were being taken to comfort stations, having been deceived by recruiters, who would pretend to be helping them earn good money by telling them lies about a better life and training for jobs by the Japanese army. The girls thought that they were going to be trained as nurses or for other needed jobs, and they went willingly with the recruiters but found themselves in brothels.

He also said that town officials, *Chosun sunsa* (Korean police), as well as Japanese military were involved in kidnapping young girls. Father panicked; he was cursing and walking back and forth. He swore to my uncle that if the Korean collaborators or the Japanese would lay a hand on his daughters he would kill them all.

Silent Marionette
침묵의꼭두각시

I had never seen my father so angry. He seemed never to really care what happened to us girls. I had never thought he would be so upset at the possibility that we would get hurt.

Father never paid much attention to us girls. We were there to help mother and our duty was to work and be quiet. Father could not handle mother very well and for him another female was just another headache. We were there to help in the field, peal the vegetables, work the gilssam, and clean the rice. Father never showed any interest in us, and many times I wondered if he noticed us at all.

In the photos: The Pil family.

Mother, Father, Pil-nyo, Pil-sun, Pil-ku, Pil-nam, Pil-sok, my young sisters, aunts, uncles and cousins

Silent Marionette
침묵의꼭두각시

Silent Marionette
침묵의꼭두각시

Saeya, Saeya

My life as a comfort woman (慰安婦), started at 4:00 in the morning that day. The sound of the falling rain clashed with the gunfire. The villagers jumped out of bed and gazed out their doors, listening to the distant thundering of guns and the stomping of boots. Over the horizon they beheld the sight of blazing destruction, and the earth trembled beneath them.

Father closed the door hastily. . "*Eminaidol nalne sumki rau!*" (Hide the girls!) he shouted to mother. We all knew that the Japanese soldiers would be after the young girls before scavenging for food. Everyone would hide the girls in their houses until the danger would pass.

Mother pushed me into the kitchen storage, and Pil-sun was hidden in the linen crate. We were told not to move and not to make a sound. My other two sisters were hidden behind the house, under haystacks, because they were younger than we were and would comfort one another when frightened.

From my hiding place, I could hear my father's anxious voice and nervous footsteps pacing the floor. This made me happy; it sounded as though he really cared and was frightened for my sisters and me. It was the first time that I felt my father valued me as a human being. I smiled to myself at the thought that it would be worth it for the Japanese to find me and kill me in this glorious moment.

Father told the three boys to run to the mountains and hide there until it would be safe to return. Many young men and boys had been kidnapped and sent into slavery in Japan. Father would never take the chance that it would happen to his boys.

Then we heard the rough voices shouting in Japanese, accompanied by the barking of dogs and the burst of guns mixed with screaming. The soldiers kicked our door open, I heard furniture being overturned, pots and pans falling in the kitchen, and water jars breaking. Father's commanding voice that I had become accustomed to was now pleading and very frightened.

This was a new sensation for me. Father was only human after all. He was scared...my father, the highest authority figure in my life, was just a scared little man. I was glad I could not see him from the closet; father would not have liked me seeing how he had been stripped of his pride.

Then I heard the shot. It was short and loud. I could smell the smoke of the shotgun coming into the closet through the narrow space between the doors. I could hear his body dropping on the wooden floor and I knew this was the end of father's sorry life.

My mother was screaming. Somebody was barking "*Asio akenasai!*" (Spread your legs!) I could hear her dress torn up wildly. I was wondering where my brothers were. They always had a mouthful to say and always acted brave. They were the neighborhood bullies. The kids in the village were afraid of them, and I knew that as much as they liked to make fun of me, they would kill any of the boys if they ever tried to hurt us.

I whispered in fear, "Pil-ku!" But Pil-ku was not there, neither were Pil-nam and Pil-sok. Then the closet door opened at once. I was squinting at the sudden light and trying to curl into my body like a snail.

"Ha, look what I found!" a Japanese soldier was digging into my shoulder with his sword. "Come out! *Ima tzuru!*" (Now!) I crawled out of the closet. The room was full of soldiers; they were laughing aloud.

Mother was on the floor, and on top of her was a soldier. She was completely naked. At this point, she did not cry or scream. She was just lying there under the soldier, her eyes dead and staring into space. In the other corner of the room, Pil-sun was sitting on top of a soldier, also naked, and he was rocking her up and down on top of him.

I could not see her face, only her skinny behind and her long black hair covering her back. The soldier would slap her on her behind and her back as if she were a horse, while moaning and sometimes cursing. Pil-sun did not cry. I could see that she was in terrible pain and shame, but she was quiet, as if accepting her fate gracefully.

I was standing there frozen, feeling my life slowly leaking out of my body like water. All I could do was stare in horror at my mother and sister, my arms lying lifeless against my body. I opened my mouth, I wanted to scream, but nothing came out of my wide-open mouth. The scream became stuck somewhere inside me, and all I could do now was shake my head in disbelief.

"Come here, *Gireides*" (pretty,) the officer said, looking at me up and down. I felt the shiver in my spine.

"How old are you, girl?"

"Fourteen," I said

"This one is mine!" he nodded to the other soldiers.

"Where're the rest of the girls? I know you are hiding more girls!"

"I don't know. "

"Tell me, *Mereiyo*!" (It is an order!)

I looked at father's body on the floor. The blood was streaming out of his head and there was a huge red puddle around him. "Abazi," (father) I mumbled.

The officer touched my head and commanded in a calm but threatening tone, "Answer me while I'm asking you nicely: Where are the other girls?" He started waving his pistol.

"I don't know," I said again. He put the pistol to my forehead. I could feel the cold metal. Somehow, it was not a scary sensation; it was actually comforting. The cool touch of the gun calmed me down and focused my thoughts. The officer looked me in the eye as if examining my thoughts.

"It would be a shame to kill a pretty little beauty like you." The soldier got up from my mother and the next one unzipped his pants. Life came back to her eyes for a second, and she said, "Tell him, Pil-nyo, or he will kill you."

Pil-sun was screaming now, and the soldier had his hand around her neck. I could see his thick, heavy fingers squeezing the life out of her, as he came to his final satisfaction. Her scream became hollow now, and died down like the sound of a dying siren. Pil-sun's life was squeezed out of her in slow motion, ending shamefully and painfully. I could hear her neck being cracked and broken. Like a piece of glass, it shattered.

Silent Marionette
침묵의 꼭두각시

He pushed her off his knees and she fell to the floor like a rag doll. Pil-sun was dead and the other soldiers jeered. One jokingly said, "Hey Mifune, you always take everything for yourself. Why didn't you leave us a piece?"

I started crying. Another soldier was raping mother wildly and she was moaning quietly from pain. The officer touched my hair again. "*Wulzi mara* (Don't cry)," he said in a surprisingly soft voice. "Your mother will soon meet Buddha." He then pulled me to the door. "Now you will show me where the other girls are."

I was dragged after him to the back of the house and stood in front of the haystack. One of the soldiers started laughing and plunged his arm into the hay. He felt around and pulled out nothing. Then he circled the haystack repeatedly. He jumped back suddenly and gasped. "Aha!"

He lifted the straw. My heart froze. There they were, my little sisters, the pride and joy of my family, the love of mother's life, hiding in the dirt like two little frightened rabbits.

I could see my little sisters holding each other's hands. I could feel their terrible fear, their terror. My poor little sisters were so alone, so innocent. The soldier smirked again and shoved his bayonet into the haystack, stabbing my sisters at random. They were crying in pain. I jumped forward, my fists clenched. I would stop him; I would make him stab me, not my sisters.

The officer pinned me down to the ground so I would not be able to move. The girls started screaming, not resisting, just screaming like wounded animals. Their screams froze the blood in my veins. They were still just lying there in the straw. The soldier examined his bayonet slowly and showed it to the officer. Blood stained the entire length of the blade.

The officer shouted an order, and a soldier emerged from the house, carrying a can of kerosene, and sprinkled it on the haystack. He then struck a match, igniting the hay in a towering flame. My sisters were shrieking from agony.

I broke free from the officer's hold ready to jump into the flames, but he caught me by the collar of my shirt. "Stop right there, *Gireides*. You will die when I give you the order to die!"

I was hitting and scratching, trying to get loose. "Let me go," I cried, "please, please let me go." Nevertheless, the officer held me tight.
He then said, "Tell me your name."

I was silent while the tears streamed down my face.
"I asked you your name!"

Silent Marionette
침묵의꼭두각시

"Maikko," I murmured.

"Sing for me," he ordered.

I looked at him in disbelief. He sat down on a stone and put his pistol on the ground.

"Sing, Maikko, sing."

I looked at the smoke, the thick smoke emanating from the burned straw mixed with the dead little bodies of my sisters, and started singing, choking up with tears:

Saeya saeya parang saeya,
(Bird, bird, a blue bird)
Nokdu batte anzi mara,
(Do not take a rest on the green gram field)
Nokdu kkochi ttoro zimyun,
(When the green gram flower leaf falls,)
Chongpo zangsu wulgo ganda.
(Then, the bluish hemp cloth peddler goes, crying.)

The officer clapped his hands, "You sing well…pleasant voice," he said.

"*Hai wakari masida.*"

He touched my hair, then my breasts. His fingers went down my dress, "Such beauty, such a treasure….." he was mumbling, his breath becoming heavier, "What a waste of beauty…"
He grabbed me and pulled me to his body.   I could smell the cigarette odor from his mouth and clothes. He passed his finger on my lips; he was in a mellower mood now. "I will not kill you; don't be afraid," he said, his voice becoming hoarse.

"Yong-soo," I mumbled, "Yong-soo help me!" I knew what was going to happen next. I expected him to take me apart now. He opened his zipper, said, "I don't waste sperm on Korean filth, little one!", and pushed my face down to his genitals. "If you bite me, I will blow your head off, Maikko san!"

It was terrible. I was choking as he was pulling my hair, pushing my head back and forth, up and down. My mouth was full of his stinking, sweaty flesh. "Yong-soo," I kept thinking *"Nere zom salnyo zurama!"* (Help me please!) I closed my eyes and I was rolling on the hill, giggling with Yong-soo. *"Bora Pil-nyo ya, nabi aniga."* (Look Pil-nyo, it's a butterfly.) I stop and bend down. *"Zong mal gop zzan ne!"* (It is so perfect!) He exclaims.

The little yellow butterfly is landing on my arm. It flaps its wings and then stretches them as if ready to go for a long nap. Yong-soo is smiling at me. "You will be my wife, Pil-nyo!"

I let the butterfly go high up, high in the blue sky, and then my mouth was filled with disgusting goo. The officer let go of my hair and sighed.

He was still holding me firm, his goo in my mouth. I was frozen under his hand, feeling the horrible nausea shaking my body. My head was exploding. I closed my eyes tight, just not to swallow the disgusting goo. I could see sharp lights, yellow and red, out of my blindness, and I started singing in my mind.

Saeya saeya parang saeya,
(Bird, bird, a blue bird)

He let go now, and I pushed him out of my mouth and set my head aside to spit the goo, but he caught that and insisted, "Swallow."

I shook my head. "Please no!" I begged with my eyes.

"Swallow!"

Silent Marionette
침묵의꼭두각시

I shook my head again. He held my neck now and squeezed. "To the count of three, you either swallow or die!" he said very calmly. "Ichi, ni, san," as he was counting, his fingers tightened around my neck. I swallowed the goo and he let go. "Good girl," he said, and gave me a narrow victory smile. "You will be of good service to the Imperial Army of Japan." He got up now and zipped up his pants.

"You will not die; you will go to a good place where you can work and live a good life." He measured my body, as if he was an expert.
"I will get you a new dress, and some makeup. You will get new high heel shoes." He was proud of himself. Then he straightened his ironed uniform and said, "Don't leave this spot! I will be back for you!"

I collapsed on my knees watching his back disappearing, and then I started vomiting. I vomited my guts, I vomited my soul, I vomited my pride, my lost innocence, my sorrow. I vomited everything I had ever had to eat, my entire life, I just could not stop. I felt faint. My throat was burning. "Omani, Abazi" (Mother, father") I was hacking out. Then I sat, empty, on the stone. My knees were scratched and bleeding. I must have forced them to the ground very hard.

Mother was dead, father was dead, all my sisters turned to ashes in a split second. My brothers had disappeared and Yong-soo, my Yong-soo, was nowhere around. I would never be able to look in his eyes, never! I was a traitor. I should have been faster. I should have jumped into the fire. I would never be able to marry my Yong-soo. The Japanese had defiled me, molested me! I was dirty, I was filth, I was a *chang nyo* (prostitute) (娼女)!

I slapped my face as hard as I could, "*Chang nyo!*" repeatedly. I was hitting my face, slapping, beating, "*Chang nyo! Chang nyo!*" Slow moving shadows of light and dark were mixed with the heavy dust of fire in the air. The stink of the burnt bodies surrounded me. *"Bingshin ganna emi nai!"* (Foolish girl).

I was hitting the ground now, my fists digging hard into the stony, rough earth, the earth I loved so much. I had known that earth from inside out. I had worked it since I was a baby. I treated that rough earth like a human being. We had mutual respect, the earth and I. When I planted the earth always gave me something in return.

The earth and I understood each other; we were dependent on each other, but this time it was cold and heartless to the touch of my knuckles. I could feel the pain as my skin was scraping off when I dug my fists in the ground. Even my loyal earth hated me. I had betrayed it. I had betrayed my family, my honor, and my Yong-soo. I was a dirty *chang nyo*!

My eyes wandered toward my house. I should get up and do something about my parents' bodies, my sisters. I cannot just let them lie there like garbage. I tried to get up, but the weakness in my knees dropped me right back on the floor. Once I asked mother how she could bear all the hard work, with father's yelling and nagging, the boys always demanding and complaining, and the neighbors' pressure.

She told me that there was a place deep, deep in her soul where everything was beautiful. There was a rainbow, sunlight, flowers and butterflies, delightful birds and a prince, a handsome prince who was always waiting just for her. That place was sealed under millions of layers and only she had the key. Whenever things got too tough for her, she would rush there and open the door with her special key, and stay there until she felt better. Nobody could touch or enter that place; it was only hers.

I asked mother many times if I could go there, if I could find that place and hide there too when I felt bad. Mother always answered, "One day you will find your own special place and it is going to be as wonderful as mine is. Then you will know exactly where to go when the time comes."

"*Gogiro galna mon od roke ham nekka Omani?*" (Where do I get a key to that place mother?)

"*Gogen nere memso ge wonze go in nen giran da.*" (The key is going to be always in your heart) mother would answer, and a single tiny tear would drop down on her cheek.

Maybe it was time now to look for that place. With effort, I got up again and dragged my heavy feet toward the burnt haystack. I had to do something about my little sisters. I was walking as if crossing a desert full of broken glass.

The wind swept across my face, bringing with it the thick, heavy fumes from the still smoldering haystack. I breathed the smoke deep into my nostrils and choked on it. Picking up a stick, I started poking in the black pile, calling my sisters' names.

Their charred bones, all that remained of two little, lively, beautiful girls, were so tangled together that I could not tell where one body began and the other ended. I could see that while the flames were devouring them, they had clung to each other in pain, and decided to die together. I tried to pick up a surviving piece of flesh, but it fell apart in my hand, like overcooked meat.

Silent Marionette
침묵의꼭두각시

"I should scream and cry. I should give the poor souls a farewell ceremony." My burning thoughts fired my heart. I knelt on the ground and tried to scream and cry, but nothing came, no tears, no sound. At this point, I was sure that I had heard my voice calling my sisters a second before; I knew I had heard it!

Now my lips were moving and no sound was coming out. I tried to scream again, but nothing. I started hitting my chest, my neck. "Talk Pil-nyo!" I tried to yell at myself; but although my mouth was wide open, all that came out was a faint, splitting sound like that of a breaking guitar string.

I have become mute! I said to myself in horror. There was a new sensation in my throat, dryness, swelling, and nausea. Maybe it is a bad cold, I was thinking. I tried to talk again, but my voice was stuck. I tried to whisper but my tongue felt so hard and heavy that I could not form the words. My lips opened and shut like the mouth of a fish in the market. My breathing became strained and unstable. I could not control it now at all. The air would exit my lungs in a long, loud whistle and then again in a wild wave of fluttering. The breath would then slow to a stop in a prolonged snoring sound.

Heat permeated my body and pain spread through my face and neck, a paralyzing, frightening pain. My eyes hurt and nausea overtook me. My lips started shaking out of control. I tried to say something again, but all that came out was another barely heard whistle. All my efforts to make a sound were fruitless.

I eventually gave up, knowing that no words would escape my throat again. I fell to my knees and filled my dress pockets with the ashes, the only physical remains of my sisters. My fingers got burned from the embers, but the pain was sweet, oh so sweet. Then I got up from the ground and made toward my house slowly and carefully. With every step, I felt that my feet were being shattered.

Silent Marionette
침묵의꼭두각시

Where there is water, there is life.

The trees were swaying in the pleasant autumn wind, accented by the comforting ringing of the chimes. It was as if nature was blind to any pain man could inflict. What was hurting was that I could hear my coughing. I could still make that sound. This eased my mind a little. I should go to mother and ask her to mix me some medicine.

It was quiet around the house as I stood at the door. The heavy silence around the village struck me as odd. Where did everybody go, I wondered? Where were my brothers? Where were all the neighbors? I looked around wondering where the officer, Toshihiro, had disappeared.

The door was wide open, which was strange because mother always closed the door to keep the insects out. What was also strange was that the usual sounds of the animals were gone. Even in the hours of the night, I would hear the barking of dogs, ducks quacking, and cats meowing their troubles.

I felt my blood turning to ice as I entered house. Right in the middle of the kitchen lay the body of my mother. Her severed limbs were strewn about the kitchen. Her breasts looked as though they had been sawn off, and my heart stopped at the sight of them impaled on the hooks that mother once had used to place her pots. I forced myself to look into her face and saw an expression of agony and fear. Fear for me. It was as if her last thought was trying to tell me to run.

Blood was splattered all over the walls and on the ceiling, and there was not a place in the kitchen where I could walk without stepping in blood. I could see the large boot prints of the soldiers in the blood. A drop of what had been splattered on the ceiling fell onto my forehead, leaving a crimson trail down my face.

I hobbled out of the kitchen. My head was spinning; I was going to be sick. I had to go, I had to go now. In the next room, my father sat on the floor against the wall, half his head gone. Blood, brains, and fragments of bone stained the walls.

Then my eyes caught sight of my sister. They had cut a line down the middle of her body, and placed the knife in her vagina. She had a relieved smile on her face, as if to say, "Thank God, now I don't have to marry that fat obnoxious boy, and my brothers won't tease me about him having larger breasts than me." She even managed to be funny at her gruesome death.

I wanted to kneel down to touch her, to comfort her. The lump in my throat had to be released. I wanted so badly to cry, but my knees were stiff and no tears came. I could not even give her a proper sendoff with my grief. Here was my best friend, my beloved sister, lying there torn apart in a pool of blood, and I could do nothing but stand staring stupidly at her torn body. I wanted so badly to touch her, to kiss her, but my whole body was stiff.

Amidst all this, an out of place thought came to my mind. I needed to eat. I needed some food and water in my mouth. I limped back into the kitchen, avoiding stepping over strewn limbs and through the blood, to the pot where mother kept the rice. There was nearly nothing left. I barely managed to scrape a handful from the bottom. I then looked around for a water jar that had not been destroyed by the Japanese. I was able to find one that was nearly empty, and let the liquid soothe my throat.

It was strange for me to be able to swallow. The pain in my throat was intense, unbearable; it felt awfully swollen. I could not will my voice to scream and cry, and here I was standing on top of my family members' bodies in a huge puddle of blood and swallowing the food and the water like a pig.

I have no honor, I thought. I have no conscience. My ancestors are watching me angrily from heaven and will curse me for life.

Silent Marionette
침묵의꼭두각시

I grabbed my shoes and ran. I ran as I had never run before. Without looking back, I ran. I had been a fast runner all my life, but never this fast. I ran into the forest, deep among the soothing trees where all was normal and sane.

The forest looked like it was waiting for me. We knew each other, the forest and I, ever since I was a baby. Mother taught me how to identify the edible mushrooms and berries. The forest ran along the fields that stretched all the way to the mountains. There was a little narrow stream running beside the forest, which made me feel safe. "*Mulma issim moksum buzin halsu itti, gorom,*" (Wherever there is water there is life) my mother used to say.

I stopped running at one point and started walking, stopping from time to time to spit the thick saliva collected in my throat. I must be very sick, I thought to myself. Toshihiro, the filthy pig, must have transferred me Japanese germs, the likes of which we Koreans had never encountered.

I spat on the ground repeatedly. "Curse you *chokppari* (short devils)!" I did not care how sick I was. A certain death awaited me anyway, somewhere in the other end of the forest. If the Japanese will not kill me, I will kill myself anyway from the pain and shame.

Why, I wondered, had I not killed myself already. Mother's butcher knife was in the kitchen right in front of my eyes. I could have put myself on fire; I could have jumped off the cliff by the forest.

The reason was not fear, I was sure. I was not a coward. I was never afraid of anything in my life except for Abazi. Even the boys in the village were afraid of me because I was strong and never afraid to speak my mind.

I ran at the speed of light and climbed trees like a monkey. Mother used to sigh every night at bath time and say her usual line "*Eminai ga son mosm gachi gogi moiga; nere sizip gagin eryup da ya.*" (You behave like a wild animal; you will never get married!). I was never as feminine and gentle as my sisters; I was not interested in new clothes, shoes, or having my hair done.

One boy used to bother my smaller sisters. I went into his face one day, my hands at my hips, and told him to his shock that if he ever teased my sisters again I would cut off his balls with the hunting knife I always had in my pocket.

The boy was bigger than I, but he got pale and ran without answering. He never touched my sisters again, and when I used to pass by him, I would put my hand in my pocket making sure he saw my threatening look. The boy would hush his friends and move silently and respectfully to make way for me to walk.

I would never understand why I did not put an end to my life that day. It must have been my stubborn nature or my incredible sense of guilt that pushed me to continue to live so that I could pay for my sins.

It was dark in the forest; there was a silence of death above the huge old trees. They had been there for hundreds of years and still would be there long after I died. I felt a strange sense of sadness mixed with pain; I was not ready to depart from those trees. I felt at that moment that I would not mind departing from the world, just those old trees, those beautiful trees...it would be hard to say goodbye to them.

My respect for and fascination with nature was something I inherited from mother. She taught me all there was to know about the forests, the fields, the rivers and the earth. Mother respected nature more than anything in the world; she worshiped the earth. Every element of nature had a god. She would pray to the god of the rain, to the god of the sun, the god of the trees, the god of the cattle. There was even a special god for the sweet potatoes. Mother collected gods, taught me that each one of them was unique in its own way, and should be prayed to differently.

I picked a mushroom and sat down underneath a tree, biting into it. My head hurt and I felt very tired. The loneliness and the emptiness exhausted me. I have nowhere to go; I said to myself, nobody would want me anyway. I was human trash, a good for nothing traitor. I closed my eyes and fell asleep curled against a tree stump.

Being a Buddhist

I woke up to the sound of the owls. It was dark in the forest. I looked up at the sky; it seemed that the sun had set not too long ago. I licked my dry lips; the pain in my throat was gone. I was grateful for the darkness and the silence in the woods. A thought passed my mind. Maybe I could stay there forever. The forest would protect me from the *chokppari* and I would never have to face my family members and village people again. I would become a forest kid and survive here just as the animals do.

I raised my head to the owl calling me. I could see his glowing eyes right on the tree above me. I tried to give him back a call, but there was still no sound from my throat. Every time I made an honest effort to produce a sound, waving my hands, my body shaking, my breathing became squeezed and heavy and sounded like short, faint screams.

This has nothing to do with a cold, I said to myself. I had just become mute, perfectly mute. For some reason that gave me a sense of comfort. I would not have to tell anybody, not even under torture, the horrible things that I had done. My sins would stay with me forever; they would go with me to my grave.

The knowledge of my muteness had not brought me any sorrow, nor had the knowledge of my coming death. To the contrary, I felt comfortable. I was cold and hungry, and felt justified in seeking to take care of my immediate needs. The forest was now very dark. Knowing that it bordered the fields I would walk to the edge and try to find something to eat, a sweet potato or maybe a piece of corn.

Without a second thought, I started walking. I could feel the soft leaves being crushed under my feet. I was wondering how mother would react if she knew that I was running around in the forest at night. I could hear her voice, "*Nere oka mun zokan*? (What am I to do with you?) I rushed faster. The hunger was bad now; I needed food, and fast.

Silent Marionette
침묵의꼭두각시

I could sense the fields coming close. This would be south of the village, the cornfields. The corn would not be ripe yet, but I could fill my stomach with it. I walked carefully into the field, trying to feel the plants with my hands. The moonlight was kind and bright. I found some corn and collected a few cobs in my skirt, and then sat down and ate the raw, bitter pieces one by one.

The sight of the fields was sad. The glow of the moon against the trees filled the landscape with strange shadows. I felt lonely now, lonely and cold. I had never felt lonely in my life. With three sisters and three brothers, the house was always full. Grandmother and my aunts, my cousins, and my uncles were around all the time.

The village people and children all knew each other; there was never any alone time. The feeling of loneliness was a new one for me. It was painful and foreign. I walked back, deep into the forest, and lay down covering myself with leaves and cried myself to sleep.

The rain woke me, along with lightning and thunder. The sun was rising, somehow finding cracks and crevices among the clouds to cast a bit of light on the forest floor. My whole body felt itchy. I sat up and found that my legs were covered with leeches.

I looked at them curiously. They were hurting me, the fat worms. It seemed that they had a plan. I remembered Abazi always saying, "A group effort is the secret for a successful organization." Those leeches were surely working to Abazi's level of group effort. They were covering my legs and sucking my blood systematically.

Unlike my brothers and sisters, shoving, pushing, and killing each other for a bigger bite of a sweet rice cake, these hundreds of fat worms worked together in harmony. None of them shoved or pushed; each had its own spot and drank my blood equally. I started pulling them one at a time. The pain was unbearable, but I felt sorry for the little creatures struggling in my fingers. They reminded me of my two little sisters trying to hold on to each other in the fire, trying to hold on to life. My blood must have been tasty. They fought me hard and refused to depart from my flesh. By the time the sun came up I had pulled them all out.

At this point the forest was fully lit. Now my stomach was hurting from hunger; I got up and started looking for food. Mother had taught me how to survive in nature. She used to send my sisters and me to look for berries, wild grapes and arugula fruits. I opened my mouth and drank the raindrops. They tasted fresh and sweet. I must have spent a full hour collecting anything edible in a fold of my skirt.

I soon arrived at a little stream flowing through the forest. The rays of sun shining through the trees reflected on the clear water. I could hear the green leaves swaying in the wind, and the shiny smooth stones on the stream's bank looked so innocent.

I sat down by the water, taking off my shoes. I placed my feet in the water, soothing the cracked and weary skin on them. It was only then that I grew aware of how long I had been running. I also came to realize that death was not just the absence of life. It was an inevitable reality. Closing my eyes, I envisioned myself lying there by the riverbank dead. It felt so real and natural, just like life itself, if not more so.

I sat there eating the berries while the river snaked over the rocks, and wondered where this water was going. The flowing of the stream made me sigh; the endless cycle of nature gave me some kind of assurance that I was still in my right mind. As a little girl, I had been taught to believe in the cycles of nature.

Being a Buddhist (佛子), it was always emphasized to me that there was a connection between the harmony of nature and the spiritual world. The whole concept of indifference and freedom from material and emotional attachments may have come now to my rescue. Mother always told me that the afterlife consoles us for the harshness of mortal life. As I filled my stomach with food and quenched my thirst with the water, I suddenly felt a new excitement, a new feeling of wondering what would happen next. It was as if I was another person watching myself as someone else.

When I heard the dogs barking and the heavy footsteps of the Japanese soldiers, I knew my saga was only beginning. There are only a few hours between hunger and starvation, only a few seconds between life and death, my father used to say. Time suddenly moves differently when there is a situation where you know that the end is coming.

The minutes freeze, the hearing is sharpened. You can hear every little peep seven times louder. Everything is moving in slow motion now. My legs are heavy; it feels as if they are stuck in cement.

The voices are coming toward me slowly but surely, the footsteps are unmistakably approaching me. Actually, I am thinking, I still have plenty of time to hide. I could disappear in an instant behind the bushes where they will never find me, but I am not moving. I am just sitting there awaiting my fate, for some odd reason without any fear in my heart.

Fear is a strange phenomenon. It comes and goes unexpectedly. It is supposed to be an emotional response to something negative, to threat or danger. The thing is that what is negative to some is positive to others.

Most people are afraid of confrontations with danger and that is when they experience fear. However, I was never afraid of confrontation unless it was with my father. I could take on anybody in the world, even wild animals in the woods, but not my father. When people or animals are afraid, they will usually run away until their predator corners them. At this point, they will either give up and surrender, or fight for their life.

Strangely, I was totally comfortable and unafraid. I was sitting there waiting for the Japanese to take me as if I was waiting for a prize. My pupils did not open wide, my heart rate did not increase, I had no symptoms of fear whatsoever. I was thinking to myself that something was very abnormal with the way I was sitting there, waiting for them without any trace of worry to take me. I was wondering if I had started to lose my mind. I had kept surprising myself repeatedly in the last 48 hours, as if I were a completely different person born out of my new silence.

Silent Marionette
침묵의꼭두각시

Pil-goengi (Pil's cat)

You can just try to imagine you are sitting in the safest, most familiar, most earthy, innocent place in the world. You sit there under a several-thousand-year-old tree, your stomach is satisfyingly full of berries and wild grapes, and your mouth is washed with the fresh raindrops. The sun is starting to come out from behind the clouds, the squirrels are trying to catch a berry from your hand, and the birds are singing their morning songs. You are grateful for the light breeze on your face, away from any violence or judgment or pain. Everything is all about nature and yourself. The silence of the forest has worked in amazing harmony with my lost voice.

Nature and I communicate without any words, and in the midst of all that, I hear a roar, the rough roar of cruelty. In a split second, the most vicious, ugliest dogs I had ever seen surrounded me. Their teeth were bared and saliva was dripping from their mouths. Their ears were down and their bodies were arched, ready to strike at the moment I would make a sudden move.

There were at least twelve solders standing behind them holding their leashes, and their pistols were directed at my head. They were standing there staring at me, not saying a word. I thought maybe if one of them would say something, sanity would return momentarily.

I shrunk myself into a little ball like the one our old cat that Abazi hated used to do. That cat arrived to us from nowhere when he was very young, and my sister Pil-sun took to him. She swore that if her fat groom-to-be would touch it she would personally cut his throat.

Father told her to get rid of that ugly garbage; there was not enough food and space for the family in our little hut, and we surely did not need another mouth to feed. Pil-sun begged him to let her take care of him. "I never had a pet, Abazi, he will not

51

eat much!" However, father told her to stop nagging or he would kick her out of the house together with her cat. Pil-sun was stubborn, and the cat stayed in our yard. He became a fierce creature and an excellent hunter.

He could jump high and catch birds in his teeth. He was fast as lightning, and no mouse or squirrel could get away from him. He would follow us everywhere we went, to the fields, to the store, to our walks in the forest. He was a clever cat. Even Abazi had to admit that he earned his living by cleaning up the rodents in our house. Mother used to give him scraps of food and we would share all our meals with him.

In no time, he became a big grey creature, and the village was filled with his kittens and grand kittens. The village people got used to him and caught themselves, for the first time in their lives, respecting an animal that did not return them any favors.

Everybody called him *"Pil-Goengi"* (Pil's Cat). He was not afraid of anybody. The only one that scared him was Abazi. Whenever he sensed that Abazi was about to pass by him or come into the house, his body would curl into a ball and his entire face would tighten. His whiskers would stand up, and his ears would stretch to their maximum and look like bat ears.

Silent Marionette
침묵의꼭두각시

Now I reacted like the cat. I must have looked like him too. I gave the soldier a challenging gaze. In the sanctuary of my forest, it all seemed rather strange, as if it was happening to some other girl. Toshihiro was not among the soldiers. I was hoping they had come simply to kill me.

The fact that Toshihiro was not there was a relief to me; I might not be tortured before I joined my family in heaven. Two of the soldiers approached me and pulled me to my feet. They were young, my brother's age. I wondered if they understood at all what they were doing in a foreign land, chasing a little insignificant girl like me.

Was this what their commanders told them that they would do once they got to Korea? There was still no talking. I was dragged among the soldiers, back to the village. Walking silently among them I still felt like a cat; the dogs did not take their eyes off me and the soldiers wheeled me among them somehow with care, as if I was a wounded kitten. I thought to myself that this was awkward, twelve Japanese soldiers surrounding me and not hurting me. It was unexpected.

Now I clearly remembered the thoughts I had had before, that my death is certain, whether I come out or stay in the forest. I was not bothered at all by what was going to happen to me or what those soldiers had in mind to do with me. No matter what they would do, it would lead me to the great beyond where I would find Pil-sun, Omani and Abazi, and my little sisters, and have a chance to beg them for forgiveness.

That gave me strength. I could feel my steps getting lighter. I would have run among my guards if they were not holding my arms. The exhaustion left me and with it the weakness. If Toshihiro will unzip his pants again, I will bite him hard this time, I will tear his genitals apart with my teeth.

The village was quiet. It seemed to have been emptied of people. My house was still standing there in the same spot undisturbed. I was taken to the headquarters.

The Japanese had hired two Korean men to run the office. None of the villagers respected then. They were working for the Japanese for a salary, and we tried to avoid them.

Some individuals became quite wealthy under Japanese rule; we all knew they were collaborating with the Japanese military against us. These people were ready to sell their own for any price; they were greedy and as cruel as the Japanese were.

Silent Marionette
침묵의꼭두각시

Between 1910 and 1945, the Japanese empire ruled Korea. However, they would not have been able to govern successfully without the collaborators.

Sang-tae

There was a man called "Sang-tae" " (祥泰) in our village. He was almost forty years of age. He was not married, and had lived with his mother all his life. Having a big scar on his face, he looked very grim. In addition, he was a hard nut to crack and nobody wanted to talk with him, not even approach him. Because of his appearance, he behaved more and more roughly, and people became openly hostile to him and tried to avoid him in the neighborhood.

When he returned to the village after a couple of months' absence, he looked like a different man, with a Japanese hat on his head and pants of Japanese style. He had gone through a transformation, found his final destination in life, and become a Japanese soldier himself.

By and by, rumors had it that he allowed himself to become a Japanese minion, but he did not care, nor was he annoyed at being treated like a traitor. People in the village would see him giggling with Japanese soldiers or police officers in front of the police substation in town.

Whenever I used to pass by him, he would single me out with his eyes and look me over from head to toe as if he was measuring my figure again and again. His looks always gave the chills; I would feel so uneasy that I would start running as far as I could from him. My sister used to spot him from far away and say "*Oe nom apzzebi aniga, nalne gaza*" (there is the creep, lets walk fast).

I could feel his sharp stare at my back for a long time after we passed him. Abazi used to spit on the ground when he saw him and say, "Damn the traitor bastard. I can't wait for the day the *chokpparis* will leave: he will regret ever being born," and he would go on and on, describing how he would tear him limb from limb. It's "*doro bun ssiregi*" (ugly garbage) like him, that has been ruining our poor country.

My life in the village was quite difficult. I always had to work. If not in the fields, I had to do chores at home, wash my brothers' clothes, and help with the cooking and cleaning.

The Japanese had ruled my province ever since I was born. On top of the constant effort to survive, since we were very poor, we had to put up with the demanding Japanese sets of rules.

I grew up with very few choices in my life. My mind was mainly occupied by my hunger, always looking for something to eat. Food was my main concern. I was trained to watch out for Japanese, Japanese sympathizers, and getting sick. Getting sick was always on our minds since we did not really have any medical care in the village. There were no doctors available, and certainly nobody had money for medications.

We all lived on leftovers and scraps since the Japanese took most of our crops. However, with all this I never felt that I was deprived of my childhood. All girls lived like me in the village. We never had any toys or got any presents, we were not allowed to go to school, we could not write and read, and we were second-class humans in a men's world that was additionally suppressed because of the Japanese occupation. We were never frail. Korean women were known for being strong; they carried the entire men's world on their backs.

In my village a few very courageous women would risk their lives to help the resistance against the Japanese despite the strenuous objections of their husbands. This was a major concern of the Japanese troops. Freedom of the press was forbidden, and any talk of sedition resulted in use of force.

If any villagers were even suspected of hiding members of the resistance, the entirety of the village's population would be herded into large buildings, especially churches, and the

Japanese would burn them down. Whole villages had been massacred in this way, just on suspicion of aiding the resistance.

Japan had transformed Korea into a colony that was designed for the needs of the Imperial Armed Forces. The developed infrastructures were intended to facilitate all the raw materials, such as rice, meat, fish, minerals, timber, and leather, anything that could be used by the Imperial Army. Millions of sacks of rice had been exported to Japan, depriving the Korean citizens of food.

Imperial Japan shipped off all of Korea's resources, including its people, in order to satisfy its war machine. The Japanese government stole land from the Koreans and gave it for a subsidized cost to Japanese families willing to settle in Korea. Farmers were forced to work on the land that had once been theirs in order to supply rice for the Japanese authorities.

The Japanese government rounded up *millions* of Korean workers, and took them into forced labor. *Millions of* Koreans were living in Japan as immigrants. The combination of immigrants and slave laborers living in Japan brought the figure up to over two million by the end of World War II. We had no right to vote or hold office; the Japanese appointed all our politicians from the local to the federal level.

The colonial government put in an act to eradicate the Korean culture and language in an attempt to root out all elements of Korea from society. The entire field of culture and education was based on the individual ethnicity of the Korean race. In 1938, when I was twelve years old, the first Korean Voluntary unit of the Japanese Imperial Armed Forces was formed. Many Koreans were fighting for the Japanese Army.

We were absolutely disgusted and horrified to hear about those people, but in the beginning of 1944, all Korean males were drafted to serve in the Army or work in the military industrial sector. Among those Koreans that were conscripted into the Army the Japanese recruited women as well. Japanese officials and local collaborators who were kidnapping women, telling them that they were going to serve the Japanese Army, did the recruiting. The word "kidnap" sent chills through my body, and more than anything I was trained for in my life, I was trained to watch for kidnappers and collaborators who were potential kidnappers.

Now I was standing among the soldiers and the dogs on the steps to the police station staring Sang-tae the *mang hal ssiregi* (ugly garbage) right in the face. He reclined against the wall with a cigarette clasped in his large hand with very-well manicured nails, giving me a condescending smile. We all stood there silently for a full minute until Sang casually tossed away his cigarette and ran a hand down his well-ironed Japanese military uniform.

He took one step towards me and motioned to me with his finger saying, "*Iri wa bora* (come here)." He gave me another look and said, "*Ni borau* (look at yourself)... How long did you think you would be able to hide? "*Ganna emi naire!*" (Stupid girl) You will pay for this dearly! He slapped my face with all his might. I did not think he would have such power in that elegant hand of his, and I was thrown back on the floor from the unexpected force of the hit.

At that moment, Toshihiro came out the door. He observed the situation and spit out; "As I was saying!" he took a second to continue, "This one is mine!"

Sang-tae took two steps backwards, "*Hai wakarimasida*!"

"I forbid you to put your hands on her! Understood?"

"*Hai wakarimasida*!"

"Get the girl washed, groomed and fed and give her a new Kimono!"

"*Hai wakarimasida*!"

Toshihiro came near me and said "*Okkiru*!" (Get up, girl)
I stood up thinking I must look like a dirty ghost; at least that will save me from another romantic encounter with him. Nobody in his right mind would have a desire for a filthy creature like me. I could smell his sweet perfume mixed with the strong aftershave odor. He grabbed my hair in his fist and pulled my head close to his face.

"Told you to wait for me! Didn't I?"
The strong pull in my hair hurt me. I gave a yell that sounded strange; the voice came out thick and loud to my ears. It was not my voice; it was a voice of some wounded animal. Toshihiro then let go and pushed me forward.

"Take her, Sang-tae, and make sure to do as I said!"

"*Hai wakarimasida*"

I was pulled by Sang-tae away into the building. He did not say a word. He gave me a dirty, lustful look. I knew very well that if not for his fear of Toshihiro he would brutally rape me, right there, without even blinking.

Silent Marionette
침묵의꼭두각시

A real bath

There were two Korean women in the building. I had never met them before; they were not residents of our village. It was strange for me to find Korean women working for the Japanese For some reason I was under the impression that only men did that. They took me into a room. Sang-tae left, to my relief. It was a big room with couches and sofas. There were some radios and lamps. I had never seen such a fancy room in my life.

One woman was preparing a bath full of warm water, which was also something I had never seen before. We used to sit on the floor naked, pouring water on ourselves. Mother would help scrub us one at a time with rough brushes. Baths are for the rich, she used to say, a human being needs water to drink and survive. No use in wasting Buddha's good water to spoil your body. One of the women approached me and tried to pull my shirt off.

I curled into my body and shook my head "No."
She tried again, but I pushed her away holding tightly to my shirt.

"Take off your clothes; I need to wash you!"

I shook my head "No!"

"*Hayakku!*" (Fast)

I shrunk even more into myself and then started waving my hands wildly, screaming. A mute scream is an interesting scream. I found that I could make all kinds of perfect animal noises.

I could sound like a slaughtered sheep, a rooster in trouble, or a dog being shot to death. I could go as high as a dying bird and as low as a dying bear. This was a new discovery for me and I went on and on screaming. The woman was really angry; she was standing there stunned by my wild sounds. She shouted as loud as she could, "*Chiara!*" (Stop)

The woman was not from our area. She had a different dialect; her pronunciation was different from what I was used to hearing.

At this point, I started crying like a baby. I did not imagine that I had so much ability to cry in me. The woman lost all her patience and yelled,
"*Ssikki rop tta goma!*" (Stop the crying)

Nevertheless, that made me feel even sorrier for myself and I was crying a river. At this point, she started hitting me and yelled, "*Uki mae!*" (Stop crying!).

But I became my fierce cat *Pil-goengi*, and I attacked her, scratching and biting. The woman left me in shock. She was surprised at my strength, turned to her friend, "This one is crazy, you take care of her!" and left the room.
The other woman had a more pleasant demeanor; she gave me a patient smile and came close to me,

"What's your name?" She asked.

She had a softer, gentler voice, and her dialect was similar to that of my village. She calmed me down a bit. I opened my mouth, trying to form the word Maikko, but only a hollow sound came out. I looked at her mouth, trying to imitate the movements of her lips, opening and closing my lips, but the imitation was not successful.

"Sh......*Ginzang hazi mare*" (relax) she said and smiled a reassuring smile.

I tried again; I breathed in deep, and then froze. My lips opened, I collected all my strength, but no words came out. I motioned to her that I could not speak, and tears started coming down my cheeks.

Silent Marionette
침묵의꼭두각시

"Are you mute?" she asked, clearly feeling sorry for me.

I nodded my head.

"*Bara*" (look) she said "*Mok ku yo ku*" (a bath).
I felt a little better and nodded my head. The feel of the water would do me good. I was sweaty and dirty, and the tub looked so comforting for my painful feet. I motioned to the direction of the door.

"*Mun zam ga dalla kko*?" (You want me to lock the door.)

I nodded.

"*Ginzang hazi mare, amudo an onda*!" (Relax, nobody will enter)

I let her take off my clothes now.

"*Ni cham mal gop dei,*" (You are a very pretty girl) she said, and placed me in the water. The warm water soothed my aches. It felt very different from what I was used to. I could not believe I had never had a bath in my life. Mother would fill up a little bucket and would scrub us fast before the water would cool off.

This felt like heaven; mother did not understand what she was missing. This was a real treat, and I was thinking that actually a bath would be perfect for poor, hard working people after a long day in the fields. I stretched my body in the comfort of the soapy water, feeling every bone in my tired body enjoying the new feeling.
The woman was sponging my body from head to toe. Nobody had ever waited on me; I was the one that always had to serve my family members. I had to wash my little sisters and scrub the backs of my brothers and Abazi. This was nice. The woman had strong hands. She was massaging my body as well as cleaning it.

I closed my eyes and hummed in pleasure like a cat. The thought of my slaughtered family was far from my mind. I did not even feel guilty indulging in that tub; everything seemed so momentary to me, so absurd, so unreal, that I could not even feel real feelings.

"It's a shame you can't talk; a pretty girl like you could be perfect if you could sing and dance," the woman sighed sadly. I closed my eyes, giving in to her hands massaging my head and washing my long hair. I could sing before the Japanese came to my village to destroy my family. Mother taught me many songs. Her favorite was Arirang. When she sang it, her eyes would get glassy and sometimes tears would appear on her cheeks. Her face came into view before me as the song started playing in my mind,

Arirang, arirang, arariyo,
Arirang gogaero noma ganda
(My love goes over the Arirang hill)
Narel borigo gasinen nimeun
(If you leave me behind you, my love)
Simrido motgaso balbyung nanda
(Your feet will hurt before long, my love)

The woman covered me with a towel and combed my hair. She sprayed me with perfume and wrapped me with a white kimono. Touching the silky material, I felt that this kind of thing on my body was something I would not see even in my dreams. I felt like I was floating on air, thinking there must be another planet and that is where I was at that moment. I put on my new white socks and my new shoes. Moreover, when the woman dragged me to the mirror, I stopped breathing for a moment.

The image in the mirror was not me. It was a strange young woman I had never met before. She was a beautiful young woman, her face as pale as the wall, looking much more mature than I had ever seen myself. The woman put lipstick on my lips and some red powder on my cheeks. If Abazi would see me like this, he would beat me senseless.

Arirang, arrirang, arariyo,
Arirang gogaero noma ganda
(My love goes over the Arirang hill)
Narel borigo gasi nen nimeun
(If you leave me behind you, my love)
Simrido mot gaso bal byung na nda
(Your feet will hurt before long, my love)

The song did not leave me now. I wanted to scream the song for mother's sake. For my own sake I tried again to make the voice come out, but it was stuck like a knot in my throat. The other woman came into the room with a tray. She stopped before me in shock, staring at me in disbelief, and then mumbled "*Ige nukko mikkizi annen dei!*" (Unbelievable)

I was seated to eat; I had no idea how hungry I was until the food was placed in front of me. I threw the food into my mouth greedily, relishing the pleasure of having real food in my stomach. I was not even paying attention to how it tasted, or to what I was eating. After living on berries for three days, one cannot imagine what it feels like to indulge in real food.

"*Chan cha hi mura*" (eat slowly) the lady said, "You are going to get sick."

The woman went and got me more. "*Mai mura*" (eat a lot) she said, "You are going on a long trip."

I choked and started coughing, motioning to her.

"*Odero marim nekka?*" (Where?)

"You'll be fine; you are going to a place where you will get a lot of food and make money."

"*Gugi odem nekka*?" (Where?) I motioned.

"*Naesa morinda*" (I don't know) she said, "You will know when you get there"

Anything was better than staying in the village with the dead bodies of my family members and the angry ghosts of my ancestors. At that point, I was convinced that the Japanese had killed my three brothers. I had nobody left in the village for me. I also felt relief that they would be sending me away from Toshihiro.

I was suspecting that all this royal treatment of bath and perfumes, the food, and the kimono were in order to prepare me for his sick pleasures. Now I understood that I was intended for something else. Since anything else would be better than Toshihiro, I was relieved for now, even though the alarm bells were ringing in my head.

I knew that whatever it was they had in mind for me was nothing as wonderful as the woman had described. I knew I was about to start a painful, tough journey. I would never see my village again. I had the feeling it was the last time I would have a perfumed bath and a good bowl of rice. I started getting ready for the worst; I was ready to depart from all I ever knew.

You are going to a good place

I never saw Toshihiro again. The next thing I knew, I was taken by a group of soldiers to a train station. I had gotten new clothes, black pants and a white shirt. The women packed up a bag for me with new underwear and the new white kimono, and the nice woman even wrapped up some rice cakes and shoved them in my bag just in case I would get hungry.

"*Zon dero galtei mem pini mugu ra kai*" (you are going to a good place, don't be afraid), she said. "They will train you to be a nurse. This is good; you would never be able to get an education if not for the Japanese imperial government. Now you are going to be an educated young lady and you don't have to worry about your future."

I looked at her eyes. She was either lying in my face or she was plain stupid. I did not know which one to choose. I gave her a faint smile; that was all I could do.

As we were standing in the train station, I was thinking that in spite of my fourteen years of life I was feeling old all of a sudden. I felt lonely, so very lonely. I knew the fields, the mountains, and the forests around my village like the palm of my hand, and it struck me very sharply that I would never see them again.

Mother always told us that Buddha loves us all. She was a passionate believer in the Buddha. Abazi would smirk every time she would light the incense and pray. Mother did not pay attention to his criticism. He would say that if there were any god, any type of Buddha, the Japanese would have left Korea a long time ago.

But mother assured us that Buddha was watching out for us. She said he loves us and protects us. Was it Buddha who took away my ability to speak? Nature does not speak words, the Korean mountains, the trees, the sweet potatoes and the rice fields, the smooth stones by the river; I was now part of nature.

Good Buddha decided to make me part of almighty nature as a compensation for my suffering from Toshihiro and the loss of my family. The thought of Buddha gave me hope that death was still there waiting for me, but I would not suffer much longer before I got to it.

The train arrived at the station. I was the only passenger boarding. A group of soldiers got off, their machine guns hanging casually on their shoulders. They avoided even looking at me. They were very young, some of them with a cigarette at the edge of their lips, and they took time to kid and joke with my guards while I was standing there like a shadow.

I might as well have been invisible to them. I looked at the long train, never having been on one in my life. Abazi used to travel from time to time, and mother went once with my little sisters to visit my aunt. I never got to go. Pil-sun and I used to walk the tracks, imagining that we were traveling on the train all the way to China.

The word China used to bring pleasant chills to my back. As far as I was concerned, China was fairyland. Pil-sun told me that there were little, good-natured people in China, and that the rice was growing in the streets. All you had to do was bend down and pick it. The Chinese people were all geniuses in calligraphy and drawing, and they had the most beautiful river in the world, the Yellow River.

My brothers once showed me a world map in their study books; I remember that as a big discovery. I had thought Korea and Japan were the only countries in the world. I could not believe how big the world was, and when my brother showed me China, I was so surprised to see how big it was in comparison to Korea or Japan.

Silent Marionette
침묵의꼭두각시

Once I asked my brother to count with me how many countries were in the world, but after twelve countries, he told me to stop bothering him since I was asking too many questions. That was when I learned that people speak different languages in each country, that there were brown people and black people and white people and of course yellow people. There were round eyed people and slant eyed people, there were straight haired people and curly haired people and fuzzy haired people.

I was always wondering where these people of the world were when my country was invaded and devastated by the Japanese. I could not ever understand how it is that every country is concerned only about its own business, why when all people are made from the same flesh and blood, they are not there for each other no matter which country they are from.

If the entire world was round like a ball, as my brother explained to me, then we should all be there guaranteeing each other's well being. My simple logic told me that if you throw a ball, it would fall on a different spot every time. That meant for me that the likes of the Japanese could land on any part of the globe, in any country, and we should be there protecting each other from this evil.

I gave a last look back at my village when the soldiers dragged me up on the train. I was wondering where Young-soo was at that moment, whether he would ever look for me, his future wife. Would he ever go after me to find me, wherever they might take me? It was strange that my last thought when I boarded the train was of Yong-soo, not my family, not the beloved views of the countryside in my village. I was crying inside, "I am sorry Yong-soo, I am so sorry. Please forgive my sins. There will never be another in my heart; it is you I will love until the last day of my life."

The train felt familiar to me even though I had never been on one. I walked through the long lines of seats full of Japanese soldiers. Some of them were sleeping, others just staring ahead.

They did not look like a happy bunch, just tired, dirty kids who looked like they had lost their mothers.

I walked to the end of the train, into a car that was half-empty. There were other young girls like me, who to my surprise were wearing the same clothes that I was wearing. I understood immediately that we were all going to the same destination for the same purposes.

The Japanese soldiers yelled, "No talking!" and sat me down in an empty seat beside another girl. Even she looked familiar. Had I been there in my previous life? Was I just experiencing a strange state of mind as can happen after extreme tragedy? All I

Silent Marionette
침묵의꾹두각시

knew was that nothing had surprised me ever since I left my village; I would accept the events that came to me from now on as if I had experienced them before.

The girl gave me a little nod and a shadow of a smile appeared at the edge of her mouth. She was a bit older than I, maybe seventeen, a very pretty girl, her clothes and even her bag were identical to mine. We were not allowed to talk or to even exchange looks.

The Japanese guards were standing on top of us the entire trip. Unlike the girl next to me, who looked very anxious from the way she was turning her head constantly and sitting on the edge of her seat very uncomfortably, I felt at peace. I closed my eyes and fell asleep as the train moved along.

Nily Naiman

Manchuria, July- 1943

"Talk! Korean whore!"

Saeya saeya parang saeya,
(Bird, bird, a blue bird)
Nokdu batte anzi mara,
(Don't take a rest on the green gram field)
Nokdu kkochi ttorozimyun,
(When the green gram flower leaf falls,)
Chongpo zangsu wulgo ganda.
(Then, the bluish hemp cloth peddler goes crying.)

The poem came to me just before I opened my eyes. I must have slept a good ten hours. I heard this poem once from my mother as a little girl and I memorized it. Now I recited it to myself and made a wish to open my eyes and find some cure for my pain. I looked out the window and saw landscapes that were new to me. The mountains looked different, as did the trees. Abazi had trained us when we were very young how to define directions. If we were ever to get lost, we should know our way back home without a compass.

I was trained to look at the stars when I was lost in the forests or on the mountain in the nighttime. I knew how to navigate by recognizing the plants, trees, texture of stones, and the direction of the rivers' flow. Now I knew that we were going northwest; I was convinced at that.

The scenery became pale yellowish and buff color. I could see right away that the rocks had become very fine, unlike the rocks in Korea. The blowing dust in the air was getting thicker as we went fast forward, and I felt the climate turning hotter and the humidity in the air getting heavier by the second.

I was convinced that we had left Korea. Remembering now the maps my brothers had shown me, my heart started beating fast. Could it be? Am I going to my fairyland? When I saw the incredible Yalu River (鴨綠江) coming toward us, the slow peaceful movement of the water, I exclaimed with excitement. My voice came out thick and broken like a man's cry. The girl next to me gave me a warning look, and the guard near me barked "Shut up!"

The rice fields stretch out endlessly into the night. For one long minute the entire world is lost in the dark silvery lines of crops. I know what is going to happen next. Everything that is happening now happened before. I remember seeing all these sights before, even the pretty girl beside me pulling nervously on the edges of her shirt.

I remember being as thirsty as I am now. My eyes are looking around. Is there any water on the train? The dryness is heating my throat. I get up and the guards jump.

"Sit!"

I motion for a drink. One of the guards looks at me curiously and says, "Talk, what you want?"

I motion again, bringing the shape of a cup to my lips.

"Talk! Korean whore!"

I open my mouth, my lips are shaking. My breathing is not normal. It sounds like a whistle. I feel the pain shooting all over my body, the pressure in my neck and on my tongue is as heavy as large sack of rice.

The noise in my brain hurts my ears. My neck muscles are stretching; I start breathing loudly and swallowing my spit. I feel dizzy, as if on a raft on a stormy ocean. My lips are shaking like those of an old woman, my face twisted in pain. I stretch my body and stand now on my toes from the effort. My lips are dried out, my eyes closed; now I am angry and I give a long, loud roar.

The soldier is looking at me frightened; he is scared of the loud, horrendous sounds that are coming out of my mouth. He opens his eyes wide and I can see him shivering. I sound like a big black bear calling out his pain. I myself cannot believe my own ears. The soldier steps backwards. He is trying to get away from me.

Funny thing, the reaction of people to mutes. It makes them very uncomfortable. They stare at you as if you came from another planet. They suffer from the mute's presence; they want him to go away. Some of them get upset or angry; they cannot bear the fact that the mutes have an advantage over them since they do not need to answer questions.

Some people think that mutes are mentally ill; some that if you are mute, you are deaf too. "Sit!" the other soldier yells in apparent fear.
I sit down, a smirk on my face, with a sense of victory. I have managed to disturb the Japanese order, and to my surprise, the soldier hands me his water bottle. Now I am at peace; I know the Buddha of the silence is with me.

I opened my bag. I was hungry now, and started chewing on my rice cake. The girl beside me watched from the corner of her eye. She was hungry; I could feel it. I looked at my guards; they were rocking on their feet half-asleep.

I cut half of my cake and sneaked it to her as quickly as I could. The girl smiled again at the edge of her mouth. I could see a dimple forming in her cheek. She reminded me of my sister Pil-sun as she was taking big bits of the food in her hand. I felt a painful pinch in my heart. I missed Pil-sun now so much, and my tears started falling uncontrollably down my face.

Silent Marionette
침묵의꼭두각시

The girl looked at the guards and squeezed my hand, and then started humming quietly,

"Ask how many friends I have?
Water and stone, bamboo and pine.
The moon rising over the eastern hill is a joyful comrade.
Beside these five companions,
What other pleasure should I ask?"

I smiled gratefully and stopped crying. I had been there before I remembered this girl, the trip, the song. I was going to China. My dreamland and the angel of death were waiting for me patiently there.

He would open his comforting arms and receive me with mercy. He would take me to the great beyond where silence rules and the human needs are just a joke. The angel of death would walk me to my forgiving family and let me have eternal rest.

Little pretty girl getting off a train

The main problem for a mute is not the fact that he cannot speak and express himself, but the refusal of people to accept and comply with the muteness. People who are mute are generally considered handicapped or mentally impeded. However, with it they have an advantage over the rest of the world; they're allowed to keep their opinions to themselves.

That is a scary scenario to people, especially insecure people. A mute is usually very quick to get comfortable with his silence and come to peace with it; it is the public that has problems accepting it. The mute then needs to turn his back on people and run away from their demanding looks and merciful attempts at communication. Nobody understands a mute but the mute himself.

Little pretty girl, getting off the train, breathing deep the Promised Land's air. Manchuria (滿 洲) has a different climate from what I am used to. Manchuria sits on the boundary between the great Eurasian subcontinent and the big Pacific Ocean (太平洋). That is why the climate has extreme characteristics. In the summer, it is very hot and humid, and the winters are freezing cold. The little girl is feeling the sweat dripping down her neck; she is licking her dry lips as she is being shoved forward by the guards.

The girls are pushed onto the back of a truck. They sit curled and shrunken into themselves and nobody talks, as if the heart does not want to reveal to the mouth the incredible fear of what is coming next. Each one is into her own self, beloved faces pass in the minds, you can hear their cries, you can touch your loved ones, you can kiss them and hug them in your quiet solitude, and nobody will come and separate you. For the next few minutes, nobody will disturb your goodbyes.

Silent Marionette
침묵의꼭두각시

A new day starts showing itself outside the flaps of the truck's covering. The girls do not raise their heads, as if they refuse to see and be seen by a new day and a new place. Each girl is deep in her own bitter desperation that is freezing her heart.

The guards are now looking at each one of them, a smirk on the edge of their lips.

One of them is touching my train partner between her legs. She throws his hand away contesting, and the guard laughs. He is amused and pulls the girl to him forcefully. His face is drunk with self-power, and he says, "The Japanese soldiers will teach you how to push away a man my little kitten. The Japanese will teach you a thing or two!"

One by one the heads are stretching. Each one is looking at the other. The eyes are looking for a familiar face, or at least a friendly face. At times like this, it is good to hook up with an understanding soul.

Where are they taking me? Some girls are trying to look out through the cracks in the flaps. The sun is now up and there is full daylight in a distant world that does not belong to them.

One girl dares to ask, "*Yoga oden gyo*?" (Where are we?)

And the guard laughs and says, "You are in Manchuria, girl!"

The girls are panicking, "Zungguge wannen gapda!" (We are in China!)

Now they are getting hysterical; a girl who doesn't look more then thirteen years old starts crying, "*Omeyo, Abuziye, salni zuso*!" (Ma! Dad! Help me!).

Another one starts shaking and vomiting, and one starts pulling her hair out and screaming, "*Zibe bone zui soya*!" (Let me go!)

The guards get up and start beating us, "Shut your mouth!"

I can feel the fists and the cold metal of the pistols on my back; I curl like an animal into a ball.

The girl from the train squeezes my hand, "Let's be always together from now on. No matter what happens, let us not leave each other. We will stick together from now on!"

I squeeze her hand in return and give her a reassuring smile, and as the truck stops, the echo of the guard is still in my ears, "*Ilbon guini galcho zunda aiga...*" (The Japanese soldiers will teach you...)

Yelling, screaming, and dogs barking welcome us, "Get off, fast, get off!"

The girls are lining up, the Japanese soldiers reading the names from a list, making sure they have us all. The girl squeezes my fingers in her hand and says, as if to herself quietly, "Now it's the end, all is lost."

"March!"

The soldier yells, and we march in a row. Where? I am asking myself, did I finally reach death? Chinese people are walking on the sidewalks, some pretending they are very busy so as not to meet the Japanese soldiers' eyes, some smiling to them pleasantly.

A couple of women walk by and I look them in the eye, but they turn their faces to the sky in shame. We march in a perfectly straight line, as if we are sheep marching to be slaughtered.

We walk by a building. I can hear loud voices, wild laughs, and drunken yells from the wooden door. The soldiers are having a good time; it was obviously a party. I am thinking that the world has cause to be happy in spite of the horrible things that are happening to us.

The Manchurian morning is striking the streets. It is hot and the humidity is unbearable. There are rice and cornfields on both sides of the way.

We are marching past the farmers' huts. I could run fast into one of these huts. I could show them how well I know how to work the field. I will teach them new tricks that Abazi taught me. I am a trained farmer. I have a magic touch with the land; my plants never die. If they would just let me in their homes, I would cook, clean, and grow the best crops in the land.

Nevertheless, I do not run, and I know I will not run. I am just marching the street, toward my gloomy destiny.

My friend is mumbling behind me constantly, as if she is talking to someone that listens, "How could I be so stupid? They cheated me. All of them cheated me, the bastards. They lied to me and trapped me like a mouse. I let them catch me like a stupid fish in a net. How could I not know it from the beginning? The bastards told me they will take me to a nursing school, they promised money, the crooks. 'Kumikko, you will be a rich woman! The Japanese will teach you in the best nursing school in Korea.' What an idiot I am!"

It is hard for me to see the sorrow on Kumikko's beautiful face; she is walking mumbling, cursing to herself. A look of despair is on her beautiful face. I am trying to catch her attention, to give her some reassurance, but she keeps her eyes to the ground and continues mumbling, "Like a mouse in a trap, liars, bastards, like a fish in a net..."

All the girls here are marching to their deaths. It is as clear to me as the sun in the sky. Nobody will stay alive. A broken ceramic dish can most likely be glued and fixed once or twice, but then its fate is the garbage pail.

Silent Marionette
침묵의꼭두각시

The Japanese guards are in a good mood; they are joking and laughing. Some are sitting on benches in front of a big house, smoking and chatting. They jump up when they see us coming, and welcome our guards as if they are welcoming their brothers.

That was strange for me, since I did not think that the Japanese were really human like us. They obviously felt relieved to see my guards alive, and they looked like they could understand camaraderie. They were very complex people, the Japanese, I thought to myself. One minute they could be the most brutal animals on earth, and the next minute become childish, playful, and friendly like your next-door neighbors.

We were taken into the lobby of a big house. A couple received us, and immediately identified themselves as Korean with a very cheerful, out of place, "*Oso dul osi rayo!*" (Hello).

If I had been able to talk, I would have risked my life and asked them what is the big, cheerful welcome for? How dare they even look in our eyes or talk to us, these traitors? Were they aware of what we girls were going through?
I wanted to take those phony, flattering faces and crush both their heads together as hard as I could.

There was also a Chinese man and four Japanese women guards. Some Japanese soldiers were sitting on couches. They did not look like monsters. They were exhausted, sweaty and dirty, sitting with their legs stretched tiredly forward, holding their hats and looking like a bunch of tired school kids who had lost their way.

The Korean man read our names now from a list he had. Every girl had to say *Hai*! (Yes). When he got to my name, I was silent. He read my name again and I raised my hand.

"Say *Hai*," The woman said.

I was silent. The Japanese women started moving toward me with their clubs.

"Say *Hai,*" the Korean woman said again.

I opened my mouth trying to search, to select the right sounds, but all that came out was a broken scream. One of the Japanese women raised her club. "Talk or I will break your head!"

This time the loud humming sounds came out of my mouth one after another. They were thick, loud hums, like the voice of a dying moose. The people around were staring at me in shock and the head Japanese guard looked startled. She was one of those people who react to muteness, or any disability for that matter, impatiently and with great annoyance.

She was one of those who would hate anyone who was different from the usual shipment of girls. She hit me with her club with all her might. The club landed close to my ear. I could hear the loud, whistling sound of the strike echoing all over my brain. My face was burning and my shoulder went numb. I fell on the floor. The pain was unbearable, and I started screaming like an animal.

The scream of a mute is different from a normal scream. It is a scream that comes from the guts, from the depths of the soul. It does not sound like a regular scream. It is an indescribable, inhuman sound, one that freezes your blood in your veins.

Normal talking, and even screaming, does not come from the throat, the tongue or the teeth. They are the work of the brain. The minute the brain refuses to communicate with the physical features of the throat and mouth, all is lost. Nothing sounds normal any more.

Silent Marionette
침묵의꼭두각시

The other guards raised their clubs and came closer; they were probably ready to kill me, as long as they could shut off my frightening sounds.   Unexpectedly, Kumikko stepped forward. "She is mute. Have mercy!"

The guards stopped. "Mute?"

Kumikko then looked at me and said,
"I know this girl. She was born mute."

The Korean woman responded, "*Oke alzi? Nimza re ttan deso wa zzanne.*" (How do you know her? You come from another village)

"*Mon chin chok iraye.*" (She is a distant relative)

The Japanese guards looked at each other,
"How does a mute girl get here? There must be a mistake!"

"Get up!" one of them yelled. She was obviously uncomfortable with my muteness, but more so by what had been done to me,

"Can she hear?" she asked Kumikko.

"She can! Hai!"

"Is she mute from birth?"

"Hai!"

The guards appeared confused. I was still on the floor. The time-wheel stood still. My knees were shaking. I was angry at Kumikko for not letting them kill me; I wanted so badly to die. I was also angry with her for talking and risking her life. All the girls were staring at me in fear. They were probably annoyed with me for disturbing and slowing the process of finding out the reason why they had been brought here.

Neither the girls nor the guards could accept my muteness. They could not agree with this new scenario. This was a new concept, a person that does not speak. Was this prisoner now supposed to get special treatment? Mercy? Mercy was nowhere to be found in the Japanese dictionary, at least as applied to Korean prisoners.

Was I somebody they were supposed to ignore now? On the other hand, maybe they should watch out for me. They were all standing there, regarding me, clueless and nervous.

"Pick her up!" one of the guards told Kumikko.
Kumikko helped me up. They finished reading the list of names and then announced,

"Line up!"

"March!"

"Move!"

We walked in a straight row behind the guards into a large bathroom. The head guard barked,

"Strip!"

"Strip!"

"Strip!"

The head guard was a quiet one, but her quiet could be heard loudly. She was clearly in charge. The murderous look in her eyes, the narrow line of her tightly closed, thin lips, and the way she was swinging her club back and forth were so sharp that it seemed to me that even her friends were scared to death of her.

Silent Marionette
침묵의꼭두각시

We were all removing our clothes. The girls were trying to hide their private parts with their hands while the guards were smirking. I was wearing a simple silver necklace that Yong-soo had given me once when we were very young. I promised him never to take it off and now I was wondering what I should do with it. Perhaps I could I hide it. I took it off and held it in my closed palm, but where could I hide it?

The head guard looked at me over. "Have you ever been sick?"

I shook my head "No."

"Were there any sicknesses in the family?"

I shook "No."

"Did you ever have intercourse with a man?"

Was Toshihiro considered intercourse? I did not know. I shook my head "No," very uncertain.
The head guard came and checked my teeth. She touched my body as if she was examining a horse. She passed her hands on my breasts, my stomach, and my behind. She looked quite satisfied, but then she asked, "Were you born with a closed fist?"

I stood there silently with my head down.

"Show me what you have in your hand! Now!"

I opened my palm. She looked at the necklace. Her mouth now opened; she had lips somewhere there I could tell. The murderous look now turned to disgust.

"Throw away the dirt!"

Throw away the dirt, the only remaining object; the only proof of the fact that I had once lived some kind of a normal life. My shoulder was hurting, the ear was still ringing, and my back was aching.

"I said," she barked, "Throw away the dirt!"

Her club was ready to hit me again. It was hard to open my hand. It seemed that my fingers had been glued to the necklace.

Silent Marionette
침묵의꼭두각시

I tried to open them, but somehow my brain stopped cooperating with my body altogether. "Throw away the dirt!"

A thought came suddenly to mind. I was not stripped of everything. I still had my silence. Now I could open the palm of my hand just before she breaks my other shoulder apart and the necklace leaks out of my hand to the garbage.

I cannot tell if she is satisfied that she choked off my will power, my defiance, or whether she is just sorry for the lost opportunity to beat me up and let go of her frustrations. I just stood there naked in front of her, studying the expression on her face as if I once studied my brothers' maps.

She was uncomfortable with my stare. I could see the muscles on her face jumping nervously. *"Nugu na yak zomi in nen giya"* (Everybody has a weak point), I was thinking of Abazi's favorite saying. In addition, the knowledge hit me at that moment; this beast of a woman would be either death for me, or my only chance to live.

"Stop staring, pig! Get into the shower!" she shouted at me.
I had never been in a shower before. It felt good on my achy body. Each one of us got a bar of soap and a towel.

"Handal gan sayong hal begupu mi ni kkini gioka ra!" (Better remember this is your supply for a month!) The Korean woman said repeatedly as she handed them to the girls.

In the shower next to me, Kumikko was standing under the water. Her eyes closed, her hands stretched up above her pale, thin body, Kumikko was in another world. Her charcoal black hair lay on her back like a blanket. Her pretty, sculpted face was as white as the wall.

Kumikko wanted to live. She for sure had not had her last word. She had dreams and hopes. For sixteen years, she had planned her life carefully. She knew whom she would marry and how many children she would have.

Kumikko knew she was the best-looking girl in her village. She would rule the world with her beauty and clever way of looking at life. She had always gotten away with everything at home. She was her father's favorite, her mother's best friend, and her brothers and sisters were always there to always fulfill her wishes.

When her father used to get angry with her brothers, he would say four boys I have in this family, but the only one with balls is Mi-za (Kumikko). She always felt safe and sound. She was always in control. There were always people to love her, to comfort her, to hold her if she fell.

Now she was in turmoil. Her heart told her that she was not in a good place. Remarks she heard on the train, the smirks of the soldiers, it all rang wrong. She saw that each of the girls on the train looked healthy and very beautiful. Even a person who never went to school could add one and one.

They had lied to her, the bastards; they had lured her like a mouse into a trap! Nobody ever lied to Mi-za; she was the smartest girl in her village. She could read you inside out with just one look. However, this time, this one time, she was fooled, and she was running around in the trap aimlessly, looking for an escape route.

Nevertheless, Kumikko would not give up! She would show the bastards. The short devils would be sorry. She would show them what she was made of. Kumikko felt my stare and opened her eyes, and smiled to me an uncertain smile.

"*Wuzza denzi ham kke hazei....*" (Let's be always together.....), her voice echoed in my mind. I smiled back. What I would give to have my sister Pil-sun with me right now. I closed my eyes under the pouring water; my hand was touching the spot on my chest where the necklace had been hanging.

Yong-soo's beautiful, dark, almond shaped eyes were looking at me, "*Bora, Pil-nyoya, nabi aniga!*" (Look Pil-nyo it's a butterfly!) A single tear rolled down my cheek, under the shower's water. "*Naere nabiga delkki guman, nalgero naraso nere boro gagomal gaso.*" (I will soon be a butterfly Yong-soo; I will soon stretch my wings and fly to see you.)

My death is near. I can feel his desire for me. I hear his light footsteps behind my back. It will not be long now, Yong-soo; I will become a butterfly and fly straight to your arms. Up there in heaven all butterflies are free as the wind, free to love, free to sing, free to feel.

Three barks for each order

"Ilnare"!
 "Pottuk"!
"Ilnagre"!
(Get up! Get up! Get up!) Three screams from the guard's mouth. Kumikko was calling me from my sleep, to save me from the club's hit again. "*Yaya, bong bin dang hagi zone, ppottuk gazei*!" (Move faster or we are in trouble!)

The morning came cruel and bitter. It came as a surprise to me that I had slept all night without any nightmare. I had been so tired and weary that I had not moved all night.

Each one of us was given a cell, a small room more like a large cage. The cells were lined along both sides of the corridor in the building, and there were a Japanese style mattress (dadami), a blanket, a mirror, lipstick, condoms (sakku), toilet paper, and a comb. In front of each cell, the Japanese name of the comfort woman was written.   In the middle of the wall inside the entrance to the comfort station building regulations were posted along with a bar graph showing how many soldiers each of us had served during the day.

On top of it were slogans written in Japanese such as "Welcome victorious warriors of the sacred war," and "Comfort ladies serve you with all of our body and heart." There was a reception area inside the building, where yellow stamps, military scrip, or money was handed over.

I get up and put the dress on my body, and look at myself in the mirror. This person in front of me is a different person. I look so small, thin and pale. I apply the lipstick to my dry lips. Abazi would kill me if he would see lipstick on my face.   Only bad women used make up, he would say. I brush my hair slowly; my mind is wandering to the forests near the village. I am flying there with the butterflies. The mornings in the forests are so lush and fresh. "Bora Pil-nyoya nabi aniga." (Look Pil-nyo it is a butterfly!)

"Fast,
 Fast
Go fast!"

The guards yell and we are all running out to line up. Order is important for the Japanese. No matter what you do, or where you go, order is crucial. You have to always be in line, always march in line, always think in line. They take us to a dining area where each one of us gets a small bowl of rice mixed with millet, and a small cup of tea. An older woman seats me.

The women look at the newcomers with hatred. It is clear that they are not happy with us. The older prisoners feel uncomfortable around all of us new girls. We are a threat; we look healthier and fresher. Why it is that the old always clashes with the new? What is the source of this disconnection? Why is there the lack of confidence of the old?

We new ones are scared, deathly scared. We do not know what to expect; we have not learned the routine yet. Why would the others feel threatened by us?

I am looking for Kumikko but she is seated in another section, her back to me. There is a small comfort with every evil. At least her cell is right next to mine.

The woman next to me looks like she is my mother's age or even older. She gives me a nasty scowl and then focuses totally on her bowl. She is using her chopsticks as close as she can to her mouth and swallowing the food so fast; I never saw a woman eat like this.

I look at my bowl and nausea chokes me. There is knot in my throat; I cannot eat. She finishes her bowl, licks it dry, and then looks at mine with burning eyes. I pass my chopsticks to my ball and put one grain at the time in my mouth slowly. I chew unwillingly. I do not have any appetite; I cannot even swallow. I take small sips from my tea and look around confused and surprised. Is this reality?

The facial expression of the woman next to me has now completely changed; her eyes are no longer regarding me with hate, but with a begging expression. She is fixated on my food, following my hand that is moving from the bowl to my mouth, and then lifting her eyes, watching me chew slowly on each single grain. She looks so neglected and lonely. Our eyes meet and she sighs a heavy sigh.

My heart is shrinking and I push my bowl to her, changing it with her empty one. Slowly, slowly, she raises her head suspiciously, surprised. She cannot believe it. She passes her eyes from the bowl to me, and then in one quick move she grabs the chopsticks and swallows everything. She looks at me again and grabs her tea, but as if she is thinking about it again, she places it back on the table and bursts out in a loud, horrible cry.

"Quiet!" The guard barks.
The woman is loosening up helplessly, and then calms down. I squeeze her hand under the table to comfort her. The woman whispers, "*Nin nugo*?" (What is your name?)

I form my lips "Maikko"

"*Missa rigo*?" (How old are you?)

I show her with my fingers fourteen.

"*Naen malbong ira, nain yoril gop igo*" (My name is Mal-bong (末峰), I am seventeen.)

I shake my head in disbelief, and motion with my hand, "What?"

"*Yerilgo bi ra kai*" (Seventeen)

My all body freezes, now I want to get up and run away, to scream a bitter scream. As if I am in a nightmare I am trying to get up, but my body is paralyzed. It does not want to listen to me.

She is three years older than I am, and I thought she was older than my mother was... "They will show you, the Japanese, they will teach you a thing or two..." I remember the soldier saying to Kumikko. My body is in chills; I feel my head burning hot. I look at her again in disbelief. I move to pat her knee, to comfort her; I cannot make myself touch her.

At the edge of the dining room one of the guards is beating a girl. She is waving her club up and down on the girl's back. I am looking at the guard's face as she is totally focused on the beating that she is applying, and I am thinking maybe she comes from a nice home somewhere in Japan. Maybe she has a cute little cat with green eyes. Maybe she has a beautiful bird in a cage. Maybe she planted nice flowers behind her house. She was a baby once; she nursed at her mother's breasts just like the girl she is beating now. From where all the cruelty? From where all the anger? The Japanese's authorities did not tell her to break Innocent girls' bones, and even if they did, she could bend the rules a bit.

I never understood the motives for human cruelty and nastiness, especially from those whose lives were in order and who were not missing anything. I could never figure out why the sick, the poor, the hungry, and the homeless were the nice ones, and those who had their fame, their belly full, and who slept safely at night knowing that they'd never a lack a thing, were nasty and cruel.

Get up!
Get up!
Get up!

Always three times. I noticed they always barked their orders three times in a row.

Fast!
Fast!
Fast!
In line!
Make a line!
Line up!

We stand in line, a long line of shadows of women. The head guard Namie is passing among us, her club waving back and forth. She examines each of us with disdain as if she is trying to guess who will survive her torture and who will fall down and die. She is looking at us as if we were fish. When you bring fish out of the water some of them die right away, some of them live a little longer…

Silent Marionette
침묵의꼭두각시

Doctor Visit! she barks,
Doctor!
Doctor!
The other guards echo her. We walk in a straight line to the edge
of the building.
Stand still!
Quiet!
Don't move!

We stand silently, our eyes on the floor. The girls go in one by
one in turn. They are all bent down as if they want to melt into
the ground, as if they are all praying to the Buddha of the floor,
"Please great Buddha, save us! Please great Buddha love us!
Please great Buddha, make this all go away! Please great Buddha
of the floor open up and swallow us now!"

Screaming and yelling wake us up from our prayers. All heads
turn. Namie is dragging a girl out of the doctor's room. What
had she done, poor little thing, to anger her so? Namie is
standing above the girl's body and slams the club into her
without stopping, without even taking a break to breathe. She
seems to be exercising a special religious ritual.

She beats the girl for the goal of beating, not for the goal of
teaching her a lesson. The guard's eyes are dead, her arm
movements are mechanical, and it is all beyond my
understanding. My mouth opens to breathe some air, my ears
are ringing loudly, and my heart is bursting. Ho! Death, what
takes you so long? Come and take me, please come!

The girl is lying on the floor and the slams are falling hard on her
legs, on her head, or her hands. The girl is howling to God. She
twitches, she shakes all over, she bites her lips until they bleed,
and she tears her hair out of her scalp. Her teeth are exposed in
her wide-open mouth; her eyes are coming out of their sockets.
She is screaming, "*Omeyo! Omeyo!*"

But Namie San, the head guard, is standing above her quiet, composed, no screaming, and no yelling any more, and keeps the club going up and down, her face in a craze. There are no mommies here in Namie's establishment, no daddies, no mercy. Namie is the full authority; she is your mom, your dad, your absolute god.

The girl is praying now to Buddha, "*Zibal zil dekko gai so, zi moksim ga ga sigo imi chin zitkko riro, buchoni mi kkin ne zusoye.*" (Take me please, let me die, good great Buddha let this madness stop!), But Namie will not let her faint. She is now having a personal fight with Buddha; she will not let him have her victim yet. She is as stubborn as a donkey. She will let that girl scream and cry a very long time before she will let her die.

Next!
Next!
Next!

Hai Oisa Sensei- Mr. Doctor

It was my turn. I entered the doctor's office. On my way, I stepped over the beaten girl. She was quiet now, lying there very silent, empty, and dead. Only the echoes of her screams were hanging in the air like a heavy cloud of black fog.

The doctor, a middle-aged man, was sitting behind his desk. His nose was in his books, and he was writing something.

Strip!
Strip!
Strip!

The doctor looked up annoyed and said to the Korean guard, "I told you not to raise your voice in my office!"

"But she is mute, Oisa Sensei, Mister Doctor!"

"Is she deaf too?"

"No Oisa Sensei, Mister Doctor"

"So stop screaming." he snapped at her. The Korean guard closed her lips, and her face reddened. She froze to her spot at attention and put her head down.

The doctor got up from his chair and came toward me slowly. "Take off your clothes, child." The doctor had a pleasant, calming voice. He was a nice man, I was sure of that. If not for the damn war he would probably have been saving lives in a hospital and then going to his cozy home to play soccer with his little children.

He stepped around me looking at my naked body and then stopped at once. He was examining the long black and blue mark on my shoulder that Namie had stamped on me with her club.

"What's this?" he demanded.

The guard was silent now.

"When did this happen?"

"Oisa Sensei, Doctor Sir "she stammered, "I did not hit her, Doctor Sir"

"Then who did it?" his voice raised now impatiently.

"It was Namie San sir!"

"Namie again, may I ask why?" he stepped now close to the guard's face; her lips were shaking nervously,

"We did not know she was mute; we thought she just refused to answer when we called her name Doctor, sir!"

The doctor sighed a deep sigh; he was obviously tired and annoyed. It seemed to me that he hated being there in his little hospital room. He hated Namie, the guards, the place and maybe even himself. The doctor was clearly out of place there.

This was certainly not what he ever dreamed about when he went to medical school; it was far from what he ever thought that he would do with his life. He touched my shoulder and applied some ointment on it silently. He was clearly unhappy. He checked my eyes and my breasts, and then told me to open my mouth.

"Were you born mute?"

I shook my head no.

"When did you stop talking, child?"

Silent Marionette
침묵의꼭두각시

He had pleasant face, the doctor. He reminded me of my uncle; something in his face brought my uncle Joong-gu to mind. He was my father's youngest brother, but unlike my father, he loved kids. He never got married and treated us as his own. There was always something in his pockets for us, a cheap candy, a toy he had made out of wood, a unique stone.

I then started crying a loud cry of a baby in pain. The tears came out like a rainstorm and the doctor was standing there watching me. His eyes were so sad, oh so sad. Sometimes a mute needs to cry. Most mutes are not used to seeing sympathetic faces. It is usually nervous, annoyed, angry, uncomfortable and distressed faces around us.

So I cried now, loudly and without shame. I could not stop crying. My tears were streaming down like river. The doctor turned to the guard and said anxiously, "This one, nobody touches! If anybody hits her again he or she will have to answer me personally!"

"Hai Oisa Sensei, Doctor Sir!"

"Sit on the chair, child."

I wiped my tears with the back of my hand. The guard was opening my legs wide and tying them to poles on both sides. My insides were exposed before the world. *"Dariro in nen dero boli rei, gire ya dol apuni kkane"* (Stretch your feet as much as you can; you will not feel the pain as much) the Korean woman said to me with unexpected softness.

I stretch my legs, big drops of sweat coming out of my naked body; my teeth are biting my lower lip without mercy. "Buddha, dear good Buddha, please save me!" My lower spine is hurting like hell. The doctor covers his hands with rubber gloves and then sticks a metal instrument inside me.

The pain is so sharp, my body shakes wildly. I want to scream, but the voice is stuck somewhere in my insides. I can feel my blood streaming out without stopping *"Omani! Omani! Nere zuko malga siyo!"* (Mom! Mom! I want to die!)

The sharp pain is crawling from my forehead to my toes. Everything is burning, everything is shaking. The blood is now streaming out of my lips. I tear my lips apart biting on them. He finally takes the instrument out of me, and puts some cotton between my legs. Then he unties my legs and sits me straight up. He gives me a comforting look and says, "Don't be afraid, child, the pain will be gone in a few days."

He turns to the guard and tells her to bring me water; I drink the water willingly. The guard then says, "Get up Maikko San!"
I am surprised; I did not think any guard would ever call me by my name.
I am trying to get up, but I drop right back on the chair in pain. Whatever the doctor did to me tore me apart. I give a loud groan and start weeping again. What kind of loathsome, abhorrent, detestable thing has been done to me?

"Please get up, Maikko San," she says, partly begging now.
I give her a loud groan again, and then a scream.
She takes two steps backwards frightened.

"Let her rest here for a while; leave her be!" the doctor complains in anger, and then sits in his chair, tired. He puts his head in his hands, as if he has a tremendous headache.

Meng-Sun (盟順) drops her arms helplessly; she will have to answer to Namie now. What kind of mess had her husband gotten her into, taking her from her family and her village and selling their souls to the Japanese for money that was not worth even bragging about?

Silent Marionette
침묵의꼭두각시

If she thought that his bad habits would be gone in Manchuria, it was a very big mistake. He was the same aggressive, violent, bad creature he had always been. Nothing changes when you move from one place to another. It just gets worse. Here she was all alone, with no relatives or friends, slaving for his needs and dealing with the likes of Namie.

All she has for a bit of affection is her cat. Cats too are ungrateful creatures, but they at least let you pet their soft fur and greet you with respect. If she thought to finish the doctor visits early, and go and relax in her room for a good afternoon nap with her beloved cat, well the doctor had now ruined it for her.

"The Japanese soldiers will teach you a thing or two…." I hear the voice in my head again. I am now officially a *Jong gun wian bu*" (Japanese comfort lady – 從軍慰安婦). There is no way back. I will never be a proper woman, never be a mother. The stamp of evil, the great Japanese machine, has stamped me for good. The great monster that controls this planet owns me now. I look through the window. The apathetic, indifferent sky is watching me. A strong Chinese sun is boiling out there, and the trees are moving slowly in the light wind. Nature is still nature.

The brothel

Back in our cells, the new girls were whining on their mattresses. None of them really knew what the doctor had done to them with his instrument. They were all in pain, all bleeding heavily. I was lying like a torn up bird, my insides burning, and the whole body in agony. The Korean lady came in to change the pads between my legs and said, "*Gumsi nal kkira, mechil man zinama tongzing do sara zil kkira.*" (It will go away; in few days, you will not have any pain.)

I gave a cry, a painful cry, and she said quietly, "*Naedo zoson sare mida, ode zoaso izi kkori hagen no*" (I am a Korean too, don't you think for a minute that I am enjoying this!)
And then before she left the room she said, "*Nen Meng-sunira, nin nas nen dero ganho won sikin da kade. Zon saramin gapda*"
(My name is Meng-sun (盟順). When you will feel better, you will be trained as a nurse. You can work at the doctor's office; he is a very nice man.)

That was good news; I was going to do real work. The doctor was a good man; he would be good to me, I thought; but my doubts did not leave me. Mother told me that there are instincts and then there is that third instinct you should rely on, when you are confused. Now my third instinct warned me not to start calming down.

Kumikko asked one of the women who were there before us what the doctor had done to us, and that one smirked and laughed a bitter laugh. "He put a tattoo inside you; you now belong to Imperial Japan. "*Zonzeng kki kkazi wurin oenomdul norige sinsen gira.*" (We will belong to the Japanese until the end of the war) said Kumikko to me.

Kumikko now was crying in her blanket; the bastards had gotten her badly. "The Japanese soldiers will teach you how to push a man, my little kitten. ..." She was bleeding heavily. They had tattooed her, the bastards. Kumikko was the smartest, prettiest girl on earth, and here she was lying on the floor like a little slaughtered animal. She was trying to stop her crying, but the pain was shooting needles in her spine.

Her guts were turning upside down. "This one is very pretty'." Namie said to her guards when she saw her. "The soldiers will be satisfied." Her voice echoed in Kumikko's ears. "The soldiers will be satisfied..." Namie's voice did not leave her as she was curling her body all the way to her forehead in excruciating pain. "The bastards," she mumbled repeatedly. Then she covered her face. *"Omui, Abazi ye, nae zzom salido..."* (Mom, dad, help me..)

The guards are coming back and forth to the newcomers' cells, with cotton and food and drinks. We can hear the other women complain grumpily, all the way, from the other side, "Those little whores are eating and drinking like cows while we are starving here".... Then the doors open to the footsteps of heavy boots, the sound of the metal of guns. The soldiers are laughing; some of them are drunk.

We cannot see what is going on in the cells on the other side of the building. We can just imagine. Some girls are crying, some screaming from pain. There are heavy sounds of moaning. Some screams are painful.

We can hear the soldiers' orders. "Lie down! Bend down!" Some curse, "Chinese whore! Korean whore!" Now we know where we are; now we know who we are. We belong to Imperial Japan; we are marionettes for the Japanese soldiers to play with.

Every day at the same time, the doors open and the new girls are lying on the mattresses. Hiding their faces under the blankets, they push their fingers in their ears, not to hear what they dread hearing. The screaming of the celebrating Japanese is reaching me from far away.

I am wondering if I am losing my hearing too. My ears seem to be blocked. "The Japanese soldiers will teach you a thing or two..." At night, Namie and her friends are cleaning up the cages. You can hear a desperate cry and then the dragging of a body.

"Too many complaints!" Namie's voice is raised, or "Too used!" I am wondering in my fifth day in the cell if Mal-bong is still there.

Namie holds the key for each one of us for life or death. She is the high authority, the final decision maker as to who will live and who will disappear one night and never be seen again. Namie is like a god. She can give us life and then again she can kill us in an instant.

Namie is a short thick woman. Her uniforms are snug and smooth on her, as if she was born in them. Her lips are thin and contracted to a tight circle, her eyes are two narrow passes, and in spite of her age, acne ravages her face. It is a high probability that all her life men have ignored her in disgust. She would examine the young soldiers, her eyes wandering down to their genitals, as if she was trying to measure their size.

She would flatter the good-looking ones, hoping for attention, but they always stepped aside, uncomfortable with her presence. Some of them would not even be shy about showing their disdain. None of them gives her a second look. They all prefer to go to the cells and get the service of the lowly marionettes.

Namie is unhappy; her sexual desires, her lust for a man's arms, for comfort, for a bit of affection, are growing in her body like a cancer. Like a lioness in heat she strolls around the cells, listening to the moans of the soldiers. She is looking carefully at each cell, officially checking that the girls are doing their jobs right.

Silent Marionette
침묵의꼭두각시

She is stopping, looking in great envy at the well built behind of a soldier, going up and down on top of a marionette, crying, moaning his joy. That particular girl will suffer from Namie's jealousy later. She will direct her unfulfilled desires into the body of that girl with her club; she will beat her until the girl loses consciousness.

In the cell near me, Kumikko is singing quietly, as if it is the last thing she can do before losing her mind,

"Ask how many friends I have?
Water and stone, bamboo and pine.
The moon rising over the eastern hill is a joyful comrade.
Beside these five companions,
What other pleasure should I ask?"

Namie had already eyed Kumikko. Now there was a girl she would love to fight. The Korean garbage for a whore had everything Namie did not have. She was pretty, smart, witty, and had a great body with long, long legs. Her figure was the figure of a ballet dancer. Namie did not yell at Kumikko. Ever since the first day of our arrival she had plans to take care of Kumikko in a different way.

Knowing that the pretty girl would turn out to be a hit in the comfort house, she will fight her with her own very special strategy. This one will not get the screaming and the club. Namie has a plan; she hates pretty little desirable marionettes, especially the smart ones. She has something very unique in mind for Kumikko. She will wait for her quietly in the corner like a beast waiting for her victim.

I hear Kumikko as she raises her voice singing louder, as usual whenever she hears Namie's footsteps by her cell. Kumikko knows, she feels the jealousy. She knows very well that Namie has special plans for her, but she will show her who is stronger. She will fight her fight; she will show all of those bastards what she is made of. She will sing, dance, and live her life. She will come out on top; she will teach the bastards a thing or two....

Namie likes to come and let a girl know that she has had too many complaints. She also likes it when a marionette is getting too used and is not desired by the soldiers anymore. She arrives at the undesirable girl's cell, her club swinging side to side, an expression of total satisfaction on her face.

The narrow openings that are her eyes are glowing with the special light of excitement. The girl gets up without being asked to, and stands before Namie. She stares at her quietly, as if she is hypnotized. They are both beasts, and her prisoner knows that the victim belongs only to Namie now, in body and soul.

Namie's lips are tightening. Her mouth has shrunk into a tiny, nasty hole. Then she opens her lips with delight. Her sharp little rat's teeth are exposed; she is looking at the girl with the eyes of a cobra before it decides to strike.

Very peacefully and quietly she says to the girl, "Pick up all your things; you are coming with me." She passes her tongue slowly over her thin, pale lips.
The girl looks like she is in shock; she does not scream, she does not cry, knowing that her death is now finally coming. She is mumbling to herself. It may be a prayer to Buddha, or possibly she is saying her last goodbyes. Whoever is dragged to the basement by Namie never comes back.

They are both marching slowly downstairs. There Namie will satisfy all her secret wild sexual fantasies with the girl before she does her the favor of choking her to death.

I look at their backs and my soul is bleeding. She could be my sister, my mother, that pale, little, skinny, shivering girl who is marching to her painful death behind Namie-San.

Silent Marionette
침묵의꼭두각시

My tears are coming down my face; each tear is bigger than the other. I am crying, mourning the poor soul long before she is dead. Namie-San will take her sweet time with her today, since this one is a pretty girl. I am wondering, where is Buddha? Is he watching us right now; is he looking at the poor girl going to her death? How can he allow this to be happening? What wrong did this young girl ever do in her life?

Maybe Buddha himself is feeling as useless and helpless as I do. Maybe he is rolling in his pain, sobbing, watching our horrendous fate and turning his face away, not to watch the outcome.

A silent marionette

The day the doors opened to our cells and the screaming came:
Get up!
Get up!
Get up!
We knew that we were ready to start working. The pain had gone, the body had healed, and we had gotten stronger. Only the burning was still there. Later one of the girls told me that most of the girls were not sterilized in the past. They would put them right to work and whoever got pregnant would be killed with her baby, or, if she was exceptionally talented as a comfort woman, she would be sterilized and then put back to work.

There was no fear in my heart. The doctor would take me to his office. He was a nice man. How could I entertain the soldiers if I could not talk? He understood it very well, I thought.

Even Namie was not interested in me. I was no match for her since I could not scream from pain properly and could not beg her for my life. What thrill could she get from me? Mutes were not exactly her cup of tea; mutes were no fun, no challenge. She liked them loud; she liked them dramatic and talkative. She would take the Koreans, she would take those Chinese, and she would even take Japanese as long as they were not mute.

We got our bowl of rice again for breakfast and a cup of tea. The good days were over. When we were recovering in our cells, we got white rice three times a day, sometimes even vegetables and soup. Now when we were ready to work it was back to the hunger diet. I was seated by two new Chinese girls and looking for Mal-bong. To my relief she was still there. Our eyes met, and she raised her brows as a sign that she recognized me.

The two Chinese girls looked like they could be twins. They were small and skinny, and hung onto each other desperately. Nausea was choking me again; now I knew better than to give my food away. I forced myself to swallow. The rice was mixed with millet; I could feel each grain in my throat, and I was trying to wash them down with the tea.

One of the Chinese girls was looking at me now and smiled sadly. I smiled back. *"Nizhiao shonn ma ming tz?"* (What is your name?) She whispered. She could not speak Japanese very well. They looked like peasant girls, beautiful as newborn butterflies. My heart soured. I was wondering if they had any idea what they were there for.

I signed to her that I could not talk. The girl was horrified, and whispered frantically to her friend, who now turned to me and gave me a sympathetic look.

"Maikko," I formed with my lips.

"Maikko san," she repeated.

The girls both repeated my name successfully. They did not look older than thirteen. They held each other's hands under the table as if they were afraid that any minute a guard would tear them apart.

"Wo shi (my name is) Lee-ping," one girl whispered, and then pointed to her friend, "Liu-fang."
I nodded my head; both Lee-ping and Liu-fang looked like little frightened rabbits. I felt a shiver in my spine; those little things would not survive long.

I closed my eyes,
"Arirang, arirang, arariyo.
Arirang gogaero noma ganda..."

Abazi, a proud Korean, was now looking at me from heaven. "I am here suffering for my country, Abazi. I am a victim of war, Abazi. I am not a *chokppari chang nyo"* (Short devil's prostitute).

Yong-soo told me that when we grew up and got married he would take me all the way to China and build me a pretty house. Yong-soo said that in China, "You don't have to work; all you have to do is to walk around the streets and pick the food from the trees."

The Yangtze River (揚子江) is full of fat fish and sweet water, and the rice fields are blessed. Young-soo told me that China, unlike Korea, had the best earth for growing crops and that is why we would have an easy, happy life. Yong-soo too dreamed about leaving the village. He felt that he could stretch his wings if he could just get away from his simple family, away from the heavy expectations. He felt that he would be able to bring the moon to me, if we could just get away.

Once, Young-soo went to see his family in Pyongyang (平壤). When he came back, he gave me the silver necklace. He said he had been thinking only of me there, and when his uncle gave him some money for candy, he had spent it on a present for me. Now here I was in China, his dreamland, and there was no Yong-soo, no house, and my necklace had gone to the trash.

"Throw away the dirt!" My tears were leaking into my tea now. Mal-bong was looking at me from the other end of the room, worried, and Liu-fang was wiping my tears with her gentle finger. *"Ppuya oku"* (do not cry) she whispered. Then, without any connection to anything, she said, "They raped my sisters, and then cut their breasts off!" Her face was blank; her mouth moved as if she were talking about the weather.

"They raped my mother and then cut off her head!" echoed Lee-ping.

I kept weeping; my head started hurting. I was getting one of my terrible migraines.

"Then," she went on, not blinking an eye, "they pushed a stick in between her legs."

I now raised my head in shock and looked at the two rabbits. I was touching their hands that were trapped in each other, and Liu-fang was whispering as if to herself, "*Woxiangs*" (I want to die).

"Line up!"
"Line up!"
"Line up!"

I wipe my tears. It is the scariest time of the day. The marionettes have to clean their cells and arrange the mattresses so that not a wrinkle is shown. The dishes have to sit on the upper shelf sparkling clean; God forbid the guards will find a spot on them. The smell of perfume has to be spread all over the room and sprayed on the linens. The girls are standing straight at attention. They are pale and tense; their hands are trembling, and their legs shaking.

The guards arrive, a group of seven, but all you can hear are Namie's decisive boot steps. She never wears shoes; only boots. It makes her feel her authority. She is the absolute queen in her little palace.

Namie never amounted to anything out in the world. Here was her domain, her property, a place where she could feel like a powerful human being. Her boots were heavy leather. They gave more weight to the kicking in the girls' stomachs or thighs.

Namie and her flock stop by each cell, and the girls' hearts are beating loudly. "Please Buddha, Buddha, please help me!"

Namie bends down and shuts her right eye. She measures the blanket on both sides, as if she is a trained mattress engineer, to see If one side hangs lower than the other. Namie was hand picked for this job and she will do it well. She will show the miserable whores what Japanese order is.

If one of the girls makes a mistake, immediately she orders Meng-sun to write her up. Then she looks at her victim, her hands crossed on her chest, one booted leg stepping forward. She now exposes her rat's teeth, and if the victim is a pretty girl, her joy will be seven times greater.

Then she punishes the girl with her club, making sure it lands on her back, her behind, and the inner thighs, all the body parts that the lowly marionette needs for work. The girl's body will turn to one mass of pain. She will not be able to move, not even spread her legs.

Then the guest will make a complaint. The girl did not fulfill his wishes; she could not act on his fantasies. Namie then will have another reason to beat the pretty little marionette to death.

Now it is time. The doors are opened to the second floor; very soon the girls will dress their faces with a smile. They will act the joy, the carefree air that the Japanese soldiers want to see. The soldiers are nervous and worried. They are going to the front to die. This might be the last time they will have fun, and the last time they will be with a girl. They are coming here as if coming to say goodbye to life.

The comfort women's job is to make them happy, to send them off to kill or to be killed peacefully. Now all the new girls know why they are here, and what exactly their mission is.

It is silent on the second floor; the girls are sitting on their mattresses waiting for their fate. The soldiers' voices are getting louder and louder, their heavy boot steps up the stairs are closer and closer.

Now the second floor is full of noises, screaming, laughing, and moaning. The girls are smiling but their smiles are crying. A young soldier comes into my cell and takes off his hat. There is a misunderstanding; there must be a mistake. I am not a regular marionette. I am supposed to be working for the doctor. I jump up on my feet and sign him frantically "No! Go away!"

The soldier looks at me confused, "What do you want?"
"No" I shake my head.
"You want to play with me? Now that is a new game," the soldier frowns.

I try to go to the door, but he catches me. "I got you, little kitten," he laughs and throws me on the dadami. I try to push him away but that makes him more determined. He pins me down. I am not able to move now, I cannot run away. He is lying on top of me. I cannot breathe. "Oh good Buddha, help me!"

I stop fighting now. I have been trapped. I close my eyes. I can feel the beast somewhere in my body. I do not feel pain, just the lack of oxygen. The screaming from the cells around his heavy breathing and me are mixing in my mind, and I can hear the soldier whining in my ear. I can smell his sweaty body. His mouth now opens; his brownish teeth are exposed like a dog's fangs. "You wait and see what the Japanese soldiers will do to you! They will teach you a thing or two...."

He is pushing himself inside me, inside my most personal private space. My brain is rushing blood into my guts, everything is burning, and even the mattress is burning. He is holding my breasts tight; it is hurting like hell. He squeezes them more and more, as if he is trying to tear them apart.

I retaliate now. I try to fight. I scratch and hit. I try to kick, but that makes him even more interested. He pins me down and laughs.

Now I stop fighting. There is no use. I accept my fate. I will never be a nurse; I will never work for the nice doctor. Meng-sun lied to me, the lousy bitch traitor. I feel his hand now on my neck; he will kill me now. "Die, Pil-nyo, die. Please, Buddha, make me die!" I am screaming in the silence of my heart. When is it going to be over? Make him stop. He is inside my most private space, the center of my innocence. Now whatever remains of my purity, my pride, are invaded, humiliated, raped to pieces.

Silent Marionette
침묵의꼭두각시

Korean people are brave people

In the cell across from me Kumikko is lying quietly, pale and helpless under a heavy, fat officer. I can see his big behind going up and down above her; I can see her nails digging in his back. She is quiet; she is cooperating, my poor Kumikko.

Next to her cell, Mal-bong is bending over a man; her head is pushing forward and back, like the top of an air pump. Then the man gets up to leave. Mal-bong stops him her arms, holding onto him, worried to death. "Was the master happy with my service?" The Japanese pushes her away, spits and turns to go. Mal-bong drops on the dadami wondering, "Was he happy?" and washes the condom for the next one.

The new girls do not have to worry about condoms. They will not get pregnant because they have been sterilized, but the others have to use one condom for a whole month, washing it after every service. The soldier finally leaves my body and gets up.

The air is starting to return to my lungs. Now I can feel my pain, my insides are burning and the nausea is sitting in my guts. He leaves behind the payment, some yellow stamps. "If I live to come back, I will ask for you again, little kitten. I really enjoyed our game." He smiles and takes a pack of candy from his pocket, and drops it on my naked body.

The second one comes in. I have not even washed yet from the first one. I am still lying there frozen. I am not smiling; I am just turning my head towards Kumikko's cell. She too is still lying there in shock, mumbling. A young officer is bending naked by her. Kumikko's eyes are closed. I can see her small feet stretching toward me. I feel the heavy breath on my face, the stink of his sweat mixing with mine.

He is digging in my body brutally. I do not feel the pain; I do not feel anything. It is as if my body has been separated from my nervous system. I can see Kumikko's lifeless legs moving up and down, I cannot hear her voice, but I can hear the soldier above her moaning loudly. He keeps uttering, "Mother, dear God, Mother." He is calling his mother desperately. Out of the most intimate act of his life, he is longing for his mother.

Kumikko is frozen under him; she is still in too much of a shock to play mommy to him. Namie will make sure to send her the most difficult cases, the angry, the confused, the depressed and the brutal. Those are being kept for the pretty girls. Namie has a good eye for the boys; she knows instantly, as she gives them a sharp look, which girl she will send them to. She is running a high-class brothel here, the best-reputed brothel in all of China. It is clean and efficient, the discipline is super class, and most soldiers come out happy.

Outside the trees are moving. I can see a bird landing on one of the branches. She is sitting on the edge of my window watching me curiously lying there under the third one. Namie warns the soldiers before they come in that I am mute, but pretty. "There will not be a conversation or entertainment; you can only lie with her," she says.

The line outside is too long. The soldiers have a very short vacation before they go back to the front. They cannot really choose much. They would like to sit and tell the girls about their pains, their fears, and their families. However, there is no time; they have to focus on the immediate physical relief and clear the way for the next one.

My line is going the fastest of all. Each soldier has thirty minutes to spend with a marionette and each officer has one hour, most of them spend their time talking, torturing, and thinking of ways to get out their frustrations or sexual fantasies.

Since they assume that a mute cannot hear their requests and cannot scream at the time of torture, they just do what they came to do and leave. Namie is happy. I am a clean cut, efficient marionette. They go into my cell and come out after ten minutes. I keep the line moving fast. I must have received thirty soldiers that day. Namie San blurts out at me, "Good job, mute!"

Yes, there is a big plus in being a mute; the soldiers immediately assume that I am also deaf, and in general completely disabled. They believe that if I cannot communicate with them verbally, then most likely I would not be able to communicate with them physically either.

They drop on me, do what they came to do, and leave. There is no reason to hit, to curse, or to demand special things. I am lucky I am handicapped.

Mal-bong in the next cell is screaming again from pain. Now I can tell where the noises are coming from. Once one becomes mute, the sense of hearing is sharpened. I can tell whose voice is whose. Until 8:00 pm when the comfort ladies are finished with their work day, I learn to select in my mind each cell and I listen to every little sound.

When the heavily breathing, sweating bodies are on me, I play the game of determining which cries belong to which girls. Kumikko has been quiet the whole day. She is receiving her last officer of the day. The time now is 7:00 pm; in an hour, the gong will sound and the workday will finally be over.

The officer is sitting by Kumikko's mattress; he does not take off his uniform for some reason.
"You are pretty," he says to Kumikko. "Can you please sing me a song?"
Kumikko sits down. She is in shock.

The officer does not even take off his jacket. He has a sad look; his head is down. Namie probably thought that he was depressed enough that he would beat Kumikko to death or demand some crazy sexual acts from her. An hour with a depressed man can bring a marionette almost a certain death. However, this officer is just sad, very sad.

Kumikko straightens her dress on her sweaty body. She is looking at the officer and thinking, "This is a strange thing." After passing the whole day with crazy soldiers and officers, her body no longer responds to the pains, her nervous system is shut, her heart is broken. And now this.

"Arirang, arirang, arariyo
Arirang gogaero noma ganda."

Her voice is breaking; the officer raises his head and looks at her sadly, a tear coming down his cheek.

"Narel borigo gasi nen nim eun
Simli do mot gaso bal byung nanda."

Kumikko is crying quietly now, crying like a baby. I am getting worried there under my last sweaty, moaning soldier. Crying is against procedure. Namie will come into the cell in a second and cut Kumikko's head off for this crime. However, the officer takes a handkerchief out of his pocket and wipes her tears.

"Once I was in Korea," he says. "Korean people are brave people." He is lowering his voice. Kumikko is weeping and putting her tired head on his shoulder. The officer looks at her surprised, and then his eyes fill with softness. He puts his arms around her shoulders and pets her hair gently.

"It's my first day," she says. "They cheated me, they tricked me, and like a mouse they trapped me!"

The officer is silent; he just pets her hair.
"War is a repulsive business, disgusting thing," he says, another tear rolling down his face. "Who would think that there is so

much ugliness and evil in the world; even animals don't hurt one another unless it's for survival. Here people are killing, torturing, humiliating, and raping just for the sake of doing these things." He lowers his eyes.

The gong sounds. It is time. He gets up and walks slowly out of the cell, leaving Kumikko sitting there, her face in her hands. The skies outside are now covered with black clouds. The Manchurian farmers are happy; the rain will finally come.

At attention for death!

Okkiru!
Okirru!
Okirru!

Get up!
Get up!
Get up!

I am hungry, so hungry; all I think about day and night is food, food, and food.

Line up!
Line up!
Straight line!

I grab a clean towel from Meng-sun. It has been a month now that she has been avoiding my eyes, my blaming looks. I give her a burning glare. "May you rot in hell" I am thinking. The lying bitch told me that I was being sent to the doctor's office, that I would be a nurse. She knows she is guilty.

Every day that month, I would count the soldiers and officers up to fifteen and then stop counting. Namie will one day announce me as the whore of the year. I am as fast as a rabbit. The men come and go like a stream and without any incidents. There is not one complaint on my record. All the guards are happy with me; I am the favorite mute prostitute in the building.

The shower is the only luxury of the day. The girls are standing under the water in quiet trauma. We are all silent. There is really nothing to say. Eventually every girl turns mute in the comfort women's station.

Mal-bong is standing next to me, her eyes closed as if this is her last shower. Her body looks like the body of an old woman. She is only seventeen, I have to remind myself. She is covered with bruises. Why does everybody like to hurt her so much? There is not one little inch on her body that is not scarred.

She has been here for three years now and has never learned the formula for how to protect herself from beatings. Her father was a doctor; her family was a respected, rich family in town.

Mal-bong was kidnapped on her way to the clinic one day, to bring her father his lunch. Mal-bong is considered the eldest of the girls here; most women do not last more than a year. In one month, I have seen more girls disappear than survive. You never know if the same girl you see today will still be there tomorrow.

Mal-bong's breasts look like two hollow balls; her body is swollen from hunger; her behind is two deep valleys and around them bones, just bones; her neck is veins and arteries. Nobody knows why Namie has not finished with her yet. Maybe it is one of her devious experiments to see how long a woman can live in torture, hardship, and hunger before she falls dead.

Lee-ping wraps her skinny body in a towel. She is a daughter of very well to do peasants. Her father was the head of her village. She was an only child; her mother's womb had closed for good after she had had her one daughter. The girl was the center of attention in her family. Her grandparents and her aunts and uncles just adored her. She was the flower of the village, the prettiest girl in China. That is what people would say about her.

When the Japanese came into her village to rape and murder the entire population, she was sitting frozen on the floor watching the horror. When the soldiers got her and dragged her to the floor, the officer in charge stopped them and examined her. "This one is a treasure; she will be perfect for our brothers at the front," he said, and with this sealed her fate.

We are at attention for death twenty-four hours a day. He is our master; he decides our fate, the hunger, the diseases, and the torture. The soldiers have become weary and impatient; there is no end to the war in sight. They are angry and frustrated, and from day to day, the comfort women have to deal with men who are more and more brutal.

Kumikko is looking at me now as if she is focusing on a picture book. She is so pale and thin. She is the most demanded marionette in the brothel. She has learned quickly all the tricks, all the means to make a soldier, the most unstable, mentally ill soldier, feel that he has had a good time. Her Japanese is superb, and her survival skills are on their sharpest edge when she is with a client.

She will show the bastards; she has a plan. She will come out of all this higher up than all of them. In spite of all the brutal soldiers there is not one scar or black and blue mark on her snow white, perfect body.

Namie is scratching her head in frustration. Kumikko was not supposed to last so long; a month is far too long. Namie is starting to doubt her own judgment. Is she sending Kumikko the wrong men? This phenomenon is beyond her understanding. That girl was supposed to be dead by now, at least to have committed suicide.

We line up to go to the doctor. A group of shadows, ghosts, is standing like sheep waiting for their turn to be slaughtered. Namie is on a very rare day off. The guards are very much on edge; if something goes wrong; Namie will either kill them or punish them. She will tell them to get on their knees and stay in place the entire night. Whoever moves will get the club.

Kumikko knows that this is her judgment day. It is today or never. This is her only opportunity before it is going to be too late. She will show the bastards today! An opportunity like this happens once in a blue moon.

Silent Marionette
침묵의꼭두각시

Namie never takes days off unless she is forced to. The brothel is her pride and joy; she hates being away. It the only place she can celebrate her ego, the only place where she feels that she is worth something, where she is listened to.

The girls were marching quietly to the doctor's office; I was called first this time. Meng-Sun motioned me to sit on the checkup chair. She was avoiding my eyes.

"What's her name?" the doctor asked.

"Maikko, Oisa Sensei (Doctor, sir)

"Has she been here before?"

"Yes, Oisa Sensei Doctor, sir"

He pulled out my papers. He had no great love for Meng-Sun; this was obvious. He pushed her aside while coming near me. "How are you feeling today?" he asked, his voice softened.

"She is mute, Oisa Sensei Doctor Sir," Meng-sun said.

"Did I ask you anything?" The doctor frowned at her. "Get out, leave us alone!"

Meng-sun opened her eyes twice their size. Doctor, Sir, never told her to leave him alone with a girl before. This was against procedure. She looked at him and then at me doubtfully.

"Get out!" He yelled, "Now!"

She ran out the door. The doctor sighed deeply and stood there for a minute, silent. Only now, the recollection came to him of who I was; he looked at my naked body and sighed again.

"If I were in your shoes, I would stop talking too," he said then.

He examined my body looking for bruises. "Are you in any pain?"
I shook my head, "No, I can't feel a thing," I motioned.

He took his time checking my body inch by inch, and then took a specimen. "I am ashamed," he said quietly all of a sudden with his head down; I am ashamed."

I did not think I had any tears left in me, but they came pouring out now. He sat by me on his chair and held my hand, examining it. "Such a small hand, so delicate," he sighed sadly. Then he got up and called Meng-sun, "She is sick; she is going to be hospitalized until further notice."

I could not believe my ears. I could see Meng- sun dying inside, and she was totally in shock now. "Bbbbbut …..Oisa Sensei….Doctor sir…."

"Shut up and do as you're told!" he raised his voice.

I got up now, and she dressed me gently, silently. She was very distressed. All she was thinking about was Namie. What was she going to tell Namie? What excuse was she going to give her for the loss of the best whore in the house?

I was taken into the back of the building; somebody was playing Bingo with my life.

Silent Marionette
침묵의꼭두각시

Kumikko

When Kumikko entered the doctor's office, she knew that all her cards were in that visit. Kumikko did not need to talk much. With her beautiful body, her long legs, and her burning, big black eyes, if she could just get the nice doctor to look at her face once, she would trap him for good. She dropped her gorgeous body on the chair and put one leg over the other as if she were sitting naked for a social tea.

"Open your legs!" the guard yelled.

"No yelling in my office," the doctor raises his voice, irritated.

"Open those legs!" the guard barks.

The doctor now gets up. "Get out; I am better off without any of you!"

"Hai! Oisa Sensei!" The guard was frightened. The doctor had never raised his voice before; she was not used to him being so angry.

Kumikko is the last patient of the day; the doctor is tired and weary. So many years in medical school, he could have been living a comfortable life with his wife and kids somewhere in Tokyo.

What was he doing here? He did not understand how he had been brought to this miserable place under the order of the Japanese Imperial Army.

The things that he had seen and heard during his three years of service in the comfort station were so shameful, so contrary to all logic, against anything he had been educated for. Over here, the world was divided into beasts and beasts' victims, and he, the only doctor in the place, had to meet with both.

That day in particular the doctor was irritated. He had had a troubled sleep at night; the haunting dreams had come one after another. The doctor was waking up every few minutes, sweaty and upset. At one point, he sat down on his bed and started crying against his will. He felt trapped in his little room, like an animal in a cage. He had never felt so trapped; the walls were closing in on him, threatening to swallow him.

That morning, the doctor was standing in front of the mirror, trying to stop the bleeding from where he had cut himself shaving. He was looking at the reflection of his face, and then at his hands. He had trouble deciding if it was a beast he sees or a man. He was trying to think what he would tell his children that he did in the army when he was away at war, to make them proud.

"Dear children, I sterilized a bunch of little prostitutes, little girls your age who were kidnapped from their moms and dads, and were forced to perform sick, disgusting, unspeakable sins. That is what he would tell his children? Maybe the best was not to even go back home, and never have to face his family again.

He turned to Kumikko; the strange girl was sitting there on the chair completely naked but relaxed, leg draped over leg as if she were coming to a beauty salon.
"Your name?"
"Kumikko, sir!"
"How old?"
"Seventeen, sir"

She had a pleasant voice, the girl; it reminded him his little daughter's voice.
"How long are you here"? He was looking for her papers.
"One month, sir" she said.

He sat down by her and looked at her beautiful face; there was something different in this girl. He saw thousands of girls, of all nationalities, all shapes, all colors, but this one was different. There was something hypnotizing in her face, in her voice.

"How do you feel?" his voice broke a bit.

"How do you think I feel?" the girl blurted, not making any attempt to move.

The doctor was surprised. For a minute, he forgot that he was in a brothel and talking to a marionette. Nobody ever talked to him like that, not guards and for sure not marionettes. Doctor Matsumoto was suffering now from deep depression; he missed his beautiful wife, his children, his cozy home. He was sick and tired of this cursed war. He hated China, this extreme weather, the lousy food, the people who would flatter him and kiss his feet while in their eyes was deadly hatred.

Matsumoto wanted his wife now to come to him and wash his feet, and then look up and say, "Are you really my husband?" as she was asking since the day they were married. She said she was so happy to be with him that she would ask this question every day for the rest of her life, just to make sure she was not dreaming.

Doctor Matsumoto would take the old photos of his wife and children out of his pocket and think; they may have changed so much by now. At night he would toss and turn, yearning for the soft hands of his beloved wife, and drown into terrible guilt because of what he was doing and seeing daily.

He was a peaceful man by nature, who never understood the nastiness in humanity. As far as he was concerned, if you left people in peace they should leave you in peace.

And now this. A girl that looks like an angel, sitting here defiantly and for the first time ever since he started working in the comfort station, talks to him as an equal. He looks at her, his mouth open, his eyes wide.

"Doctor, I am a prisoner, but I am really only a young woman," she dares. "They fooled me, my father's friends. They told me I was going to be sent to the Korean front as a nurse. They trapped me... I believed them... I did not know they were going to send me here....." Kumiklko now started sobbing.

The doctor, against his will, felt his hand reaching for her face. He wiped her tears slowly, his heart suddenly beating unsteadily. She put her hand now on his hand; he felt a shiver in his lower back. All these days, all these months, he was so longing for a woman's touch, for an understanding ear.

Silent Marionette
침묵의꼭두각시

Doctor Matsumoto was now completely drowned in the beautiful Korean girl, and Kumikko used all the tricks in the book to use this rare chance for life. When his lips rested on her lips and they kissed as if it were the end of the world, she knew that she had won the battle against Namie.

That very afternoon Meng-sun, who was frightened to death now at the prospect of the loss of another favorite marionette, helped Kumikko pack her few belongings. Kumikko was now officially the doctor's Geisha.

When Namie would return at night all the guards would regret the day they were born. Namie would make them all bend down on their knees and would beat them until they lost consciousness. Some of them might lose their fingernails. Namie had a particular love for pulling nails off fingers.

The supply of marionettes was no longer pouring in; fewer and fewer girls arrived. This was a bad time for the shipments to stop. The fighting had intensified at the front, and the soldiers' demands for release from tension were more desperate than ever. There were more and more orders to ship girls from the comfort house to the front and they had been losing many girls. Namie would go crazy when she got here. Heads would roll.

Kumikko, carrying her little bag, is walking toward the door to heaven past the traumatized marionettes. A miracle has occurred in the brothel. A true human prisoner, a real marionette, is walking out to freedom!

The girls regard her not in envy but in sad surprise and disbelief. Kumikko waves goodbye as if she is going on a school trip. The door opens and the Manchurian sunlight spills into the comfort house, blinding the marionettes' eyes. Then it closes behind Kumikko's straight dancer's back; darkness covers the new workday.

Jonggun wianbu (從軍慰安婦)

In the beginning of 1944, we could feel a change in the marionette comfort house. The soldiers grew weary, depressed, and impatient; some became very violent. We started hearing rumors that our comfort house would be closed and we would all be shipped to the front.

Japan's plans to invade Port Moresby were interrupted by the American and Australian forces. In order to keep face, especially after the bombing of Tokyo, the Japanese government decided to seize the Midway Atoll. At that point, Japan sent forces to occupy the Aleutian Islands. Nevertheless, the American army was aware of the plan and prevented its success by defeating the Japanese navy. Now Japan chose to focus on the overland invasion of the territory of Papua.

In mid-September, when I was still in the hospital, the Japanese army was treating the battle for Guadalcanal as a priority. They sent large numbers of troops, many battle ships, and enormous quantities of ammunition to the front. Guadalcanal became a focal point for both sides in the war. The Japanese army lost the battle and withdrew.

The Allies initiated several operations against Japan after that point. The Americans eliminated the Japanese forces from the Aleutians, and soon after that there was a massive operation to isolate Rabaul by capturing all the surrounding islands and to breach the Japanese central Pacific perimeter at the Gilbert and Marshal islands. However, morale was still high among the Japanese since their navy fleet was strong and the army did well.

Our supply of food diminished noticeably. Instead of two meals a day, we now were getting only one. We were always hungry, and many died of hunger. Some girls started looking swollen, the last stage before turning into a mass of bones and being executed. Even the most sex-starved soldier would not touch a pile of bones.

Silent Marionette
침묵의꼭두각시

The Japanese government began issuing harsh, very precise sets of rules for the treatment of slaves, including sex slaves, in order to ensure that their living conditions would be as wretched as possible.   Old rags for clothing, overcrowded sleeping conditions, primitive sanitation, hardly any medical care, minimal amounts of food and poorer quality of food, all were designed to crush the slaves' will to live.

In June 1944, the recommendation by Honma Fusakichi, who served as Kishi's deputy cabinet secretary, was to issue slave guidelines called "Reference documents for use of Chinese Workers".   He observed that if you give a slave very little food and leave him hungry, he will become tense and his work productivity will improve.

Japanese and Korean workers should be eating less and less food every day so they will get used to working on very little food. There was no need in his opinion to use any calculated methods with the Chinese, since the Chinese race had no feelings, and would not be affected by hunger, suffering or torture.   He believed that Chinese people could not understand or feel love, hate, humiliation or any other emotion that can affect a normal human being. If a Chinese was crying, it was not real tears; it was probably good acting.

The slaves' sleeping quarters should not be more than ten cm. higher than their heads when they were sitting; that way you could triple the amount of people in the rooms since they could not stand up or walk about. Slaves did not need bathing facilities since they had no respect for cleanliness.

He recommended being overpowering with harsh methods of control. When a runaway was captured, he must not be allowed to go back to his camp to work; he must be killed publicly so that the other prisoners would learn not to do the same thing. Living quarters must be made as shabby as possible.

The slaves lost any concept of sanitation. They were suffering from malnutrition. They would eat rotten, leftover foods that had been thrown away, and they died like flies.

In the beginning of April 1943, about 40.000 Chinese men between the ages of 11 and 78 were brought to Japan to advance the war effort. They had to work in very harsh circumstances in the mines, construction sites and docks from Kyushu to Hokkaido. The overall death rate was 50 percent. However, more than that died in China during hellish detention or while trying to escape before reaching the coast.

Many slaves were kidnapped from China and Korea, able-bodied males and pretty females that were treated as war booty. The conditions under which they were held were unbearable. Failure to meet demands resulted in beatings and starvation. Some slaves were reduced to wearing discarded cement sacks with armholes cut into them. They were housed behind high fences in isolated camps with armed guards.

Now we were thirty-eight women left in the comfort house. The girls came and went like lights being turned on and off. Our guards became more and more violent, especially toward the Chinese and the Korean girls. The guards would find any reason they could to beat them black and blue as a way to show their loyalty to the Japanese. The girls were starved almost to death. The only time we could find a bit more food was once a week when we were allowed to do the laundry in the river. On the way, we would find some berries.

We were there to serve the troops to keep their morale high and to prevent spreading of STDs, but we all got sick so often that many girls just died from lack of medicine. The brothel was emptied out of the old girls as fast as the new ones were kidnapped and brought in. Many of the new girls had been tricked or defrauded into joining the Japanese brothel. Some of them had arrived through an intermediary and some of them had come after the Japanese directly demanded from the local leaders to provide them with girls.

The situation worsened as the war progressed. The military did not provide enough supplies to the Japanese units, and in response, the soldiers made up for it by looting supplies from villagers and carrying out the "three alls" policy of kidnapping, raping and looting. Those girls that got to the comfort stations and brothels were now immediately raped, beaten and tortured. We were the *jonggun wianbu*, our function was to be marionettes, and we would be raped and beaten day and night. Brutality, horror and starvation was our reality,

I was lucky thanks to Kumikko; she was living in the doctor's quarters now, and would sneak me extra food. If not for her, I would have been dead long ago. I also got better treatment than the others did because I was a mute, free from Namie. In addition, thanks to Kumikko, the doctor would come out with excuses constantly to hospitalize me.

I would be brought back to the brothel and then taken out by the doctor again. Kumikko would come to visit me in the hospital with extra dishes that she had cooked for the doctor. "As long as I make the doctor happy," she would say, "I will live; but if he leaves and I have to go back to the brothel, I will die!"

More than anybody else, the Chinese girls suffered. The Japanese believed that Chinese were subhuman. Some soldiers would ask specifically not to be sent to a Chinese girl's cell. Japan had proclaimed itself as a superior culture (even though it was Chinese culture with minor modifications), and demonstrated its superiority through war.

The psychological complexity of the relations between Japan and China was evident in the aggressive and confused treatment of the Chinese girls by the Japanese officers and soldiers. Sometimes the girls would be beaten and tortured to death, their bodies a mass of black and blue marks, and sometimes they would be treated with tenderness and even given small presents.

I remember hearing the stories of "*Hwan-hyang-nyeo*" (home coming women), who were the victims whenever Korea was invaded by neighboring countries or tribes. In 1636, during the middle of the Lee Dynasty (李氏 朝鮮時代), when Ch'ing (清) invaded Korea, many young women were compulsorily taken to China as sex slaves.

The majority of the victims were from North Korea because there were many beautiful women there. When they came back years later, having suffered indescribable hardships, they were not welcome; thus, they were humiliated once again. Similar cases happened in 1592 when Japan invaded Korea, so called "*Imjin oeran*".(壬辰倭亂)

Namie loved to take the Chinese girls for a last spin in her basement. You could hear the screaming all over Manchuria. Whoever said the Chinese do not have feelings and cannot react to pain did not include the Chinese Manchurian marionettes. After a while Namie would call her gang of guards and they would drag the slaughtered carcasses to the garbage. Their cells would be cleaned and new, frightened recruits would replace them.

Korea has a long and painful history of women abuse. During its history Korea was invaded nearly nine hundred times, and in all of those invasions the women suffered the most. Young women were raped repeatedly and then were thrown like broken toys to their death.

With the Japanese invasion, young women were captured and taken away suddenly from the streets, during farm work, while cooking at home, or when washing clothes in a stream. After being loaded on trains like animals, they were sent to various front lines and were gang raped. They were used as prostitutes. An estimated four hundred thousand females were forced to become comfort women and deliver sexual services to the Japanese soldiers. This was the largest, most methodical and deadly rape of women in all recorded history.

The Japanese and their collaborators tricked and abducted females as young as eleven years old and imprisoned them in rape camps throughout Asia. The comfort women were forced to serve 50 to 70 soldiers a day. They were beaten and tortured, starved and made to endure abortions and sterilization.

In all, in addition to those who were forced to serve as comfort women, there were probably ten million women raped. Those who died were simply discarded; there were no official reports on them. As for the comfort women, the Japanese government systematically destroyed any official records of them.

Mal-bong

Every morning Kumikko came running to help me make the dadami and clean up my room for inspection. Another purpose of hands is a salvation from Buddha, My room was always ready first, and then Kumikko ran around helping the other girls. Kumikko became the angel of the comfort house. She would sneak food for the girls and help them out with chores.

Namie was burning inside from hatred and anger but she would not say a word, or touch the pretty girl for fear of the doctor. Kumikko was the doctor's private geisha. Nobody could have said that the doctor had not changed; he was happy and relaxed, had a glow in his eyes, and was always smiling and pleasant now.

Kumikko did him a lot of good. She cooked his favorite dishes, made passionate love to him and listened to him telling her about things he had never told a soul before. She was his world now; he would bring her with him to the hospital and was teaching her how to help him with the patients. Thanks to her promise to me, my monthly checkup always ended up with him saying that I was sick; and I would get a week or two of bed rest.

Kumikko gave me a notebook and pencils. I would draw now the pictures that were in my mind. I could now draw almost like Pil–sun. I found that I had quite a talent. Pil-sun had taught me many tricks; I never thought I remembered them. But now because of my lack of ability to speak, pictures of what I had been through all these days since I was captured had been collecting in my mind in the form of pictures, a huge mass of pictures. I was surprised to find how anxious I was to tell my stories. I had assumed that whatever I went through would die with me. I thought that I would not even want to tell those stories to myself. I was upset and humiliated, and felt dirty at all times. I was so angry I would suffer convulsions. However, when I held the pencil for the first time, I was so hungry to tell my stories that I filled up three whole notebooks with just the first set of pressing stories that I had to clean out of my system right away.

Now the guards would line up for me to sketch them. In return, they would leave me another piece of soap or a potato. Namie would sit down almost daily for me to sketch her. I would make her look pretty. I would change her entire face, give her fuller lips, widen her eyes. She was Namie, but a much better version in my drawings. That made her happy. "Is this really me?" she would exclaim again and again, and show the picture to everybody proudly.

That helped with the supplies. She would come up with an endless supply of papers and pencils as long as I would draw her. Once she even brought me ink and a calligraphy pen. I was really truly lucky to be a mute; otherwise, not all this would be happening and I would never be alive by now. It was very uncommon for a girl to still be alive in this brothel after more than six months. Most of the girls would be sent to the front and would never come back.

Namie never puts my name on the lists for transport to the front. I am mute, I cannot entertain much and I am her best worker. I also am an attraction now because of my talent in drawing. Namie takes pride in me as if I was her personal discovery, and she behaves like an agent. She sends me the fancy guests to be sketched, and makes sure I do not take too many soldiers so that I will have enough strength to draw.

She does not even argue with the doctor about all my sick vacations. She tried once to say something about rules and regulations with regard to Kumikko, suddenly shocking him; and he gave her a mouthful. "Don't you talk to me about rules and regulations. If I will report everything you do in that brothel that is against the rules, the court marshal will not even give you an opportunity to commit hara-kiri. You will be executed publicly in front of the all world."

Namie knows that Kumikko has won this time. This has never happened before in her marionette's house. Kumikko looks at her with a smirk on her lips when she is passing by. She sways her hips intentionally and moves her little behind, from side to side, as if she is saying, "This particular piece of marionette will never be yours!" Moreover, Namie swears to herself that she will have revenge. No miserable mouse has ever escaped her trap, especially not a Korean one.

Today in the shower, Mal-bong is not looking at me anymore. She is a pack of bones; you cannot see an inch on her body that is not scarred. Namie has always kept her for the most sadistic ones. Mal-bong has clearly lost her mind by now. She should have been shipped to the garbage long ago, but for some reason Namie does not let go. When the guards put her on the list to be killed, Namie automatically erases her name. It is some kind of sick fascination that she has with the poor soul.

Mal-bong looks strange to me today; there is something in her dead eyes that is different. There is a weird determination in her face. I feel the danger crawling up my body. Something bad is going to happen today. This morning is different from other mornings. I feel tense. Lee-ping, a shadow of a Chinese doll, is leaning on the wall pale as a ghost. She also is staring at Mal-bong. "They will teach you a thing or two, the Japanese soldiers…."

Kumikko taught me how to behave with the soldiers, how to avoid venereal diseases. I had to survive by keeping in mind what she said. How can I be like Kumikko? Kumikko is made from other materials. She does not break; she has a strong, fierce, fearless character. Never in the history of Japanese sex slavery would a slave have done what she did. Kumikko is different from the other girls; there is no other human being like her in the world. She is capable of anything.

One day she arrived in the hospital with a closed, wrapped pot. "Guess what it is?"

I shook my head; nothing would surprise me with her any more. She opened the wraps and took out a ceramic pot.

Silent Marionette
침묵의꼭두각시

"Guess again, Pil-nyo!"

I shook my head. She opened the top and the smell of the kimchi hit me and filled my nostrils. When was the last time I ate kimchi? This was unbelievable. I started crying. Every time I thought that my tears were dried forever, they kept coming again. "What are you crying for, silly girl? *Oso mura!*" (Let us eat!) She smiled.

The doctor one day became interested in Kumikko's life, her family, her village, the food she used to eat; and Kumikko volunteered the information enthusiastically. She talked so much about her mother's kimchi that the doctor took his car and went to gather the ingredients. It was not so simple to find food in Manchuria. Cabbage was rare and so was any meat.

The Japanese army emptied most of the villages of food. People died from hunger like flies. Nevertheless, the doctor did not give up until he found everything on the list that Kumikko had given him. The doctor would do anything to satisfy his Korean princess. He would even bring her the moon.

She is watching me eat, proud of herself. "Eat slowly, Pil-nyo; you will get a stomach ache." I stuff my face, spoon after spoon. "Omani," I think. Omani made the best kimchi ever. From all over the village they came to taste her cooking wonders, and the women would sigh, "Why can't I get that taste too?"

Abazi would come from the fields and wash his hands, and the whole family would sit around the kimchi pot. "*Bap mok chau*" (let us eat) he would say somewhat ceremonially; and mother would start digging the miracle out of the pot into our bowls. All you could hear around the table was the spoons knocking in the bowls and the sighs of pleasure, the tongues clicking, and the sucking of the teeth.

In the dining room, we are swallowing the few spoons of rice in our bowls. The hunger is nibbling in my guts, even though I get more food every day from Kumikko. I exist on a much richer diet than the other girls do, yet the food disappears into me as into an empty hole.

Like a starved wolf, I feel the hunger biting me. I look aside at my neighbor. Maybe she missed a grain; maybe one fell. I could sneak it to my mouth without her noticing. However, the table is empty, clean as a whistle.

On my other side, Mal-bong is licking her bowl, her face blank. I touch her arm, but she ignores me. She sucks her lips in and squeezes her forehead; then she holds her stomach and leans forward. A scream exits her mouth. "*Aigo*!"

Meng-sun turns around. "What's the matter?"

"My stomach! My stomach hurts like hell!" she yells.

Her miserable body is shrinking on the floor now; she is cramping like crazy, contracting as if she is giving birth, and the pain is tearing her apart.

"Sit quietly!" Meng-sun is clueless as to what to do. She looks fearfully at Namie, but now Mal-bong is vomiting her guts, stream upon stream of green, stinking liquids pouring out of her mouth.

Meng-sun jumps backwards horrified. Mal-Bong is laying half-dead in the puddle of foul, green goo. Her eyes are coming out of their sockets and her mouth is leaking foam.

We watch silently as Namie arrives at the scene, her club swinging from side to side. "Clean the scum!" she commands her guards. They pick up Mal-bong's broken body and take her into the showers.

"Clean the dirt!" Namie yells at us in disgust, and we are all on our knees, wiping up the last of the liquid that was in Mal-bong's stomach.

"We need to take her to the doctor," says one of the guards.

"She is receiving clients today as usual!" spits Namie.

Silent Marionette
침묵의꼭두각시

"But she is too sick," dares the guard.

Namie slaps her face with all her might. That guard will carry a mark on her face for months now.

"I make the decisions here!"

Mal-bong is dragged beck to her cell. The guards throw her cn the dadami. Her cell now is right across from me where Kumikko used to work. She is lying motionless, pale as the wall. She looks like she is dead now. The gong is sounding the beginning of the workday. The screaming of the girls and the laughter of the soldiers now fill the building.

A young soldier comes into my cell. He looks like a lost boy. He wipes his sweat and appears uncomfortable and confused. I smile to him. The soldier starts getting undressed. He is unsure of himself and tries to hide his naked body in the blanket. Then he hands me the yellow stamps.

A fat, powerfully built officer with the face of a murderer enters the cell across from me. He takes a look at Mal-bong's half-dead body and rubs his hands satisfied. He will show the Korean whore what he can do. He paid nicely to reserve her for the whole day and night. He will have many hours with the marionette and he has planned every detail of what he is going to do to her. He has paid many yellow stamps for this pleasure

The young soldier is lying on top of me, trying unsuccessfully to enter my body. I spread my legs as much as I can, but the soldier is breathing heavily, trying again, with no result.

"Help me!" he begs.

"Sh"....I sign to him, "relax."

I pull his head to my chest and I pet his hair. The soldier is calming down now. He closes his tired eyes and his breathing sounds more and more normal.

Silent Marionette
침묵의꼭두각시

In Mal-bong's cell, the officer is commanding her to bend down. His huge, heavy body is completely naked; he looks like a massive gorilla. He takes his thick leather belt in hand. The games will begin with a beating, hard beating. Mal-bong is bending, in the last of the life that she has in her bones. Her hands are touching the chair in front of her, where his clothes are lying folded carefully. He starts hitting; the belt is going up and down on her broken body. She is looking at me now, and a shadow of a mad smile comes upon her face. She is waving goodbye to me.

The officer continues to beat her. He will not quit until she spills blood, lots of blood. Now in a sharp move she suddenly grabs his pistol from the chair and at once shoves it into her mouth and shoots.

My hand is stopping frozen on my young soldier's hair. Mal-bong's head is exploding to millions of pieces.

The officer is standing above her, his arm raised high in the air; his fat, naked body is covered with thick blood and parts of Mal-bong's head, his mouth open in shock, his eyes running madly from side to side.

Namie and the guards are coming running frantically, their boots stamping hard on the wooden floor. The clubs are in a ready position. The soldier is raising his fatigued head from my chest. I smile my dead smile to him as if nothing has happened, and then he bursts out crying.

Lee-ping's birthday

The cramps are killing me, cramps of hunger. We go outside to wash in the stream; The Korean couple's fat cat is stretching lazily in the winter sun. At the end of 1943, there is now no food at all. If not for the little bit that Kumikko would sneak to me, I would be dead.

Manchuria is freezing cold. The animals are eating any leftover plants, the berries are gone, we can't even find any little fish in the half-frozen river. The trees are naked of leaves. A layer of snow is on the ground. All around is a white, freezing silence, so pure and clean, as if there are no marionettes, no sin, and no evil.

Nature stands there watching us searching for food, carrying our few pieces of clothing to be washed in the freezing water. Snowflakes are falling slowly on our heads like pieces of rice paper and covering our footsteps. I look behind me as I walk, and I see the snow erasing my footstep as if I was never there, as if my footprints were a figment of my imagination.

Liu-fang is pointing at Lee-ping, "*Sheng-ri*" (birthday). Little Lee-ping is sixteen today and she already looks like an old woman. Hatred flushes through my body, overwhelming hatred. I do not even know whom I hate. I hate them all, the Japanese, the Chinese, the Koreans. I hate so passionately that all human beings in the world seem like little ants against my powerful hate. I hate the murderers, the rapists, and the abusers, and I hate their victims just the same.

I looked around. There were no guards. They let us go to do the laundry all by ourselves now. Where would we go anyway? There was nowhere to run away to. The Manchurians had their own set of problems to deal with; they were hungry and poor. The last thing they would want would be to get in trouble with the Japanese for hiding a miserable whore.

I started gathering wooden sticks and branches as if a ghost was chasing me; I motioned to the girls, "light fire!"

Liu-fang looked at me surprised. "Why?"

"*Yinshi*" (food) I motioned. The girls by now had learned how to read my motions and the words I formed with my lips.

I ran determinedly toward the gate. It was getting late; soon the gong would sound and the soldiers would crowd the building. The Russians and the Americans were close now. The Japanese soldiers were being hit hard and their morale was down. They became more and more aggressive and demanding with the girls. We were their last station before death.

We ourselves were waiting for death to come. Death was sitting with us as a permanent guest. We all knew him and had gotten used to him. We were living constantly on the sharp edge between life and death.

Right now, it was my Chinese friend's *sheng-ri*. I was hungry as a beast and was determined to get food no matter what. I went into the yard. The guards were busy talking and laughing; who would pay attention to a little, miserable Korean whore?

I caught the cat in my arms. He was a big, huge cat, the pride and joy of Meng-sun and her husband. He got to eat all the leftovers from the kitchen; he surely ate better than any of us. The lazy cat stretched in my arms. He did not object to this sudden attention. "Meng-sun earned this when she lied to me about becoming a nurse," I thought.

I brought the cat to the edge of the stream. The girls looked at me confused. I gave the cat to Liu-fang. "Hold tight," I motioned.

I decisively held onto the cat's neck and turned it 360 degrees. The cat stopped breathing on the spot; only the crack of the neck breaking was heard.

The girls looked at me in shock; they were scared to death. However, it was Lee-ping's birthday and I wanted a party; there was no other thought in my mind. I skinned the cat in an instant, like a professional. Abazi had taught us how to skin the sheep many times. I was an expert in skinning. We threw the cat into the fire and looked at each other with sly smiles. It was the first time we had felt a sense of sisterhood.

None of us liked Meng-sun. She was a two-faced Japanese sympathizer, and her husband was a two-timing ass kisser and boot licker with no conscience whatsoever. He would come into our cells often and rape us wildly since it was free, and he would take anything free. Sometimes he would sit with the cat and pet him slowly; I saw him even kiss it. He loved his cat probably more than he ever loved a human being.

Now the meat was cooked and the delicious smell was wakening our taste buds. We pulled the black, charcoaled mass out of the fire and tore it apart like a bunch of hyenas. Lee-ping got the first honors, and she chose a leg. We were all eating the meat as if we had never had meat before in our lives. All you could hear in the silence of our party were the sighs of pleasure, the teeth clicking, and the tongues licking.

The meat melted in our mouths. It was an unbelievable taste of heaven. We had not eaten meat since we were kidnapped. Kumikko would bring me a rare piece of fish or a bit of chicken in the soup. However, to sink my teeth into a piece of meat like this, it had been ages.

We wiped our mouths with the backs of our hands and then looked at each other, and for the first time in the history of the brothel, we were laughing. Liu-fang started jumping around Lee-ping, singing happy birthday in Chinese, and the rest of the girls were giggling and went each one in her turn to hug the birthday girl.

We could hear the gong from far away. Quickly discarding all evidence of the party, we ran back with our laundry to the house. Liu-fang, with a rare expression of humor, meowed all the way. That day we serviced the soldiers with a bit of a victory feeling, as if we were above them somehow. Lee-ping told me later that she felt on that day, her special birthday, that we were not the victims, that the real tragic victims were the Japanese soldiers.

For days after that we heard Meng-sun and her husband going ksssss....pssssss..., calling their beloved cat, until one day her husband said to his crying wife, "The ungrateful beast just ran away!" Meng-sun wiped the tears from her fat cheeks, turned to us, and asked, "Have you seen my cat?" Would she ever shed a tear for any of us?

How many of us innocent girls had been beaten, tortured, and even killed right in front of her eyes? Did she ever have any compassion for us? Liu-fang gave me a smile. "No," we all shook our heads. And Liu fang went, "Meow....," quietly under her blanket.

"You ask how many friend I have"...

"One day you'll walk out on me I know,

Saying you need a change of air,

You hope I understand, you do so hate a fuss.

I suppose you would love to see me dancing,

Somewhere far away from you,

Scattering azaleas in your path, perhaps?

I can just see you there, prancing along,

Squashing those poor flowers under your foot

As you fade away into the sunset.

Oh yes, you will walk out one day, I know.

Saying you need a change of air.

You think I will mind. I won't, you know."

The year 1944, was very eventful for the Japanese forces. The winds of war were blowing sour for them. The soldiers did not seem victorious; they were quite depressed. In January of that year, the Americans were launching powerful counterattacks. Starting in March there was a series of battles that brought many failures to the Japanese. They lost 5,000 men and were slowly mopped up, closing the campaign in the Solomon Islands by the end of the year.

Silent Marionette
침묵의꼭두각시

On January 9th, 1944, British and Indian troops captured Maungdaw in Burma, and right after that on January 31 invaded Kawajalein in the Marshall Islands.

In the month of January, most of the girls were shipped to the front, leaving only twelve of us remaining in the brothel to service the soldiers. The lines were long and we were forced to work 60 to 70 soldiers a day. The only good thing about it was that the pleasure time was cut to fifteen minutes each; consequently, there was not too much time for the soldiers to torture us or ask for special treatment.

The body and the soul have no more motions left; we are just marionettes, live mattresses, and miserable sex slaves. The guards are tired too. All the screaming, yelling, and beatings are not really intended for us, but for the ears of the people in charge.

Namie needs to know that the guards are doing their jobs. The best way to show loyalty and hard work is by making as much noise as possible. I am thinking of my mother now. I cannot help it; she comes to me lately all the time whether I am asleep or awake. My mother was the prettiest of all mothers. She was the strongest, the wisest of them all.

"Who loves you the most of all in the world, Pil-nyo?"

"Omani."

"Who is the prettiest, the cutest in the world?"

"Pil-nyo."

"Who is going to get the biggest kiss ever from Pil-nyo?"

"Omani."

Mother had long, beautiful hair, and shining eyes. Her hands were gentle and soft. She is kneeling now in front of Buddha. She lights the incense. "Please, holy Buddha, guard my Pil-nyo," she begs. And Buddha, great merciful Buddha, is nodding his head to her," Pil-nyo will live."

I am holding my stomach with my two hands; today more than ever the loneliness is closing in on me. What would I want today more than anything in the world? I would want today not to exist, to disappear into time that is what I would want.

Something is wrong today; something is rotten. The guards are running around like frightened ants. Namie is screaming and raising her club on whoever is around her. The cell across from me is being prepared for a new girl. Where is Kumikko? She never came this morning to help me prepare for inspection.

The changes were coming fast to the brothel; every day there was something new happening. New people, new orders, new girls, but who cared? We were not keeping time anyway; we did not know what day it was or what time it was. We were just automatic sex dolls.

Life in the routine of horror and chaos did not consider time, only events. Years and minutes were the same for us. The world of the comfort house worked on different rules of physics, rules of a mad planet where everything that was normal became abnormal, and vice-versa.

All we knew were seasons, when it was unbearably hot and when it was freezing cold. We could make little snow balls and eat them, pretending they were rice balls in the cold winter. Springtime was particularly helpful since we could find some wild berries and vegetables to eat. In summertime we could wash in the stream and try to catch some fish.

The brothel's building is suffocating me; there are bodies of people everywhere. My cell is like a cage, no space to move. When I lie down, I can feel the ceiling coming down closer and closer to my face. The walls are shrinking and closing in on me and I start choking. My voice gets buried even deeper in my guts. My eyes are focused at the dirty window. The officer on top of me is moaning, "Mother, sweet mother..."

Silent Marionette
침묵의꼭두각시

I feel the pressure in my chest, that familiar sign of loss of oxygen. My head hurts; thousands of hammers are knocking in my brain. A deep scream is growing inside my guts. I feel like vomiting. The soldier above me is leaving me with his sticky warm liquid spread all over my legs. I get up now. I must wash myself. I am disgusted all of a sudden, as if it is my first time.

"You have a guest today!" Meng-sun is sneering at me nastily. "Your fancy friend is coming back!"

I shake my head no, it cannot be.

"No more spoiling for you, mute princess!" she blurts out her wisdom and leaves me in the shower. My heart is racing; it is a dreadful day today. Liu-fang is looking at me from the next shower, and her eyes are wide open with fear. Not Mi-za!

Liu-fang is panicked now. She is holding my hand under the shower, squeezing my fingers as hard as she can. What happened to Kumikko? I was beyond hope, beyond any feelings. I kept shaking my head under the water. No! Not Kumikko! It is all a blind game of luck, the whole madness of life, I am thinking.

From out in the lobby I can hear the Japanese officers laughing. Namie's voice is stronger than any of theirs. She is laughing aloud as if she has just won a huge prize. She wants the officers to notice her, to see who she is, and how important she is here. I wipe myself and put my dress back on. I walk back to my cell and sit on my dadami waiting for the worst.

Kumikko is dragged to the cell by the guards. Namie is pushing her down to the dadami. "Your good life is over, stupid whore! You are mine now!"

Kumikko is sitting on the floor. She does not cry; her face is cold as stone. She shows no expression, not even a sign that she knows where she is.

The gong sounds again now. A group of soldiers is lining up. The workday continues. Mother comes to me again now. She pets my hair, "Buddha promised me; Buddha, never lies Pil-nyo! Close your eyes, my lovely girl, close your weary eyes and rest in my arms."

"You ask how many friends I have.

Water and stone, bamboo and pine.

The moon that is rising above the eastern hill is a joyful comrade.

Silent Marionette
침묵의꼭두각시

Beside these five companions,

What other pleasures should I ask for?"

The soldier above me is crying out, "Love me girl, I am going to die!"

I touch his head "Sh......"

"Wadasio aiside gudasai" (Give me love), Love me, love me to death! he cries out. His fingers are clinging to mine. "Sh..., sh..."

He moans, cries, and then rests for a second. I wipe the sweat off his forehead. Kumikko is sighing now. I have no more soldiers today. The war must be at a boiling point. Fewer and fewer soldiers are coming to my cell. I grab my notebook and pencil, and I draw in panic all the monsters of the world and their victims. I draw Mal-bong and Liu-fang, Lee-ping and Kumikko. I draw the shame, the disgrace. I draw the revulsion and the hatred. I draw my lonely silence, my torn body, my disgust with myself, and with the whole world. The shame, the guilt, I draw my coming death.

My ears are sealed; now I have to draw as fast as I can. As if I am going to die any minute, I have to spill the pictures as fast as I can onto the papers. I have to draw Kumikko dragged back into her cell. I have to draw Liu-fang's fear in the shower. "The Japanese will show you a thing or two...." my hand is moving as fast as light. My lips are moving, and my entire body is in rage. Now I understand that the source of speaking is not in the need to describe or to imitate, but in the will to warn, to command, or to protect.

The more I draw, the more I understand my muteness. I understood better the mechanism of speaking. It is all about purpose; the difficulty lies in the lack of purpose. Why would it be important for me to speak if I had no purpose in speaking? How are the events that are happening to me important if they lack any logic or purpose? Why would I want to make the effort and speak about events that have no purpose to them? I would be a mute until the last day of life. My life would never have any purpose; I would never be a mother, a wife or anything useful in society.

Silent Marionette
침묵의꼭두각시

Namie

Doctor Matsumoto was moved to the front without any advance notice. An officer in a jeep just came and gave him ten minutes to pack. He did not even say good-bye to Kumikko. One minute he was there in her arms, and the next he was gone. She was sitting on the edge of the bed when Namie came for her with the guards, her sharp little teeth exposed in satisfaction.

Her little rat eyes were glowing. "You are coming with me!" she ordered, and then emptied out the house of the dishes, clothes, shoes and all the cheap jewelry the doctor had ever gotten for Kumikko. Namie had won. She had been waiting for it a whole year. She now owned the stubborn girl and everything she had. Namie was happy. Her patience had paid off; she was the last one to laugh!

Kumikko is determined; she will not let Namie get her. She will show them all! They keep fooling her, the bastards; life is fooling her. She has had enough! Her burning thoughts are putting her whole body on fire. She will win. She will be the one to strike the final strike. There is no way in the world that she will finish her life in that dirty brothel. She is not a low life marionette; she is Mi-za. She will show them all!

Strip!

Strip!

Strip!

Namie is becoming paranoid now. She is making her inspections every couple of hours. A new doctor is coming to the brothel, and she intends to start her relationship with him on the right foot. Her marionettes will be clean and healthy.

My stomach is rumbling. I am hungry; oh so hungry. My gifts from Kumikko are now finished. I will die from hunger. Only once a year on April 29, Hirohito's birthday, do we get to eat a decent meal. There are eggs and meat and the marionettes are eating until their stomachs burst. Hirohito means "*Showa*", which in Chinese means enlightened peace, which always made me wonder if the Japanese did understand Chinese.

They called themselves the *Yamoto* people, which meant great peaceful race, but they were busy killing, raping, and torturing throughout their entire fifteen years of occupation of the East. What was the source of their hatred for all other races? It was beyond me.

The Emperor himself admitted that he was Korean. The Emperor that was the god of his people talked about his Korean ancestry and said that he had a close kinship with Korea. The modern Japanese had come quite late from the mainland of China to Japan. In recent years DNA tests have confirmed their close genetic kinship to both Korea and China.

After the shower that day, Kumikko gave me an envelope. "Bring it to my parents after the war," she said.

"Why?" I motioned, the fear cutting my guts.

"Just do it!"

I am angry; she manages to annoy me with her stubbornness. I shove the envelope under my dress. Now what? What is she planning now? She is seriously getting on my nerves.

I hold her by her shoulders; I shake her, "Stop!"

"I have a plan," she says, a strange expression in her eyes. Her face is ashen. She looks like a stranger to me. Her eyes are alight with a strange flame, sharp and distant.

I hold her more firmly. "Don't you dare!" I am thinking.

However, as if she reads my thoughts, she is trying to break free, to repel me.

Silent Marionette
침묵의꼭두각시

My hands are weakening. They have all gone crazy here. The whole world has gone crazy. What is the point anyway? There is no hope; we are all going to die sooner or later. It is a matter of seconds between life and death in this world.

I released my grip on her now, and she stood still and then turned to me and said, "You must survive, Pil-nyo! The war will end soon. The doctor told me. You must survive so you can deliver the letter to my family."

I am looking at her beautiful, stubborn face; my heart is breaking. "Let's stick together from now on..." I never had a friend like Kumikko and will never have a friend like her again. I have to let go of her now. She is not the type that would let herself be crushed like a worm under Namie's boot.

She would also have a problem controlling her nerves. She would lose all control of herself and attack Namie. She would pull her ugly eyes out and would crush each pimple on her disgusting face! With that, she would bring a disaster not only on herself but on all the girls.

In the dining room, I am sitting between Lee-ping and Liu-fang swallowing the rice. Today we get a special treat, a glass of milk. We sip it slowly. The pleasure of the white liquid is spreading through my body like a fantasy. We look at each other with disbelief, our fingers wiping the table as if there are invisible drops falling, and we are licking our fingers as if there are really drops of milk there.

A sip and then a finger lick, a sip and then a finger lick, it is a heavenly taste, it is a present from Buddha; great dear holy Buddha does exist. Maybe it was a treat to impress the new doctor that we are being fed right. The new doctor is young and tall; he looks like he is in his thirties. The *chokpparis* are usually short in height, but this man was tall, which seemed strange to us.

In the middle of all the lip smacking, Kumikko gets up. She does not even touch her milk. She is walking now toward the kitchen, her back as straight as a ruler and her face eerily white. She is moving robotically, with total confidence, before the wide-open eyes of the crowd, the open mouths of the guards, and the shock of the officers.

She is walking proudly now into the kitchen, as if it is a daily thing that she's supposed to do, to just walk as a robot into the holiest of all holies of the brothel, the kitchen. Namie is frozen stiff and her mouth is open. I can see only her bottom sharp teeth. It takes her a full minute to get up and go after Kumikko who has disappeared behind the kitchen door. It is good to be a mute in cases like this. The scream gets stuck somewhere in the guts. If I would not be a mute, they would shoot me for screaming like a mad woman.

Silent Marionette
침묵의꼭두각시

Namie is rushing into the kitchen, her club already in motion. None of the guards is getting up; they are all sitting in their seats, not moving. We all know that whatever will happen now is only between Namie and Kumikko; it does not concern anybody else. It is quiet for a while; the silence in the air is heavier than a ton of bricks.

The guards, the officers, and the marionettes are all watching the closed kitchen door, their mouths wide open. Suddenly a noisy crash of heavy metal shakes the house to its roof. Nobody moves; everybody is still. No one wants to know, and no one wants to see.

There is no screaming, no wailing. All we hear is the crash of pots and pans and then a shattering, guttural cry. Moments later, after we have recovered from the paralyzing shock that has overtaken us, we slowly creep into the kitchen, where we find Namie lying lifelessly on the blood-soaked concrete floor, her throat cut wide open from ear to ear. A few feet away, leaning against the wall is Kumikko, who has a butcher knife lodged in her abdomen hara-kiri style. I press the envelope into my chest. Kumikko has a peaceful expression on her face. She has won; she has had the last word!

Outside the cold, strong wind is entering the bones. Tomorrow the big pots will be washed of the blood, and the cooks will prepare warm soup. Eating soup is a good way to warm the body in the cold bitter Manchurian winter.

I felt hungry. All that had happened had not even touched me. I was just hungry for food. I could eat an entire elephant now, I thought to myself. I went to my cell and hid Kumikko's envelope among my drawing papers. "Sayonara, Kumikko- san!"

Silent Marionette
침묵의꼭두각시

The sun never dries my tears

Saeya saeya parang saeya,

(Bird, bird, a blue bird)

Nokdu batte anzi mara,

(Do not take a rest in the green gram field)

Nokdu kkochi ttoro zimyun,

(When the green gram flower leaf falls,)

Chongpo zangsu wulgo ganda

(Then, the bluish hemp cloth peddler goes crying)

Things had gotten much worse now for the Japanese troops. In the next few months the attacks by US troops came one after another. The Japanese lost Kwajalien and Majura atolls in the Marshall Islands, the base in Turk in the Caroline Islands was destroyed; the Mariana Islands were attacked from the air, and American ground forces landed in northern Burma.

On April 17, 1944, the Japanese began their last offensive in China, attacking US air bases in the eastern part of the country. The Chinese and the Americans worked hand in hand now, and we could smell the end of the war coming. The question in our minds was, "Are they going to kill us all in order to get rid of evidence, or just leave us and run back to Japan?"

That year, after an eventful April during which the Allies invaded Aitape and Hollandria, and the Biak Island in New Guinea, it was a very quiet birthday for the emperor. We were not expecting much, knowing that the army's morale was low, but we did get white rice and soup that day. We had not eaten soup for ages, and this was a blend with some vegetables. It tasted good.

When you take fish out of the water most die right away; only the strong will survive a few more hours. Abazi used to tell us that repeatedly, particularly when my older brother Pil-ku would say that he hated the village, Korea, and everything in and out of his house, and would threaten to run away to America. I now understood what Abazi meant when he said "Fish out of water". I was one of the strong fish, but my time was up.

Death was closer than ever. Very few hours separated being full and being starved. I knew that very well, but I could not force myself to eat. I would tell myself I had to eat to survive, but the sight of Kumikko's blood leaking off the pots and pans in the kitchen would not give me rest.

The food is stuck in my throat, but if I do not eat, I will turn into a skeleton and they will execute me. No soldier wants a skeleton in his bed; they want to feel the flesh and the health. Who wants to make love to a bunch of bones? "You must survive!" Kumikko told me. I try to swallow the rice, but it hurts in the throat as much as the words that get stuck there somewhere.

The words and the food are both against me. Food will not go in and words will not come out. Both situations are bad news for a comfort woman. However, I cannot swallow; no matter how hard I try, I just cannot. I push my bowl to Liu-fang. She looks at me sadly. "Eat! You must eat Pil-nyo!"

I shake my head, "I can't."

Why am I hungry only when there is no food? The hunger is burning like an open wound. I feel I am losing my mind; I must eat! I so long to eat! But when the food is in front of my eyes, I can't even put it in my mouth.

We are hardly getting any new girls now. Maybe that is a sign that the end of the war is coming. When a new girl appears, I go near her and smell the wonderful smell of a foreign, free world that comes from her body before she becomes just another marionette. The frightened girl smells like the most wonderful smell of heaven, a smell of home and a mother and a father, of forests and fields, of freedom and distant laughter.

What would I give to go back home now to my little village, to bury my sisters and parents as they deserve to be buried. I would find my brothers, hug them, and ask them for forgiveness. I would ask them for mercy and be their slave to the day I die. I know I would never be a normal woman. I would never be loved again like before, and I would never be a mother.

There will never be a function for me back in the village. I am a prostitute. I pleasured the enemy. I am dirty; I am cursed for the rest of my life.

Where were my brothers when the Japanese animals killed my family? My mind keeps wondering about it. How did they know to hide? Did they hide? By now, maybe Pil-ku is in America, and maybe he took my younger brothers Pil-nam and Pil-sok with him. Someone once told us that in America there are money trees. All you have to do is to pick it. They might all be living there in a huge house in that magic money land, and eating meat every day, the best kind of meat.

I might have lost my mind. How many more days could I lie down on my back and receive strangers' sperm into my body? They are all killers, all murderers. The youngest of them all had raped or killed a person, no matter where they had come from. Lying day and night like this in silence, in this horrendous muteness, is as hard as death.

Life is much more bearable if you can spill your heart out to somebody. Eventually all the comfort women pair up so they will have a friend to talk to, but not me. I cannot give advice or comfort their pains. I am a mute, and therefore I am deaf. Dumbness always goes hand in hand with deafness, no matter what.

After a while, even if people know you can hear they forget it. The silence is a blessing and a curse. I can hide in my silence from all the evil, yet I can hear much better than others, things I do not want to hear. I watch the two Chinese girls licking Hirohito's birthday rice bowl. They are both still holding each other's hands under the table, looking like a couple of broken dolls.

"*Bora Pil-nyoya, nabi aniga*" (look Pil-nyo it is a butterfly!) Yong-soo's beautiful face is now looking at me. Why did you leave me? You promised to stay by my side forever and ever. There are no butterflies here, no flowers, nothing but emptiness and darkness. I will never be your wife; some other girl will hug your back at night and sing you love songs. Some other girl will bear your children and share a bowl of rice with you. Your strong arms will hold her tight, and you will never again be mine.

I never had a real friend anyway until Kumikko came along. My sister Pil-sun was the closest soul to me, but she is still on the kitchen floor at home lying down, torn apart; and her face is still sealed in an expression of "Why?"

Yong-soo was my best friend. Perhaps he is sitting now in our favorite spot on the hill, looking down at my father's field and thinking, "Where is Pil-nyo, my best friend Pil-nyo, the purest, the cleanest, and the most beautiful of them all? Where did she go, leaving me like this to pain; when will she be back to marry me?"

Doctor visit!

Doctor visit!

Doctor visit!

Ever since Namie was gone, the order was gone. The almighty queen's masculine screaming voice still echoed in the building. There were several calls made to inquire who the next supervisor of the establishment would be, but the Japanese army had more urgent things to deal with. The new doctor was no one to talk about. He was nothing like Dr. Matsumoto. Many times, he would examine a girl and then have her right there on the examination table.

Silent Marionette
침묵의꼭두각시

The brothel now was not run as meticulously as in Namie's days. The building was dirty and messy; we were spotting mice and roaches everywhere. Inspections became rare; some of the girls did not bother cleaning up their cells or their bodies.

By the summer of 1944, the building was infested with vermin. Namie had her evil minuses, but she had her pluses too, and they were missing now. The guards did not have her sharp eye as to which soldiers to engage to which marionettes. The disorder and chaos were everywhere; nobody really cared anymore, and everything was loose and unattended. A number of girls managed to find ways to commit suicide, and some of the soldiers deserted.

The soldiers now became even more impatient and violent. They were experiencing many defeats at the front. The Americans bombed the Japanese railways in Bangkok, Thailand, and then invaded the Saipan and Mariana Islands. Then the American planes bombed Yawata. On July 22 the Americans destroyed the Japanese air defenses in the Marianas and then liberated Guam.

There was a feeling of desperation and defeat for the first time among the young, tired soldiers. They started to doubt the reasons why they were not home with their families living normal lives. And of course the frustrations found their expression on the girls again; we were all constantly covered with black and blue bruises, black eyes, cuts and scratches.

The summer came with all its might, and the heat was unbearable. The fans in the tiny cells just moved around the hot air. In the brothel there was no joy. Nobody really cared about the change of seasons; we never got to be in the sun long enough to enjoy it anyway. As Liu-fang said, "The sun never dries my tears."

She was right; the tears kept coming and coming no matter what. We were all irritated, and as skinny as skeletons; it got to a point where we would catch mice and sometimes eat their meat raw out of desperation. Some girls would go out to the woods to try and find some snails and worms, and then cook them as soup.

We would find some frogs and tiny fish in the lake if we were lucky; whatever was edible we consumed. Of course, there were no stray cats or dogs left in the all of Manchuria; the locals had eaten them all. If I were lucky, a soldier would sometimes leave me a cigarette or a piece of candy. The soldiers themselves were hungry. They never got enough food either. I would trade the cigarettes with the cook or with one of the guards for a piece of bread or an extra bowl of millet, and force myself to eat.

At that point, Kumikko's room across the hall was given to Nina.

"For high officers only"

Nina was brought in under mysterious circumstances from the Philippines. She was an experienced comfort woman. Meng-sun told me of her arrival and spent more time than usual preparing her cell. A new, fancy, thick dadami was brought there, and two big, wooden, and traditional Japanese boxes for Nina's treasures. Meng-sun spread perfume on the bedding and left a lot more makeup than I ever saw her providing for the rest of us.

"This one is like a celebrity," she said. "She has been all over the front units and has made herself a name as the best, absolutely top prostitute there is. She is intended only for high officers now, and they don't pay her yellow stamps, but with expensive presents and real money." Then she hung a sign on the door saying, "For high officers only!" The entire brothel was preparing itself as if for the arrival of royalty. I could not grasp what the excitement was all about. Even if a top prostitute was arriving, what was the big deal?

When she walked into the brothel, however, we understood the excitement. Nina was the most beautiful woman we had ever seen. She actually looked like a queen, with her straight back, her beautiful, healthy, well-built body, her incredible rear-end and her sculpted breasts. Her long, wavy brown hair was well groomed and lying on her shoulders, shiny and beautiful. Nina had big eyes and lips that reminded me of cherries. Her nails were long and well groomed, as if she just walked out of a beauty salon, and her lovely figure was full.

The fragrant smell as she walked by made me dizzy. This was probably how the American movie stars looked, I thought to myself. She had a confident way about her, as if she knew that she was a celebrity. She was walking in a way that showed she was expecting the doors to be opened for her and the bags to be carried for her. The guards naturally were all over her, flattering and hustling like a bunch of busy hens.

I was wondering what Namie would say to this new phenomenon. I do not think she would have stood for this circus. I could see her thin lips vacuumed into her mouth in disgust, and spitting, "Who is that new fancy dirt? I will show her a thing or two...," but Namie was no longer there since

Kumikko had decided to take her with her to the next world. The remaining guards had their hands full now with Nina.

The Japanese were suffering one defeat after another. The soldiers were cut off from food supplies and ammunition. Thousands of dead fighters' bodies were tossed into the fire on all fronts. There were rumors of an all out war on the mainland of Japan. The Japanese citizens were prepared for the worst; they were told that the Americans were close. Nobody knew what was going to happen next. There was hardly any food; it was the worst summer ever.

We would go to the forest with slingshots to try to hunt for birds, but even the birds were rare, as if they felt that the world did not mean well for them. Fish in the stream were small and had hardly any meat on them, and the locals grabbed the berries long before we had a chance to get to them. At that time Nina's room was filled with the best of the wines and snacks and the most expensive meats.

High officers were coming from far away; they would travel sometimes a whole week just to get a night with Nina. Reservations were made a month ahead of time. The supply office sent a special, fancy leather notebook where all reservations were planned and recorded by the new head guard, Misaki, and signed by her. Misaki was the exact opposite of Namie; she really hated her job, and tried to get away as much as she could.

She understood the logic of having comfort women for the soldiers, but for the life of her, she did not understand the whole establishment of brothels. Why couldn't they just take these idiotic girls to the front as they did with the rest of them?

She hated China. She hated the weather, the lowlife Chinese, and the food. Even the water tasted rotten. However, most of all Misaki hated fancy, spoiled brats like Nina. As far as she was concerned, all Filipinos belonged in the garbage and not in a cell made up as a *washitzu* (Japanese room), with fancy makeup and perfumes.

There was not enough food for the staff, and no food for the girls. Misaki and the other Japanese guards were always looking for ways to get some more food on their plates. They would deal and sell any object they could for some more food. The Japanese guards had families back home in Japan who were starving, and brothers in the army who were either dead or wounded. Nina overall was not a great blessing for them, and they kept whispering and protesting about it.

Nina had an odor of another world, a world far gone, a smell of freedom, of laughter, of good times. I would watch her from my cell with my mouth wide open, as if I were watching a rare animal in the zoo.

She is partially sitting and partially lying on her fancy *makuru* (pillow) that was shipped just for her.

Her china bowl is full of white grains of rice that look just like shiny pearls. Nina is holding her silver spoon in her long fingers, and eating the grains of rice slowly, lazily, bringing the spoon up and down in aristocratic movements, as if she is forced to eat.

Two pieces of bread have been sitting on a plate by her since last night, as if they are begging, "Nina, please eat us; put us in your magnificent cherry lips." However, Nina eats only when she wants; those slices of bread will eventually be tossed to the garbage.

Only Nina can stop her act of lovemaking in the middle, and tell a high officer that there will not be anymore love giving unless he orders her a tray filled with beef and wine. God knows where those guards would run to get the beef. I did not think there was a single cow left in all of Manchuria.

Nina does not talk to anybody. She does not mix with the other girls. She showers and eats when she feels like it, and takes her walks under the close supervision of the male guards, who feel honored to do this job and escort her as if she is the Emperor's concubine. She jokes with the officers, stretching her long, beautiful legs, exposing her snow-white teeth, and my heart is bursting with jealousy.

Here is a happy person. How did she have her life made for the art of loving? I am hypnotized by her self-confidence, the angelic, relaxed expression on her face, her catty, fearless eyes, the way she licks those cherry lips as she sips from her royal cup of coffee.

Nina gets all the coffee and wine she wants. For The first time in the history of the brothel, a special stock room is created for one of the girls and her clients. The guards themselves never touch the meats and the coffee and wine. Those luxury Items are intended only for luxury people.

The shipment unit would itemize in meticulous detail what was shipped. In addition, every item of food or drink had to be written down and signed for by Nina or the officers. If something were missing, the guards would be punished severely and could even face execution.

Nina would ring her pretty little china bell and the guards would raise a brow. "The princess is ringing again." They would go into her cell bowing, , "Yes Nina", "No Nina", and go back and forth with trays filled with little bowls of colorful snacks, the finest of the imported wines, and the best of the rice. Who ever had had the opportunity to see all this luxury since the beginning of the history of all brothels?

The high officers would leave her expensive rings and pearl necklaces, silk robes and stockings, and endless amounts of money.

In no time, Nina has built an empire in her cell. She is a VIP, and receives only VIPs. We the prisoners are watching the celebration of Nina's ego, and we are losing our minds from hunger and thirst, from pain and despair.

Yuriko, one of the guards, would spit on the floor and blurt out, "This lousy damn whore, I will make her eat dirt; you'll see!"

Misaki would curse her mother, and the mother of the mother of her mother, every time she passed her cell. "Goddamn bitch, wait until you fall in my hands!"

Meng-sun would swear to me that one day she would wrap her fingers around Nina's fancy swan neck and choke the life out of her slowly and painfully.

At that point, I started drawing Nina. At first, I did it out of fascination at the incredible new phenomenon in the brothel, and then I started doing it to draw her attention.

Silent Marionette
침묵의꼭두각시

"As long as you draw me, you'll live!"

I was a mute and my body was a pile of bones. I looked like an old woman after more than a year in the brothel. I was never a hungry person, never ate much even if I could, but now the hunger was eating me up, boiling my bones like a raging fire. What would I give to lick even the crumbs that were falling to her feet while she was gracefully putting the spoon in her mouth.

I had to get her attention against all odds. She never talked to any of us or to any of the guards. Why would she pay attention to a mute, miserable creature like me? Ever since she had moved to Kumikko's cell, right across from me, she never once even gave me a glance.

She was the kind of woman that never looks around anyway; she never really needed to see anybody else. I would wait for her to stretch like a fat, sleepy cat and I would draw her, one sketch after another, as if I were completely enthralled with her. I must have filled up six notebooks with my sketches of her.

One good thing that remained after Namie was the silent agreement of the guards to provide me with an unlimited supply of paper and pencils.

Actually, they were proud of my ability to sketch. When soldiers refused my services after hearing that I was mute, the guards would tell them that I was an also an artist. Many times the officers and soldiers, instead of torturing me with sick requests for lovemaking, would pose for a sketch and come out happy from my cell having something to send home to their wives and mothers.

I found that the drawing was an important survival skill; it brought an extra yellow stamp, an extra cigarette, and a bit of confidence. The drawing also soothed the hunger and the pain; I had something to do other than to think about food.

It was not long before she spotted me. "What is she doing, staring at me day and night?" she demanded from Meng-sun.

"She is drawing you!"

"Ya! You there! What are you doing?" She turned to me.

"She is mute, she can't speak!"

Now she seemed interested. "Mute," she repeated and her brow furrowed.

"Take me to her cell!" she ordered Meng-sun.

I squeezed myself to the wall in my typical way of curling into a ball. This was one of the times I felt it was good to be mute. Now all depended on my performance and my drawing talent.

If I could just get one more slice of bread a day from Nina, I would shave my head and become a monk after the war, and give my life to serving Buddha until my last day on earth. Only a few hours separate between hunger and starvation. I was at the point where the starvation had reached its peak. It was Nina, or finding a fast way to end my life.

Many times I was contemplating doing exactly what Kumikko had done. If I could just have gotten my hands on a knife or anything sharp for that matter, I would have been dead a long time ago. But after the incident with Kumikko and Namie, there was a heavy guard on the kitchen doors, and no way to get into the kitchen.

The pleasure of dying was not so easy to attain, and because the shipments of marionettes had almost ended at that point, the guards made sure we stayed alive even in the form of bags of bones. As long as we were justifying their salaries, we were good enough to live.

Nina entered my cell, her fragrance filling my nostrils so powerfully that I felt my head spinning. She stood above me

Silent Marionette
침묵의꼭두각시

like a queen, examining my face and my curled up body, and then turned to Meng-sun. "Leave us alone!" she ordered.

Meng-sun turned around unwillingly, mumbling a curse under her lip. Nina extended her hand to me. "Show me your drawings!" I handed her the notebooks. Nina stood there flipping the pages, and then sat down on the edge of my dadami.

She lit a cigarette and then played with it silently, rolling it between her long fingers. I was sitting there shrunken like an empty package, looking at her, waiting for the verdict. She put away one notebook after the other, and then said suddenly, "My mother is mute."

I lowered my head.

"She is deaf, too.," she added.

I looked at her curiously; an expression of pain was brushed on her face. I had found her weak point! Things became clear to me now like they had never been before. I knew what I was going to do. I grabbed my notebook and started scratching her. I drew her for the first time from close by, only face, no body. I caught the expression of pain and exaggerated it as much as I could. I darkened the eyes, brushed her cherry lips longer, and brought the lines down for a dramatic effect. I darkened the shades around her cheek bones and made her look melancholic and gentle.

She was still sitting there as if lost in thought, her hands sitting gently on her lap. It seemed that she had forgotten my existence. I finished my work and looked at it satisfied. I was happy, even given my pitiful physical and emotional state, the burning hunger in my guts, and the pains all over my body. It was the best work I had ever done. I looked at Nina and thought, "What a beautiful creature!" I sighed loudly.

She heard me and turned her face toward me. I handed her the drawing and she glared at the paper. Her eyes stared frozen at the drawing and then a little tear, like a tiny diamond, came down her cheek. I put my hand on her hand, but she shook her head as if waking up from a dream, and pushed me away.

I shrunk again into my corner praying, "Please don't punish me, dear holy Buddha. I had bad thoughts about you. I thought you were gone. I thought you abandoned me, but I was wrong. I was a sinner to think so. Please, I will never think badly of you again; just do not leave me. I beg you, good Buddha of the mutes, the Buddha of mercy, do not punish me. Help me; please do not leave me! As soon as the war is over, I will shave my head and go to a temple, to be your servant forever and ever!

Time froze. All the clocks in the world had stopped. Abazi forgot to teach me that there are only a few seconds between heaven and hell. Nina raised her pretty head and said, "From now on, you will be my profiler; you will draw me every time I tell you to. You will draw me inside out, the way I really am!"

I pushed my fist onto Kumikko's notebook. I never dared open it. I did not know how to read anyway. I could not make myself look at her handwriting. I could not face Kumikko; I was not strong enough for that, but I understood what Nina wanted. Nina wanted me to create her own diary; she wanted me to create her story with my sketches.

I nodded my head and shrank myself into a ball again.

"Wait here!" she ordered, and left my cell with all my drawings. She came back after a minute with two slices of bread and a big piece of dried meat, and laid them on my dadami. "You will live," she said quietly. "As long as you draw me, you'll live!" Then she turned, her back as straight as a queen's, and rang the china bell. "Shower!" she spit out to Yuriko who came bowing again and again to the royal marionette.

I looked at the treasure on my dadami in disbelief. I had never seen so much food from close by since I had come to the brothel. I hid one slice of bread in my dress devoured the other one like crazy. Then I lay down on my blanket, sucking on the meat as if I was sucking on life.

The meat melted in my mouth and tasted like heaven. My body answered the pleasures of the meat like magic. I was drunk with happiness from the grace of Buddha, from the beautiful world I was lucky to live in. Buddha was alive and well; he had never disappeared. He just had to be the one to decide when to appear.

I had found the key that mother told me about, the key to my magic garden; my silence and my talent for drawing had opened the gates to the magic garden for me. Only a few seconds and a very short distance separated heaven from hell. I was on my way to heaven.

Liu-fang

In September of 1944, the American troops invaded Morotai and Paulaus, and immediately after that came the air raids against Okinawa. The people of Okinawa were starting a long, sad journey into their dark fate. The Japanese were suffering defeat after defeat, but their stubborn nature would not give up.

The more soldiers that died or committed suicide, the more warplanes that were shot down, the more stubborn the government became. It was a matter of honor, a matter of keeping face. After so many years of occupying the countries of Asia, and the feeling of being a superior nation that could do it all, it would be horrible for the Japanese to admit failure. They would fight to the last soldier and sacrifice the last citizen, but would not give up their occupation and would never admit losing the war.

The fall arrived in Manchuria that year on a full, relaxed stomach. The house became cooler, the leaves started falling from the trees, and light breezes were blowing outside. I was never hungry any more; my figure started filling out thanks to the food payments I got from Nina. I shared my food with Liu-fang. I was determined to keep her alive.

Lee-ping had died a few months earlier from lung disease. She started coughing one day and never stopped. Her cough became so persistent that Lee-ping begged Misaki to take her to the doctor, but only when she started spitting blood did Misaki finally comply. By then it was too late. Lee-ping never came back. We heard the news of her death two days later.

Poor Liu-fang was mourning so deeply she almost died. She stopped eating and could not end her crying. She wound up with a very high fever and was taken to the hospital, were she stayed for weeks until she finally recovered. When she came back to the brothel, she seemed like a ghost. She carried herself like a broken woman, her body bent and crooked. Lee-ping had been a lifeline for her, a reason to survive. Now it was over; there was no reason to stay alive.

The soldiers constantly complained about her, and she was beaten by them and by the staff. However, I was determined to keep her alive and forced her to eat half of my share of Nina's presents. "If the war ever ends" she said, "I will go far away and never come back to this continent. I will go to live on the other side of the world. My feet will never touch these cursed eastern grounds ever again!"

Liu-fang came from a village near Nanjing. When the Japanese arrived in 1937, she was a young girl. All the houses and fields that had been passed from father to son for ages were burned to ashes. Women and children were raped brutally and murdered, babies were tossed into the fire, and people were lined up by the side of the road, stabbed, and shot to death.

Liu-fang watched her mother and sister being violated and killed, just as I did. After three soldiers, one after the other, raped her, she was brought to the officer in charge, who was impressed by her beauty and kept her for himself for two weeks. As a reward, before he left for his next station, he sent her to Manchuria to the brothel.

Liu-fang received good training from her officer since he was brutal and mentally deranged. She never knew what he was going to say or do. He would torture her until she would lose consciousness, then buy her food, and tell her how much he loved her.

Liu-fang met Lee-ping on the train. They were both scared to death, and since they were seated together all the way to Manchuria, they held hands and did not let go after that.

In spite of her pitiful psychological state, Liu-fang decided to survive. Since there was no family left for her back home, and she needed to justify her strange will to survive, she decided to adopt Lee-ping to give herself purpose. Lee-ping would be her new sister and Liu-fang would have to live for her.

In this game of life and death, Liu-fang needed a reason to excuse her existence. She would be free to die only if she ran out of excuses.

Silent Marionette
침묵의꼭두각시

Now Liu-fang was my reason to tell death to wait. Nina had come when I was already starting to smell Death and feel him around me. He was close by all the time, and I was sure that he had gotten tired of my nagging and was willing to take me now. Nina's arrival was timed as it was by Buddha because he had it in mind for me to keep Liu-fang alive. And when I shoved food into her mouth, she had to eat it, no arguments.

The guards were not very happy with the situation. They could forgive the fact that the poor, dying Korean mute was being taken care of now by Nina, but there was no justification in their minds for spoiling a little Chinese whore. Like all the Japanese, they did not see the Chinese as human beings; they believed that the more you starved and tortured them, the better they were at work. That was why Liu-fang was kicked around by the guards and always abused.

Nina would come to my cell at all hours. When she demanded to be drawn, it had to be right away. The guards could not send too many soldiers to my cell since they never knew when Nina would need me. That disturbed the entire schedule and order in the brothel. Not too many girls were left, and the guards needed my services. Nina received her high officers as if there were no war out there. She built a world of her own in the brothel.

Having walked into hell through the hallway and seen the horror, the torture, the dirt and the violence, all I had to do was to open Nina's door to enter the gates of heaven. Nina's room was sparkling clean and smelled of fine perfumes. She had silk curtains on her window and silk sheets on her fancy dadami. She had no end of jewelry and robes, delicate china dishes and the finest foods.

I drew thousands of sketches of her. Sometimes she would bring one of her officers with her and ask me to draw them together. At these times, I would make her face indifferent and distant; I would never reveal her true feelings.

The officers were generous to me, and always left cigarettes and money, real money that I kept, hoping that I might be able to use it after the war.

There is no need to talk in order to get to know a person from the inside out. I never learned art; nobody ever taught me the real craft of drawing or painting, except for the tips that I got from my sister; but I guess I had a natural talent. I could catch the inner person from the expression in the eyes and face.

Nina was like a strange, fascinating book for me, her face, her moods, her feelings, her pain, and her beauty. She changed every time she came to my cell. She could come five times a day and pose for me, and each time there was a different story in her face. She hardly ever talked. She would sit on the edge of my dadami after spreading her scarf over it; there was no way she would sit on a simple, dirty, sweaty sheet.

She would stretch her long, incredible legs forward and arch her body backward, stretching like a lazy cat. Then it was my job to look in her face for the events of the day. Had something sad, funny, interesting, frustrating happened to her? My drawings were documenting the events of her days. She was captivating to me, the most beautiful and tragic creature I have ever seen.

Nina was asked numerous times by high officers to be their private geisha. She was offered her own house and as much money as she possibly wanted, as long as she would become the sole possession of one man. However, Nina refused. Repeatedly she refused. "I am a war prisoner," she said to me, "that's all I am. I am here to be a sex slave against my will, and nobody will have the pleasure of owning me of my own free will!"

Nina was a rare bird, a rare beautiful bird any man would have liked to keep in his golden cage and indulge in for his private pleasures. Nevertheless, Nina would not let anybody break her wings. She was the master of her wings; she would be the one to decide where she would fly and if she would fly.

"Talk! You know you can talk!"

Nina never spoke of the circumstances of her coming to the brothel. It was easy for me to understand Japanese and Chinese behavior, but as far as Filipinos were concerned, I knew nothing about them. I did not know where the Philippines were, what kind of culture they had, or what they believed in.

Nina was a completely new, mysterious world for me. Unlike Kumikko she did not look for ways to run away; she was passive, complete, and indifferent to where she was. It took me a long time to understand that her attitude was a mix of self-inflicted punishment and a kind of a war of her will and ego against the entire Empire of Japan.

Nina did not even work hard on her officers; they would give their lives to be with her for one night. One disappointed officer had made a reservation for a night with her four months ahead. He had arrived from the front lines on a one-night leave. When he learned that a General had come unreserved and had taken her for that night, he had committed hara-kiri right there in the brothel's lobby.

Misaki and her friends would never forgive Nina for the way men valued her more than life. A Japanese man should know better than that. A high officer should be proud of his country and position and should not even come near the brothel to splash in the dirt of the foreign whores. Misaki and her friends swore one day to take revenge against Nina and her fancy high officers, revenge that would lbe written in the history of all revenge.

Nina felt and knew all that. One day she said quietly, "Soon I'll disappear; you will keep all the drawings and bury them for me instead of my body so that I will have a grave." I would shake my head and make my loud, weird noises. "You will never die," and she would smile a painful smile. "The only one that will remain alive from all these miserable whores will be you!" I would raise a brow; I thought I would be the last of all of them that would be expected to survive.

I had no will to live anyway. I was waiting for my death like someone who was waiting for a grand prize. I was disgusted with myself and with everything I touched. I was dirty inside and out. I was a sinner, a walking rug, a prostitute, a traitor, a no good pile of bones; that is what I was. Not even death wanted me, no matter what I did to try to end my life.

How many times did I see women die around me or kill themselves? I felt so envious of them. That world in the far beyond must be so relaxing and soothing. What wouldn't I give to meet my mother and sisters and bow to their feet to beg for forgiveness? How many times had mother and Pil-sun come to my dreams to comfort me, to assure me that they were still there? How happy I would be to join them.

At the time that I was doing Nina's drawings, she arranged that I would not have to accept more than three soldiers a day. I had to be more available for her. The guards were going crazy. Misaki wrote an official complaint to headquarters, and received an answer saying that she should abide by Nina's requests because she was a great asset to the officers and the war effort. When she wrote another protest letter, she was warned by the central war office should be that she would be fired if she were to question on Nina's status again.

Misaki was fuming with anger. The only thing she could do was to spit in Nina's places or drinks when they were brought to her. However, Nina was not stupid; she demanded her drinks in a sealed bottle so that she could pour them into her cup herself. Her meals would come sealed, packaged straight from the oven. If she suspected that somebody had tampered with them, she would not touch them.

Nina used to sigh, "By next year this time, you will be free. The war will be over. Pity, I won't be here to see the beasts retreating." I would shake my head, and make my protest voices, but she would smirk and lick her incredible cherry lips, "You will be the only one to survive, Pil-nyo. As mute as you are, you'll become the biggest voice of this war one day!"

There were days that I actually felt guilty, sitting in my cell doing nothing, while the other girls were screaming from pain and receiving sometimes up to fifty soldiers a day. As the Japanese army started smelling the end of its glory days, the soldiers became more abusive and demanding.

Thanks to Nina, my figure filled out and I looked better. She taught me how to apply makeup and would do my hair sometimes when she felt generous enough. Now that I became better looking and I was limited to three a day, the soldiers started telling stories about me. I was called the "Korean mute artist," and Misaki would get requests from officers to have a turn with me, mainly for my artistic abilities and not for my performances as a sex slave.

Misaki would come into my cell and say, "She made you a celebrity, the Filipino whore! I hope you will not lose your head and forget who you are in your glory days!"

I would shake my head and smile painfully, "I will never forget, Misaki-san," I was screaming in my mind. "How the hell can I forget?"

Now that I had most of my life focused on Nina, she became a form of occupational therapy for me. I would draw her even if she were not posing for me in my room. I drew what I thought about her and my concerns and worries about her. I drew my dreams, my hopes, and my wishes for her. She had become the focus of my life.

Toward the end of the year, the Americans invaded Mindoro in the Philippines. Nina's officers told her that in a matter of few months the Philippines would be free of Japanese. When she told me that, I smiled and opened my eyes wide. I clapped my hands. This was good news; if the Americans were to free the Philippines, then it would not be long before there would be prisoner of war exchanges, and Nina could be freed.

Silent Marionette
침묵의꼭두각시

However, Nina was not happy. She smiled a bitter smile and said, "You just keep drawing and remember your promise to me!" I held her hands desperately, shaking my head. I had never tried so hard to talk since I had become mute. "What do you want to say to me? Talk!" she said in a wave of wickedness, "you know you can talk!"

I would do it! Just for her I would do it!! I started breathing heavily, my lips opened wide. A very weak, whistling sound began, grew stronger, weakened again. I breathed deep, raised my head up, stretched my neck muscles as much as I could, and tried another time, now barely coming up with a purring sound. My face was twitching, and I waved my hands and stamped my feet helplessly. Then I started crying.

Nina got up with a disgusted expression on her face, said, "What a display of dramatic weakness!", and left my cell. However, later that night, when I was lying on my dadami half-asleep, she came and knelt by me. Thinking that I was asleep, she passed her hand gently over my face and sighed. I could feel a single tear falling on my face. She then covered me with the blanket, like a mother tucking her baby to sleep, and left quietly.

Silent Marionette
침묵의꼭두각시

Artist

Between life and death lie only few seconds, Abazi said. I am still here against all odds. Even if I am locked up in a cell and cannot count how many times I was close to death, I am still here. Buddha must not be ready for me. Nina might have a point; maybe I am still here for a reason. As I realize it more clearly every day, I put more and more work into my drawings.

Now I start drawing the brothel, the cells, and the lobby. I draw the other girls, my memories of Kumikko and Mal-bong, Lee-ping and evil Namie. I draw the mice, the rats, the roaches. I draw it all as if I am in a panic attack. I must draw what I have seen and what I see, as fast as I can, before I run out of time. Every additional day that Buddha lets me live cannot be wasted. It must be useful; it must be purposeful.

I had a stock of thousands of notebooks and loose papers in my cell. Misaki kept telling me that the mess had to end and that I had to do something about the way my cell looked; how could I host a respectable officer beneath all those papers?

One day out of the blue all the guards, Japanese, Korean and Chinese, chipped in and bought me a present, a huge wooden box, to store all my work. Meng-sun had convinced her husband after many loud fights to buy me a special box for my pencils and charcoals. I was overwhelmed; I received the gifts from the women in disbelief. Who would ever guess that those tough, violent, hard-nosed women had a soft spot somewhere for any of us?

My fingers rubbed the wooden box. I had never actually gotten a present before, except from Yong-soo who always came up with little gifts for me. I assumed they had taken to me since I was quiet. I never complained, never made a big deal out of myself or anything else for that matter. I never had made problems for them or gotten them in trouble.

My neck muscles tightened and stretched, and my fingers whitened from the pressure of the rubbing. I started breathing heavily, and deep sighs came from my chest. My face and lips shook in a terrible spasm, but I could not make myself say thanks.

Meng-sun, with a rare display of affection, hugged me and said, "Your cell will look neat now, right?" I bowed to each of the guards, a dirty body doing dirty work, with dirty people in a neat place. Yes, it will be neat from now on. The hypocrisy of the whole situation was ridiculous, but I had to admit to myself that even though they were all getting very small pay for their work, they had gone out of their way to buy me the presents. It was a very exceptional event to treat a marionette like this.

I could not help but feel a stupid sense of pride, too, since it meant that they appreciated my talent in drawing. I was not wasting my time; I was serious in what I was doing and I did it well. Now that I had become somewhat precious, and I was useful to the brothel as an artist, the guards from then on would brag about the mute marionette: She can draw your face to the smallest detail; she can even guess your thoughts and feelings while she draws you.

The officers that came to me would get a night and a sketch to remember, and would leave behind a generous amount of yellow stamps, money and gifts. It was almost as if I had become the second best choice next to Nina. Some officers would say, "If I can't get Nina give me the mute artist." Art became a strange complement to sex for some of the officers, bringing a different atmosphere to the brothel.

It was strange to feel valued after such a long time of being considered just a hollow bucket to collect unwanted sperm, a walking garbage can, a wooden marionette, a punching bag to pound and kick around. In these circumstances, my throat would constrict and I would become nauseated and confused. Now that food was available daily, my appetite gave up on me.

My body had filled out, my hair had become healthy and shiny, and my figure looked like a young woman's figure and not like an empty sack anymore. However, at that point, just to anger me, the food got stuck in my throat again. My stubborn guts were rejecting the need to eat.

Nina would get angry looking at her dishes sitting on the table untouched. "You'd better eat, stupid cow! You owe me; you have to live!" Nina would yell at me repeatedly. I would sneak food to Liu-fang and the other girls; I would also push some food to the guards, as long as I could keep Nina's anger down, as long as I could keep those dishes empty when she came in.

I tell myself I need to eat; it will end very badly, the business of my nausea. For the life of me I cannot understand the craziness of not being able to even swallow one spoon of rice when I have all this food in front of me. When I have nothing to eat, I am ready to swallow mud and snow; all I think about is food, I am going crazy, craving it. Now, when I finally have plenty to eat, I just want to vomit.

I sit and stare at my bowl of rice. "Save the life of Pil-nyo! Please, Buddha, make me eat!" I cannot swallow even one bite. Plenty of eyes are watching every movement of mine, hungry burning eyes; they all know that I will push the bowl away any minute. The question is in which direction; who will be the lucky girl who will get my rice. "The crazy mute is at it again," they must be thinking. They all jump as I push the bowl away, to grab it.

"Why is it that the boys get the big portions?" Pil-sun whispers in my ear, "We work so much harder…."

"Sh…. Stop, Pil-sun, Abazi will hear you."

"It is unfair, Pil-nyo, why aren't you eating? You will become a skeleton again and the soldiers will complain. Who wants a skeleton in bed?"

"I can't eat, Pil-sun, have mercy, I can't eat!"

"The guards will come one day and take you away; you'll disappear like all the other marionettes. Eat, Pil-nyo!"

"They were not like me. I have a function; I am an artist!"

"You are nothing, my sister. You are just a marionette. They never had an artist in the brothel, and they will live without one in the future. Any minute they will come to take you. Eat now!"

"I can't eat, my beloved sister, help me! Save me, Pil-sun. My body will not receive the food. My lips are sealed to the touch of the chopsticks. I want to throw up; I can't stand the sensation of food in my mouth."

"Eat, Pil-nyo, eat for me, eat!"

It is too late now to listen to my inner voices. The hungry tongues of the girls have already licked my bowl dry. I swear I will eat tomorrow, I swear to Buddha. Tomorrow I will force myself to swallow even if my throat will burst!

Silent Marionette
침묵의꼭두각시

Nina

When the New Year arrived, the winter turned brutal and cold. Nina now came to my cell to be sketched almost every hour. Her moods changed constantly. One minute she was in a black hole; the next she was smiling. She would bring me the news from the front as she had heard it from her generals.

On days when she had news of her country, she would act like a little girl. In the month of January of 1945, the US army invaded Lingayen Gulf on Luzon in the Philippines, and then attacked the Japanese in Manila, Nina's hometown. Later that month they recaptured Bataan and Corregidor. It would be not long before the Filipino troops and the US airborne would take back Manila.

Those were strange days for Nina. She wanted to be sketched repeatedly, and would tell me her family stories. I would use my pencil until my hand hurt, drawing page after page, rubbing with my fingers on the drawings repeatedly to get the right effects of shadow and light. My fingers were black at all times, and my dadami was covered with charcoal and ink stains.

I never worked so hard as I worked during those days. With every piece of news of failure on the part of Japanese troops in the Philippines, with every rumor of more gains by the American troops in her country, she became increasingly demanding of me and sometimes posed in my cell for sketching for a whole day at a time.

Nina was the only girl among nine children in the family. Growing up with eight brothers was not an easy task. She needed to know how to mark her territory among all those males; otherwise, she would disappear, or in the best case become a lifetime servant for them. Her father was a hard working repairperson, always looking for jobs and ways to put some food on the table. Her mother was a very beautiful young girl from a large family, but she had been born deaf and dumb.

Silent Marionette
침묵의꼭두각시

Nina's grandfather had decided to marry her mother off as quickly as possible. It would be hard for him to do that, even though at the age of sixteen she was a real beauty and men would turn their heads after her whenever she passed by. Even with all this beauty, she was deaf and dumb, and there were no families that would want to match their boys to a disabled girl.

Finally, he found a family in Manila through a matchmaker. The son was in his thirties. He was hard to be matched since he was paralyzed in one leg. It was a great honor for a girl from a remote village to be matched to a well-to-do family from the city. Nina's grandfather was very proud of himself for this arrangement. The family he had found had money; they were well respected and the young man was educated.

Nina's mother disliked this match from the very beginning. The young man was arrogant and nasty, and he thought that a disabled country girl like her was not a good enough wife for him. He was rough and unpleasant, and he treated her as he treated his servants. Eventually she had enough. She took off and disappeared from the household.

Three days later, they found her at her aunt's house in Manila. She had told her aunt in sign language that she would not go back to her husband unless he would come personally and beg her forgiveness.

Nina's mother was a stubborn girl. Being disabled in a harsh, Philippine village environment, she was always considered an outsider, a nuisance, an unnecessary burden on the family. This type of upbringing had made her tough. She had to learn to survive at a very young age. She had to learn to be decisive and assertive. It was a matter of life or death for her.

The whole family came to the aunt's house in Manila to deal with the problem, but no talking, begging, or yelling helped. After everyone was completely exhausted, her husband then came and sat with her. It might have been the first time in his life that he had seen a woman showing strong will.

Nina's mother was calm but firm. She counted her complaints on her fingers, and counted her demands, while her aunt translated her sign language. She made him write everything down and sign his name on every promise that was written. That was when he fell in love with her.

Nina's father always told her mother that what would make him the happiest of men would be for her to bring him a daughter just like herself. Five boys were born before Nina came to the world. When she was born, after a very difficult delivery, her mother looked at her beautiful big eyes, checked that there were ten little fingers on her hands then checked her toes. When she finished cleaning the little bundle, she wrapped it up and gave it proudly to her glowing husband; it was his personal present from her.

Nina was the spitting image of her mother. She had her face, her figure, and her character. She was the pride and joy of her father. Everywhere he went, she tagged along behind him. She was the center of attention wherever she went. She learned how to dance and had private tutors for her piano lessons and for her English and Japanese education. She had house cleaners cleaning after her and nannies to dress her and do her hair.

Her father worked for the Japanese, and made quite a bit of money from them. He had a factory that contracted with the Japanese to make tents and camping materials for the army.

On December 8, 1941, the Japanese launched an attack on the Philippines, just ten hours after the attack on Pearl Harbor. They were bombing repeatedly, and ground forces were landing north and south of Manila. On January 2, 1942, the Japanese occupied Manila officially. The Philippine defense continued until the surrender on the Bataan peninsula in April 1942.

Silent Marionette
침묵의꼭두각시

Most of the 80,000 prisoners of war captured by the Japanese at Bataan were forced to walk the "Death March" to a prison camp 105 kilometers to the north. About 10,000 men, weak, sick and malnourished, died before reaching the camp. The Japanese authorities began organizing a new government in the Philippines, even though they had promised independence for the islands after the occupation. They organized a Council of State. They were the sole authority on all civil affairs until October 1943.

At that time, they declared the Philippines an independent Republic. Most of the Philippine elite, with only few exceptions, served under the Japanese government. The collaboration with the Japanese was for the protection of the people from the harshness of Japanese rulers and to protect the personal affairs of people and their families. In addition, they believed that Philippine nationalism would be advanced by solidarity with fellow Asians. Many collaborators passed information to the Japanese, thereby raising considerable anger.

Underground and guerrilla organizations were formed; about 260,000 people participated in guerilla activities. Their effectiveness was such that by the end of the war Japan could control only 12 of the 48 provinces in the Philippines.

The major resistance in the Central Luzon area was the Huks, Hukbalahap, (people's anti-Japanese Army). Luis Taruc, a communist party member, formed this organization. He was able to arm 30,000 people and gave them control over much of the Luzon. Many other members were attached to the American allies and fought with them all through the Far East.

Nina would never forget the day the Japanese aircraft arrived suddenly over the center of the city, targeting the ships in the bay and the port facilities. Many government buildings, among them the treasury building, were bombed. The harrowing experiences of some people who happened to be close to where the bombs fell were told over and over afterwards.

Nina had eight brothers, four of them older and four younger. Her mother was always busy and her father was at work and often out of town. James was the oldest; he wanted to become an engineer. All the boys went to a private Christian school. They were good students, but they were bullies, always getting into trouble and coming home with black eyes and scratches.

Other children would tease them for being Japanese sympathizers and would tell them that their father was a traitor. Some laughed at their mother for being deaf and dumb and at their father because of his limp. There was always a reason for her brothers to fight, and if there was no fight with other kids that day, they fought among themselves.

The family lived a lavish lifestyle, and Nina's father was not happy with it. He argued with his wife constantly about reducing the level of expenses. He was not stupid. He knew what his fellow citizens thought about him. With all the flattering and bows around him he knew that they called him a traitor for dealing with the Japanese, and that they hated him for it.

Since Nina was the only girl, she was quite lonely. Out of boredom, she learned how to divide and conquer. She would cause trouble among the brothers for the joy of seeing them beating each other up. She would make up stories to tell her mother or father about the boys. The parents would not stop to check her stories. They would punish the boys severely. The brothers just tried to avoid her at all times, and in general, they related to her as the brat in the family.

When Nina became sixteen years old, the family was invited to a party in the army headquarters in Manila. There was no choice but to go for the sake of business relations. Nina's mother bought her a pretty dress and arranged her hair in the latest style. She was wearing high heel shoes, and looked like a doll. When she entered the party, a sigh of appreciation was heard; people looked at her and their jaws dropped. Even though she was only sixteen, she was the center of attention; men asked to be introduced to her, and were drawn to her like bees to honey.

She got compliments all night about how attractive and pretty she was. It was the first time Nina was aware of her beauty. It was an eye-opening event for her. Since her brothers always tried to avoid her and her father treated her like a live doll, she had never thought that she was someone in whom men would be interested.

This was a new sensation, the men's desirous looks, the sexual tension in the air, the way they bowed to her, the manner in which they held her when dancing with her. Nina realized that she was no longer a child. She checked herself long and hard in the mirror and realized that she was a beautiful young woman now.

From then on, she was invited to all the Japanese functions, and her father became restless. He noticed the looks that the Japanese men gave her. It was easy to forget how old she was. She carried herself as a woman. She had a sexy figure and full hips. Her breasts had grown now and were showing through her dress. Her beauty was amazing. This was a time when young girls disappeared by the thousands. They were snapped up in the streets, from schools, and even from their homes.

Her father now tried to prevent her from leaving the house; he came up with all kinds of excuses not to let her go to the parties. Her mother spent many sleepless nights because of her fears for her only daughter.

Nina's father was dealing on a daily basis with the Japanese; he knew all the high generals stationed in Manila. It was not easy to refuse invitations. Too many times he resorted to excuses such as Nina does not feel well, or Nina has to stay home to watch her little brothers. The Japanese could turn from a partner to an enemy in an instant.

Silent Marionette
침묵의꼭두각시

It was not long before the Japanese started checking Nina's father's books on a regular basis, making strange remarks that the income shown was not high enough in their opinion.

New winds of suspicion started blowing around him. The Filipinos used to say that the Japanese trust no one but the devil. They could be polite and friendly one day, and the next day could cut off your head.

Nina's father sensed the troubles coming ahead of time, and he decided to get prepared. After much argument, Nina's mother agreed to send three of the boys, Henry, Peter and Samuel, to a boarding school in England. Even though England was in a war situation with Germany, the father felt at that point that they would be safer there. Nina's two older brothers got married and moved to live with their brides' families. Nina was at home now with her mother and three smaller brothers. The servants were fired, the cook was sent away, and the father insisted on selling half of the house to another family.

In 1943, the Japanese claimed her father's factory. It was taken in the name of the war effort, and there was nothing he could do about it. Because of his old relationships with the Japanese, they allowed him to continue to work in the factory as a manager on a very small salary. Nina was eighteen, and from then on, the family lived in constant uneasiness.

The people of Manila who had always flattered them, bowed, and smiled were now happy to hear that Nina's family had lost their fortune. Nina's father had helped the people of his town with their personal problems and had given a lot of money to families in need during the period when he owned the factory. Nevertheless, the people now turned their backs on him.

Nina's two older brothers, who had suffered a lot from the neighbors' abuse because of the father's collaboration with the Japanese, joined the guerilla fighters, the Hukbalanap "Hukbong

Bayan Laban SA mga Hapon (people's army against the Japanese), determined to prove the world that they were not traitors.

Nina's father lost all his money, all his savings and assets. He felt that the end was near for all of them. He would walk every day to the factory that he loved so much. Remembering how hard it had been to build it and establish it, he would cry for hours, asking forgiveness from his dead father who had worked so hard to create it. He was full of frustration, guilt and heartache. He had gotten deeper and deeper into desperation and had become irritated and weak.

One morning his assistant came into the office and found him dead, swinging from a rope. Nina's father had committed suicide. A short note asked his family for forgiveness for leaving them behind. He was cremated that same day while the family was in disbelief and shock.

The remaining money was gone a short time after he died. Nina's mother had nothing left. She pulled the boys out of the private schools and sold all her jewelry in order to try to survive, but in the end, she was forced to sell their beautiful house for a ridiculously cheap price. The family then boarded the train and left Manila for the mother's village.

Nina's mother bought a small house on a little farm, and new life began for them. There was a little sugar cane field and a few cows and goats. Nina's mother bought a few chicks and the boys were taught how to tend to them. Nina was an outsider in the village from the minute she got there. Girls of her age were married already with children.

None of the girls in the village looked like her. By the age of eighteen, they appeared much older than their years. They had been farming the land since they were little girls. Their hands were rough and they looked like hardworking young women.

Silent Marionette
침묵의꼭두각시

Their hair would be wrapped up in the back and most likely would be hidden under a shawl. They never wore makeup or walked in high heel shoes.

Nina was a different type; she drew attention wherever she went. The men in the village were fascinated with her and the women all hated her instantly. She was a threat to them, a phenomenon they had never experienced before. She was confident and pretty, and moved like a queen. She acted as if the whole world was at her feet.

She was not arrogant, but she had an arrogant appearance. She always looked as if she was above everybody else. On the rare occasions that she would go out to help with the sugar cane or the laundry, unlike the rest of the farmers, she always wore hat and gloves to protect her skin. Nina looked different and carried herself differently. She was not cut out for life in the village. Her cousins were indifferent to her; she had not a soul to talk to or to be with.

When Nina had had enough of the village life, she told her mother that it was time for her to return to Manila and find her lost life there. She would find her brothers and join the Hukbalanap. She knew she could help by gathering information from high officers who would remember her father and would remember her too, thanks to her beauty.

Nina could speak fluent Japanese. She also had had English and Chinese lessons. She was confident that there was an honorable job she could do for the Philippines guerrillas. Nina's mother was so distressed over her idea that she was crying and pulling her own hair and scratching her face in frustration. However, she knew that once Nina decided to do something, nothing would help to change her mind. And so, after many arguments and a lot of screaming and crying, Nina boarded the train back to Manila.

The General's rare diamond

When Nina got to Manila, she was surprised to see the ruins of the city. This was not her Manila, her beloved city that she remembered. The Japanese army was everywhere. Buildings had been destroyed, and people walked around with their heads down. It was quiet; you could cut the heavy silence with a knife. The sights of the city hit her like a brick in the face. There was not a sound in the streets other than the noises of army vehicles and stray, skinny dogs.

There were no children in the streets, no young couples walking hand in hand, no elderly on the benches. It was as if a heavy black cloud covered the city. Nina went to a relative that she knew who had connections with the guerillas, and he arranged a meeting with them. The commanders took one look at her and knew that they had a treasure in their hands. Nina's irresistible beauty, her incredible body and her fluent Japanese would serve them well.

The next morning Nina entered the Japanese headquarters and asked to speak to the officer in charge. There was that authoritarian thing about Nina. What Filipina had ever dared walk like this into that office and demanded to speak to the officer in charge? The Japanese officer at the desk looked at her from top to bottom, his mouth wide open, and turned as if hypnotized and led her to the main office.

Nina entered the office headquarters commander and sat down on a chair slowly, crossing one long leg over the other, and after five minutes of very little talking she got the job. She officially became a personal translator for the headquarters commander.

The commander was an older general. He had a wife and three sons in Japan, and he had not seen them for a very long time.

Nina came into his life at the right time. She was different from any other woman he had ever met; never in his life had he seen such a lovely creature. He remembered her father and some of his officers remembered Nina, even if they had seen her only at a party. Once having seen Nina, one could not erase her from one's memory.

Nina would escort the general as his private secretary and translator wherever he went in the Philippines, like a shadow. She gave her reports to the guerilla fighters on a daily basis by messengers, phone and Morse code. She would risk her life twenty-four hours a day doing what she did. She would constantly spy and search the general's files, listen to his phone conversations, and sneak out at night to make her reports.

Nina had no idea about sex. She had never been touched by a man, and had always been protected and shielded by her family. A week after she started working for the general, while on a trip with him, he entered her hotel room and got into her bed. Nina knew she was being raped, but she did not scream or object.

She decided that playing the most willing geisha would benefit her more. Her intuition told her what to do to please the man, and he swore to himself that he had never had been in the arms of such an excellent lovemaking young woman. The general was in shock to find that Nina was a virgin; he was so touched and so incredibly moved that he decided to keep her for himself. Nobody else would touch her; the beautiful girl would belong to him as long as he lived.

Nina moved into his house in Manila and again started living the good life. She would leave for work every morning in his fancy car and eat in the best restaurants. She was welcomed as a translator in all the most highly secret meetings, and then reported the details to the Hukbalanap.

The general was a rich man and an art collector. He was not about to waste his time in the Philippines. Every home that was destroyed, every public or private building, was searched according to his orders for sculptures and paintings.

Nina was one of his rare art finds. He would take her to the most expensive stores to buy her clothes and shoes, as if he was dressing a rare doll. He would spend a lot of money on perfumes and jewelry for her. He wanted her to be the most beautiful woman on earth, since she belonged to him. When Nina got any money from him, she would send it right away to her mother.

The General treated Nina like a rare diamond. He took her everywhere with him and she met the highest, the most decorated officers of the Japanese army. They all craved her; they all tossed around in bed sweating, calling her name. If they could have snatched her from the general, they would have done it a second. How they wanted to look as happy and satisfied as their general, to lie with her in bed and make love to the most gorgeous woman on earth.

The general liked the fact that he owned rare things; Nina was definitely one of them. The general treated his rare things with the utmost respect and gentleness. He cherished his collections. During the day he would cut off Filipino prisoners' heads in a matter of a seconds without blinking an eye, but when he was at home with his stolen art collections or with Nina, who was another art object, he was a totally a different man.

Nina was living with the general almost a whole year. The guerrillas benefited from her reports so much that she became their chief double agent. After years of being called a traitor by her fellow Filipinos, Nina felt that she was getting her family pride back. She was able to see her brothers from time to time in the field, and she felt fulfilled. Nina was smart; she would listen to her general's phone calls and conversations, and would report the most important details to the guerillas.

One night she let down her guard. She was sure that the general was sleeping, and left the house to meet members of the Hukbalanap.

Apparently, the general's deputy had been suspicious of her for a while. He desired her just like all the other men in the world. Since she never gave him a second look, his lust turned to hate.

He started spying on her, determined to catch her in a wrongdoing. Nina was caught with her brother and another member of the Philippines guerillas; the two men were executed on the spot.

The general was so hurt and angry that he decided to leave her alive in the cruelest and most vicious way he could imagine. He sent her far away from the Philippines, her family, her very reason to live, to the front to be used as a high-class comfort woman.

Nina swore to herself that she would survive until the Philippines were free and she could take revenge on her general, the one who had taken her freedom and then her dignity.

Silent Marionette
침묵의꼭두각시

Buddha always forgives

By March of 1945, there were no more new women in the brothel. They were all sent now to the front, to serve the defeated soldiers. We were only fifteen comfort women left in the brothel, not counting Nina, and no matter how many soldiers were lining up out there, we had to work them all. The workdays now were twelve to fourteen hour shifts, many days without breaks or food. Even though I was officially limited to only three soldiers a day, I decided to take as many as I could to help the girls, or they would die of exhaustion.

Misaki understood that, and sent nonviolent soldiers to my cell one after another. Nina was angry that I was not available enough for her. Misaki at that point was so irritated that she told her to go ahead and make an official complaint. She told her that it was my choice and she would not argue with a mute.

Nina came to my cell fuming after the conversation with Misaki. She yelled at me, saying that I was an ungrateful brat. Here she was trying her best to protect me and get me away from the beasts, and I choose to kill myself.

I knew that she was frightened that I would stop sketching her. It had become very important to her in the last few months. I was the only lifeline she had now, the only string that tied her to reality, to some kind of sanity. It was vital to her that I would work as much as I could. I was Nina's biographer, and she knew that her days are numbered.

Nina was not a fool. She knew how to get information from the high officers and translate it to reality. Soon enough the war would be over. Her family had all been executed by the general's order. Nina had nowhere to go. Her part in this world was over.

On March 10, the U.S. army invaded Zamboanga Peninsula on Mindanao in the Philippines. On the 20th the British army liberated Mandalay, Burma, and a week later the U.S. tenth army invaded Okinawa.

The terrible stories about Okinawa came to the brothel as a shock. Two of the guards were from that island. They were hysterical at the news that apparently 90,000 Japanese had been killed. In the two months of the battle, the Japanese flew 1,900 kamikaze missions. There were 140,000 Okinawan civilian dead and more than a third of the population were wounded.

Okinawan women were raped, tortured, and murdered. Long before the Americans came in; some civilians were committing suicide, having heard about the terrible things that the Americans might do to them. The Japanese government through its propaganda was urging them to die before the enemy entered Okinawa. At that point, the Japanese started pulling out of China.

The guards were angry and confused enough to lose their patience for all of us. The beatings became intense, and the yelling and screaming were heard all day long. I packed up all the drawings I had made since Kumikko was alive, and stored them in waterproof oilcloth wrapping so they would be preserved. I felt that the end was near; the angel of death was still waiting for me patiently. He had time. He was in no rush. Moreover, he knew that I would come to him willingly when he was ready for me.

Nina had become mostly silent. She seemed distant and reserved, and stopped talking to me about herself or her family. I was the only soul in the brothel that she spent any time with. I knew her so well that I could read her mind, or at least guess her thoughts.

I knew that Nina was getting ready to die. I saw it in her eyes, her body movements, the way she looked around, and the changed eating habits. Nina no longer ordered special foods; she mostly ordered a lot of rice wine. In fact, she hardly ate, and she lost some weight. My sketches of her became darker and darker with time; she looked very lonely and depressed in all of them.

When I saw her whispering one day to one of the generals who had been visiting her often, I knew it was the begging of the end. I saw them arguing for a while, and then he nodded his head. He reserved her for the next day and I saw him slipping her a small bottle that she hid immediately. I felt nauseated.

It did not look good to me. I could guess what was in the bottle and I could guess what was in Nina's mind, but it was hard for me to expect it. I did not realize how much I had become attached to that girl. As demanding and conceited as she was, egomaniacal and abusive at times, in a strange way I had been hooked to her.

Later in life, I learn that when even if you become a biographer or a profiler of the most twisted personality in the world, you become attached to him, whether you like it or not. In the process of trying to understand and learn the person, the attachment is unpreventable.

The Emperor's birthday was coming soon. The situation was bad for the Japanese, worse than ever. In the beginning of April, just before the Emperor's birthday, The Americans flew a mission against Japan with their new P-51 Mustangs based in Iwo Jima. They sunk the super battleship Yamato and several escort vessels which had planned to attack US forces in Okinawa.

At that point, a secret meeting was called for all the high officers in the Pacific and Manchuria. The Japanese had always called for the tactic of fighting to the end, fighting to the death. Now that policy had to be changed.

Nina knew about this meeting a long time ahead from her officers. She smelled the opportunity she had longed for and she was ready for it. Most of the high officers reserved a night in the brothel, but Nina knew that her general from Manila would be the one to get her. She knew very well that as much as she had hurt his pride, as much as he hated her for betraying him, he would not give up a chance to come and see her again. He would want to see her suffer; he would want to make sure his punishment had paid off. He would want to see her in her misery, at her lowest point.

Silent Marionette
침묵의꼭두각시

Nina had been waiting for him for a long time. Now was the opportunity to close the circle. The secret meeting had been scheduled a long time ahead, and every detail was planned carefully. High-ranking officers from all over the Pacific were flown to the Manchurian headquarters. There was a total silence as to this meeting.

Those who spent the night could choose to come to the brothel, or to invite a comfort woman to their room in their hotel. Nina was not surprised when her general insisted on reserving a night with her in the brothel. He had to seek revenge; he had to see her humiliated, in the lowest and dirtiest place on earth. He had to see her trapped in her cage in the brothel.

That morning when she sat on my dadmi, I knew it was the last time I was drawing her. She looked like a princess that day. She wore her best kimono, a white satin with gentle, printed lilies. That was the kimono she had gotten from the general, the one she was caught with at the time of her arrest. She had a gold headband in her hand, and she let me brush her long thick black tresses. I then carefully placed the headband on her beautiful hair, and chose tiny pearl earrings for her to wear.

"You are beautiful," I signed to her. I drew her this time as an angel, her face alight with a heavenly glow as if she were the Madonna that I had seen in paintings. Her eyes had a different gleam, a distant, pure look. I had never drawn so well. Buddha himself helped me with that sketch, as if he were guiding my hand. I was working in a kind of hysteria and panic, mumbling to myself the whole time.

I could taste my sweat dripping down my neck, and from time to time, I would wipe it with my sleeve. When I was finally finished, I served the paper to Nina. She gazed at the sketch in disbelief and sighed in wonder. Then she handed me a big thick envelope, and said, "This is for you, Pil-nyo. I won't need this where I am going." Nina touched my shoulder for a second and looked at me, a shadow of a smile at the edge of her cherry lips, and then left.

That evening, Yuriko asked me to wear a clean kimono. "You have to look presentable, Maikko. You are hosting a very high general for the night. He chose you because he heard about your artistic abilities, do-zo! Wash your hands and clean yourself up! Don't embarrass us!"

I nodded my head, and cleaned myself up. There was no limit to the hypocrisy. I would embarrass the establishment by not washing my hands, when the dirtiest, most filthy things on earth were done to us.

From the corner of my eye, I saw Nina turning off the lights in her cell and lighting small candles as if she were preparing to worship a god. I hid the envelope she gave me; I did not dare look inside. I prepared the papers and pencils and straightened the sheets and blankets on my dadami.

That evening the preparations were different, as if I was preparing for a special event. After more than a year in the brothel, being a sex toy, a ball to kick, a marionette to torture, my body was numb. There was no connection whatsoever between my body and my soul. I hated myself; I had never hated being a woman as much as I hated it now. I wished every day that I could cut off all my private parts so that nobody would identify me as a woman.

No matter how many times I took showers or washed my hands, I always felt dirty and always was disgusted with myself. Now the only excuse I gave myself to live was my drawings, as if Buddha had given me a mission to remain alive at least until I could show the world what had been done to us.

I knew I would never talk again; I had no will to talk again. I was comfortable in my world of silence. I would never have to explain anything tc anybody. The only one I had to report to was Buddha. Mother had said Buddha always forgives. He would be my only partner for conversations.

Nina's General

A strong odor of expensive perfume filled my nostrils when
Nina's general walked into our hallway. He stood there at the
entrance of her cell and looked at her. I could feel from my cell
the heavy mass of emotion. He was a man of medium build,
very well dressed and groomed. He was clearly a man of good
taste, with an admiration for the good life.

Right away I concluded that he and Nina had been born for each
other; they could have made the ultimate couple. I could sense
his stubbornness, his sense of self-value, and his pride.

It is a shame, I thought to myself. In another time, another life,
these two would be a perfect couple.

The two examined each other quietly and he said, "*Anatta!*"
(You).

Nina smiled lightly. I could see her hand touching her hip, her
fingers getting whiter and whiter as she squeezed her Kimono.
She bowed to him "*Arigatto wakarimasida*" (thank you sir). He
entered her cell and sat on her dadami. He looked around and
then said sadly, "It's like looking at the most beautiful butterfly
in the world in a cage."

Nina did not answer, but I could read her thoughts. She would
be a butterfly in a cage anywhere she would go. The general
knew that; in his own twisted way, he loved her. Nina fascinated
him. He knew she was like a rare gem. One could own it, but
could not really wear it. There would be the constant fear that it
would be lost or stolen.

The general now felt that all his anger was melting. The
questions that tormented his mind, whether she ever liked him or
not, whether she was just using him or not, how much did she lie
to him, how many times did she fake her pleasures with him, all

this just disappeared. He examined her now at length. She looked thinner and older, and he felt the craving to hold her in his arms to comfort her, and to beg her for forgiveness.

He was angry with himself for his hasty decision not to kill her. He was angry that he had sent her to be shared with other men. He then sighed and said, "*Tottemo ippai desyo!*" (It is painful).

Nina looked over his shoulder at me. I was still sitting there waiting for my officer. I saw her lips tightening. Nina bowed again. "*Hai wakarimasida.*"

My officer came into my cell. He was an older man; his hair was completely white. He was short and muscular, and was looking at the wonders of the world that were locked in a cage. This was a new scenario for him, a little handicapped Korean prostitute who could draw. There was a shadow of appreciation on his face. He was not in a rush. He was touching my stock of paper and nodding his head. He had not expected to find rice papers in a brothel. Then he checked my ink, charcoal, and pencils. He was satisfied that I had the right tools.

"*Onama ewa nan deskka?*" (What is your name?)

I nodded my head and showed him the silence in my mouth.

"A mute prostitute?" He was impressed.

I nodded my head.

"Show me your drawings, Do-zo"

I give him some of my notebooks. He is stinking from cheap aftershave. His nails are polished and manicured. I feel nauseated; there is something truly rotten about this man.

In the cell across from mine, Nina is asking the general, "Sake?" (Wine?)

The general is nodding his head, and starting to take off his shirt. Nina goes to her table and pours two glasses of wine. In a quick movement, she grabs the little bottle from under her kimono and pours half of it to his glass and half to hers. She glances at me and closes her beautiful almond eyes. Her lips are mumbling something,

"*Sayonara*, Nina," I whisper in my head. I am staring at her hypnotized. The night is fully covering Manchuria. A full moon is hanging by my window, and a light spring wind is blowing outside.

Nina and the general are now sitting on the dadami, slowly drinking their death sake. They are not talking now. The general slowly puts his hand on her incredible leg and then starts to move up. He parts her Kimono. "Golden skin," he mumbles, "no woman has your golden skin!" He finishes his drink to the last drop and mumbles again sadly, "Golden doll."

Now he stands up and takes off his pants. Nina is stretching like a Siamese cat on the dadami.

He turns around to her, his face as pale as the wall, and then starts to vomit blood. Nina is touching his head mercifully "*Sayonara*, General" she says loud and clear, and closes her eyes. My officer starts screaming in terror; the guards are running, their clubs swinging from side to side. Nevertheless, Nina and the general are already dead, both their faces peaceful as if they both know where they are going together, as if they both planned the whole ordeal. Souls, Nina's and the general's, are flying up to heaven holding on to each other for eternity.

Silent Marionette
침묵의꼭두각시

Machiko

I am the only marionette the guards are not hassling with searches. I am lucky since I have many secrets to keep, Kumikko's diary, Nina's biography, Nina's thick envelope, all my drawings of the brothel, the money the officers gave me, the little presents. I could never bring myself to look at any of them. Nina's sketches remained tied up and wrapped in oilcloth, Kumikko's diary was hidden under all my papers and so was Nina's envelope. The money and the little presents were tucked under the dadami; I never had any interest in them.

Now when food was not available anymore, I was hungry all the time. The emperor's birthday passed by almost unmentioned that year. We did not even get an extra piece of bread. I would roam around the woods with Liu-fang and find some spring plants and berries to eat. If we were lucky, we would catch a fish or very rarely a rabbit.

The hunger is eating at me like a colony of ants biting and crawling all over my body. I am too weak now and have stopped drawing altogether. I am just lying there in my cell as a frozen marionette with my legs spread, and I let the soldiers do with me whatever they want. I am totally numb to any pain, any feeling. I obey orders automatically, as if I am a robot. My body is a separate unit from my being; it is a pile of bones and holes. I feel at all times like a dying, insignificant bug.

Now there were no more reasons to live. I did not draw anymore; there were no more gifts of food. I was far too weak. I felt that my body was floating somewhere without any weight to it. My head was empty and for the first time I started having nightmares.

Silent Marionette
침묵의꼭두각시

Mother and father came to me in my dreams screaming, my two little sisters huddled together in a big blaze of fire, Pil-sun begging for her poor life. I was walking in my village, and then I stumbled over something. I looked down and there were millions and millions of dead bodies; the entire earth was full of them. I could recognize all the dead people's faces. There were my grandparents, aunts and uncles, and neighbors. I was walking on top of the bodies, calling my brothers' names and my Yong-soo.

The bones are crunching under my feet; it is an ocean of dead bodies. I cannot find my brothers anywhere, and then Yong-soo appears in the distance. He is calling my name. "*Pil-nyo ya, naere yotae gida rizan, ode inne*?"(Pil-nyo, I have been waiting for you all the way, where have you been?) I start running towards him but the dead bodies are awakening now. They are raising their hands and catching my dress. They will not let me run. They stop me and pull me back; some of them scratch me. I can feel the pain. Some of them hit me and then they all pull me down, and I am drowning slowly into the mountains of bodies, into the darkness.

I do not know where my body begins and where it ends. I am a walking sack of air. My head, my brain and my heart are empty. It is getting warmer in Manchuria. I am smiling bitterly to myself to think that my life's dream was to see China. I am watching fat Machiko the Japanese guard, closing her fat little fingers with her bitten nails, on a fat sandwich. My eyes escort her every move, her every bite. Here I am again going crazy at the sight of food. I stare at Machiko in desperation; I can feel my face twitching. But her callousness is at its peak now. The sandwich, the most beautiful sandwich I have ever seen, belongs to Machiko. And when I had it I just could not eat.

I pull on Machiko's sleeve, my eyes begging for a bite; but she has forgotten that I am an artist; she has forgotten that I have a function. She kicks me in my stomach. I roll backwards on the ground, and she spits out, "Dissolve! *Zosenzing*!" (Korean filth).

Machiko has forgotten already how many times I made sketches of her to send to her family. I always made her look thinner and prettier. Machiko is careful to stuff her face right in front of us. I look at the other girls holding their tiny bowls of rice, their mouths leaking, watching Machiko.

She is wiping her hands and mouth with a towel. Oh! How much I wish I could be that towel right now. I could at least lick the remains of the fat from her face. I am so hungry now I want to die. As I am looking around at the other miserable marionettes, suddenly Abazi's famous saying comes to mind. "A group work is the secret for a successful organization."

In my confused, befuddled mind, I see the light. I will get all the girls together and we will have a proper feast for the beloved Japanese emperor's birthday. A mysterious, wonderful joy comes over me now, a feeling of sweet revenge, of self-confidence, of total superiority. I now fall on my knees and thank Buddha for having mercy on my desperate soul.

The night of the emperor's birthday was a quiet one. Machiko was the only guard on night shift. The others had the night off because of the holiday. They were all in their rooms drinking. The line of soldiers was very short that day. Since there were too many troubles at the front, very few soldiers had the night off.

We were waiting until Machiko had shut off all the lights and had gone to her desk in the lobby with a bottle of wine. Machiko was angry. She was the black sheep. All the other guards were having a good time partying and drinking for the holiday. Machiko always was stuck on shift at the worst times.

We all sat in our cells, hungry like rats in their holes, waiting silently. We could hear some music coming from the guards' quarters. From time to time there was wild laughter. Machiko finished her bottle. Soon her head landed on the desk and she started snoring loudly. We all came out quietly from our cells.

Silent Marionette
침묵의꼭두각시

Dong-shu had a metal cable in her hand. She had gone through hell long before landing in the brothel. She was one of six girls in her family. Her father was a scrap metal collector. Her whole house and yard were one big metal junk pile. Her father used to sell the scrap metal and fix wire fences and machinery for the farmers in the area.

Dong-shu was raped for days by a whole battalion of soldiers, along with her sisters and her mother, before being brought to the brothel. She had a compulsion about metal. Whenever she found anything lying on the ground made out of metal she would keep it or hide it. Now it came to use. Dong-shu was proud to participate in my plan. She had a long-standing account with the Japanese, and especially with fat Machiko. This was her glorious opportunity to exact her sweet revenge.

We quietly circled the desk; I felt a burst of energy coursing through my weak bones. Liu-fang squeezed my arm. She was in seventh heaven. *"Tzdo-Hongsi"* (food), she whispered, her face flushed.

Dong-shu wrapped her metal wire around Machiko's neck in a move that was as fast as a panther's attack. Any assassin would have been proud of such a quick-encircling move as Dong-shu preformed. Then she pulled; she choked Machiko silently, not saying a word, her face steady and calm as if she were used to doing this every day of her life.

Machiko began suffocating, coughing and struggling. Now her face turned blue. Foam oozed from her mouth. Her chubby arms waved to all directions. Dong-Shu silently squeezed the wire with all her might around Machiko's flabby neck until the guard's last breath had sputtered out.

"Between life and death there are only few seconds," Abazi used to say. All we are, actually, I was thinking while watching Machiko saying *sayonara* to life, all we amount to, is just walking food bags. Some are bigger than the others are, some are full, and some are empty, just bags, walking food bags. What is the value of any of us? One minute we are here and a split second later, we are dead. The only thing that is important is to fill up the stomach; nothing is more important.

A strange sensation of nastiness comes over me. Just to eat and drink until my heart is content, that is all I want. Sang-mi and Dong-shu drag Machiko's body into the kitchen and close the door. We all are standing behind to guard. Sang-mi's father was a butcher in Pusan; she had learned the craft from him. I can hear her saying to Dong-shu, "Cut it to very small slices so it will look like pork steaks."

But I am not laughing. None of the girls are laughing. Now the sweet revenge is turning bitter. The girls are slicing Machiko and filling up the icebox with her meat. The cooks will come tomorrow and will be so surprised and happy. Dear Emperor did not forget the brothel after all. Meat was sent, and the best of the meat too. All the guards, the officers, and the top personalities in the brothel will celebrate on the finest meat available.

We are cleaning up the remains of Machiko and packing the garbage bags with unnecessary body parts. Dong-shu and Sang-mi are excellent butchers; they are doing an outstanding job. We are cleaning the floor and the tables, and leaving the kitchen spotless. Then we sneak back to our cells quietly. The music is still playing from the guards' quarters. Machiko's desk is empty and lonely. Now we can hear loud voices. They are all obviously drunk.

Liu-fang was pulling my sleeve. "Wouldn't it be the perfect time to run away, Pil-nyo?" I nodded my head sadly. "But then again, we have nowhere to run away to," she concluded, and went to her cell. I dropped on my dadami, the nausea choking me. My headache was growing to a monster of a migraine; the voices in my mind were becoming louder and louder. I could hear a sickening hum; my ears were about to burst. The hell with this! I was thinking, and then lay down, fighting the anger, the fear, the guilt and the hunger; I fell into a restless sleep.

Steak dinner for the Emperor's birthday

The next day we awoke to the smell of meat cooking. It was, as expected, a perfect day for the staff. They had the meal of a lifetime. They all went down on their knees and wished the emperor happy birthday. They sang the Japanese national anthem and agreed that it was a good day to be Japanese.

The cooks were so proud of their meat supply that had arrived overnight that they cooked extra rice and vegetables for the marionettes too. We could hear them bragging about the quality of the meat that they had received. The emperor had not forgotten our war efforts in Manchuria. We all were part of the beloved nation of Japan and were appreciated too; the best pork steaks were shipped to the brothel.

The nausea from the strong odor of the meat cooking shook my body. I pushed my head out the window to get some fresh air. I dragged myself to the dining room with the other girls. I felt my head burning hot and my heart beat rapid and irregular. I was sure I was going to vomit any second.

Now I was having thoughts about Machiko's mother and father. Maybe she had siblings who would miss her. Maybe in real life, outside of this hell, she was actually pleasant and funny.

I remembered that she had chipped in with the other guards to buy me the wooden box. I was uncertain now about my brilliant idea of feeding the Japanese high-ranking officers and guards with Machiko. At this point I was wondering what my mother would say other than *"Eminai ga son mosm gatti gogi moiga!"* *(You behave like a wild animal)* *"Nere oka mon zoken nanzi?"* (What am I to do with you?) "Look at yourself!"

Silent Marionette
침묵의꼭두각시

I was laughing and crying in my mind. There was no limit to the ridiculous way the wheel of life was turning. I looked around the dining room. Dong-shu looked pale and sad, with none of the victorious feeling from the previous night remaining in her. Sang-mi was the only one who was smirking at the edge of her lips. Our eyes met and she winked at me. I was not amused and turned my face away. Liu-fang held my hand under the table, and when the meat was served, she squeezed my fingers as hard as she could. "If they find out, we are all dead." she said.

I squeezed her fingers back, to calm her down. We all stared hypnotized as the highest ranking general took the first bite into his mouth. We watched him chew on it for a while, and then he swallowed and said, "Delicious!" There were hands clapping and they all started eating. We were lucky that even though Machiko was fat, the meat was barely enough for fifteen people. We never got a share of it, thank goodness. However, we did get extra rice and some Chinese cabbage.

I kept thinking about the rest of Machiko's body parts that had been cut up and thrown in the garbage in small bags. The vultures must be having a feast on them. None of the guards had noticed that she was missing yet. They all had awoken with hangovers after the night of drinking, and assumed that she had finished her night shift and had gone to sleep. They were eating now with so much pleasure; it had been a long time since they had had real pork meat. They smacked their lips and sucked the leftovers between their teeth, and agreed that it was the best meal ever.

I was poking in my rice; there I was again looking at the food in front of me and could not put it in my mouth. Liu-fang shoved me with her elbow. "Now what, stupid?" I pushed my bowl away and then ran to the bathroom and threw up my guts. There was no end to my suffering; I felt that what I wanted most of all, my greatest wish, was to die. I stamped my foot angrily and cursed the life out of me.

On my way back to the dining area, I stumbled and fell. It had been weeks since I had had a decent meal. I was weak and tired. I lay there on the floor pretending to have fainted; it would be perfect if they would take me to the hospital, at least until the building would be free of the smell of Machiko's cooked, dead body. The guards were unhappy that I had interrupted their feast. As I predicted, they sent me to the hospital in order to get rid of me fast.

Meng-sun and her husband put me on a stretcher and wheeled me to the hospital. The doctor was at the feast in the brothel. The nurse took one look at me and said, "She is malnourished. Leave her here." I had fever, and at that point, I started shaking from weakness. The nurse put me on a clean dadami and gave me a shot, and then hooked me to intravenous fluid. I closed my eyes and breathed in the hospital smell deeply. Now the nausea was gone. Machiko was far away.

The Russians

In May of 1945, the Japanese army started withdrawing from China. The Soviet forces deployed double the number of divisions that they had had in Manchuria before. They sent eighty divisions to the border, along with forty infantry tanks and mechanized divisions plus artillery and combat support units.

The Japanese would not admit to the Soviets or to themselves that they were weakening. They started redeploying troops to Manchuria. They also started military constructions projects. Our brothel was now considered part of the front line effort, and we had to service hundreds of soldiers and construction workers.

Because of this change, new girls were being kidnapped and brought to help us. Some of them were eleven or twelve years old, still babies. There was no time to operate on them or train them. They were just thrown into the cells and raped from their first day, by large groups of soldiers. Those little girls knew nothing about sexual intercourse or pleasuring men, and consequently would be beaten up violently for not cooperating.

From then on, the horror never stopped. The screaming, crying and begging were constant. It was a nightmare twenty-four hours a day. The guards were understaffed; they had no patience or strength to deal with the little girls. They already concluded that Machiko had deserted. The Japanese army looked for her for a while, but very soon gave up. They had more serious problems to deal with.

In August of 1945, the Russians launched a surprise attack on the Japanese army that was still in the process of organizing its military and construction activities in Manchuria. The Soviets used tanks for their offensive and stormed into Manchuria finding the Japanese completely unguarded. Over 650,000 men formed one tank army, four combined-arms armies, a soviet Mongolian cavalry mechanized group, and air army.

There were about 50.000 vehicles and 2,500 tanks. The Russians found very little resistance from the Japanese. From then on they rapidly advanced into Manchuria encountering very little fighting and few kamikaze air attacks. By radio on August 14, the Japanese notified the allies that Japan would accept the Potsdam offer for surrender, but since there was no official cease-fire order the fighting went on. By August 19, there was an official surrender.

When the news came to the brothel, I knew that once the Soviets captured us they would treat us as collaborators with the Japanese. The rapes would be much more severe and they would probably kill us. I made sure all my drawings and my few possessions were in the wooden box, and performed another fainting show. This time I made sure that Meng-sun took my wooden box with us when I was transferred to the hospital.

Silent Marionette
침묵의꼭두각시

When the Russians came in the next day, they attacked the brothel, raping and brutalizing as I had expected. I escaped the torture thanks to the fact that when they took over the hospital they thought that I was just one of the prisoners of the Japanese. I was still there when they brought their wounded soldiers in for treatment; they had their own doctors and nurses. It was the first time that I got adequate medication and food in the hospital. Two weeks later, I was free to go.

Omani

The Russians just told me to go. That was it.

All the guards including the Koreans and the Chinese were taken prisoner or were killed. The girls were raped and tortured, as I knew they would be, and then were left in the brothel like pieces of trash. I found Liu-fang in the woods, after having giving up on ever finding her. She was curled up under an old tree. She looked like she was part of it.

I sat by her and held her hand; she opened her eyes, not surprised at all and smiled a weak smile. "You always know when to run away." I nodded my head. Buddha still wants me alive, I thought. I handed her a loaf of bread that the Russians had given me, and she grabbed it and took big bites, hardly chewing on it. I pulled her sleeve and motioned to her to slow down, the war is over, take it easy or you will throw up. "You're always there for me" she mumbled, and calmed down.

I watched Liu-fang quietly eating the entire loaf of bread. "Where will you go now?" she asked.

I shrugged my shoulders. Where would I go?

Liu-fang looked at my wooden box. "At least you have some luggage."

I gave her a faint smile.

"I am not going back to Nanjing!" she said, "I am going far away from this cursed land!"

Silent Marionette
침묵의꼭두각시

I held her hand, my fingers squeezing hers. For the first time in my life, I was truly terrified. I had nowhere to go. Korea was not free yet, and anyway I would feel like stranger now in Korea. Eventually I would have to explain where I had been and how I had survived. I would immediately become an outcast. My own fellow citizens might even kill me, mistaking me for a willing prostitute, a collaborator with the enemy. I did not realize how hard I was squeezing Liu-fang's fingers. She let out a scream.

"I never saw you scared, Pil-nyo!"

I lowered my head and touched the wooden box with my fingers. One day I would have to start looking for Kumikko's family, to give them her diary. I would have to search for Nina's relatives to give them her biographical drawings.

"Pil-nyo, you and I should stick together from now on," Liu-fang said suddenly.

I stared at her. I had heard that sentence before, a long time ago, when we had gotten off the train in Manchuria, my hand in Kumikko's hand. Kumikko had said that to me, meaning every word of it. My brave Kumikko was gone to Buddha now, and she was watching us from heaven with sadness.

We both looked like broken dolls. After all this time in the world of the marionettes, both of us were hollow, empty of life, devoid of feeling. We appeared much older than our ages; we were skinny and looked like used up rags. We were all alone in the world now, with nowhere to go and no one to turn to. All of a sudden, the freedom we had been longing for so badly seemed much bitterer than life in the brothel.

We felt dirty and sick. We were not even women anymore; we would never be able to get married and have children as normal women would. We were outcasts and we would die outcasts. What was the point in going anywhere? Why go on living? Liu-fang swore she would never go back to Nanjing and I swore to myself that I would never go back to my village.

We got up and went deeper into the woods, walking silently as the evening turned to night. We shared another loaf of bread and lay down under a tree. The heavy darkness spread over the forest. We could hear distant explosions and faded gunshots. "Let's sleep, Pil-nyo." Liu-fang stretched on the ground. "Tomorrow we'll decide what to do with ourselves."

Liu-fang had the ability to put her head down and fall asleep anywhere, anytime, no matter what the circumstances were. It was a cloudy, starless night. I was not tired; I could not fall asleep. I listened to Liu-fang breathing monotonically and I lay down staring into the thick darkness. I could not focus my thoughts. The darkness swallowed me in. I wished I could become part of that black void and just disappear.

A strange nervousness spread through me. I started humming to myself, to soothe my nerves.

Saeya saeya parang saeya,
(Bird, bird, a blue bird)
Nokdu batte anzi mara,
(Do not take a rest on the green gram field)
Nokdu kkochi ttoro zimyun,
(When the green gram flower leaf falls,)
Chongpo zangsu wulgo ganda.
(Then, the bluish hemp cloth peddler goes crying.)

I was sweating from the effort to calm myself down. I closed my eyes but then opened them right away; something was not right. I had been trained in the woods since I was born. My intuition gave me the warning signals again. I felt thirsty. My throat hurt; I needed water right away. The heavy darkness around me was too threatening. Silence. All I heard was Liu-fang's restless movements. The darkness was choking me. I felt my breathing getting heavier and harder. I could hear the whistle in my lungs. I am losing my mind, I thought. Now when it is all over I am finally losing my mind. Deep in the woods, I heard the owls calling. That calmed me down a little. Wherever there is life, there is water. I would wait until first light and go look for a stream. I had to have a drop of water; I was never so thirsty in my life.

Maybe I could pass the night thanks to the owls; they would keep calling and keep me sane. As long as I could hear nature functioning, I would be all right. I had the usual feeling that there was not too much time left for me. I had just sung my last song.

I wiped the sweat from my forehead and breathed deeply. Mother suddenly appeared from the darkness out of nowhere. "Omani, hold me!" I cried. Mother bent down and picked me up. She was big and strong, much more so than I ever remembered her to be. She held me like a baby and rocked me in her arms. Her face was shining; she was the prettiest of women.
"Where is Abazi, where are my sisters, Omani?"

"Sh.... Go to sleep Pil-nyo, they are fine; they're with Buddha now."

"Omani, forgive me, Omani! None of it was my fault!'

"Sh....sleep now child, I forgive you...."

"I love you Omani!"

"Sh... close your eyes child, sh....."

I closed my eyes now, and felt much better in my mother's arms. She kept on rocking me in her arms until I fell asleep.

Silent Marionette
침묵의꼭두각시

Haru

I woke up at first light. Mother was not there anymore, and Liufang was still asleep. I felt better, spotting a bit of light cutting through the darkness. My throat was still dry. I got up and stretched; I had to find some water.

I started walking deeper into the woods, trying to memorize the trail. In all the time that I had spent in the brothel, I never really knew how big that forest was. I now saw that it stretched over a vast area of land, and that it would take us days to cross to the other side.

The sun came up quickly, much quicker than it used to come up in Korea. There were no stages in the sunrise. One minute it was pitch dark and the next the sun was up.

The forests in Manchuria were different too. The trees, the bushes, the flies, the small animals in the woods, they were different in size and color. The laws of nature were the same, though. As I was walking barefoot on the ground as carefully as a cat, my steps were light and slow. I could feel the ground getting cooler and wetter, the plants and bushes greener and healthier. Water! My head was bursting, I was getting excited, water!

I was sniffing. There is a special smell to incoming water. "Where there is water there is life!" If there is water, there must be animals that drink and use the water. I could smell the animal droppings on the ground, and now my sharp ears could hear the mosquitoes' buzz and the frogs jumping from leaf to leaf. I could even hear standing water.

When there is a problem with any of the senses, the others function at a higher level. Ever since I had become mute, my senses of smell and hearing were as good as an animal's senses. I could finally see the stream ahead. I stepped carefully toward it, and almost stumbled over a Japanese soldier's body lying right by the water.

I stopped at once. The soldier was alive. He moved a bit out of sleep, and mumbled something. I was standing there frozen until I was sure that he was back to heavy sleep. Then I bent down and grabbed the pistol and the knife that were right by his head.

The soldier yawned and started moving. It was strange, but there was no fear in my heart. At this point, I had nothing to lose; besides, I had a gun and a knife in my hand, and I knew that I would gladly use them if he were to start problems.

Now that the Japanese had lost the war and were not in charge any more, I would not hesitate to kill. The soldier was young, in his twenties. He actually had a pleasant face. His hands lay close to the sides of his body. He had clean, long fingers. His entire appearance was quite gentle.

I directed the pistol to his head and stood still above him. The young man opened his eyes and gazed at me quietly for a minute. Then he wiped his eyes and begged, "Don't shoot me do-zo!"

I motioned to him to get on his knees. I pushed the pistol hard into his forehead. I seemed to myself like another person; it was not me there. I was never emotionless, cold-hearted, or calculating. I never liked hurting people or any creatures. When Abazi had to shoot a sick animal, I would cry for days after that.

I had difficulty understanding what had become of me, what had happened to my Buddhist education, to my values, my morals. I was full of hate, bitterness, and anger. Looking at the young man, I grasped all that had been done to me. The confusion of feelings hit me hard; the rage shook me in a merciless wave. The wrath and the desire for vengeance were so great that I had to hold myself back with all my might not to kill him.

The soldier sensed it and did what I told him to do; he got on his knees, his head down. I tied his hands behind his back with my shawl, as tightly as I could. He had an army backpack with him. I emptied it and found a water jug, rice cakes, some money, extra underwear, and clothes.

There was a photo of a family posing in front of some tower; I figured it must be his family. Once upon a time I had a family too, brothers and sisters, mother and father. We lived peacefully; we never bothered anyone. We never hurt a soul, we worked our land, we tended to our animals, and we took care of each other until that day those beasts came out of nowhere and destroyed us. I wished I could speak at that moment; for the first time in a very long time, I wished I were not mute.

"Don't kill me do-zo, I am a deserter," he begged again.
I took a long slow drink of water from his jug. What do I do now? I was in charge; the decision was mine whether to keep him alive or not. This was a brand new feeling after all this time of having my life in the hands of others. I thought I should feel

the sweet revenge, the will to hit back, but that was not at all what I felt.

I had new energy now. I felt strong, and there was no fear in my heart. I looked at the Japanese and just felt tired and sad. I tapped on his shoulder to get up, and I shoved the knife in my pocket. I pushed him forward to pick up his belongings. He walked in front of me. I kept holding the gun to his back as I was pushing him in front of me, into the woods.

Liu-fang will question him and then we will decide if he can be of any use to us, I thought. It was good news that there were some money and rice cakes in his bag. The money could get us a boat trip out of Manchuria. I understood now that I had a real prisoner in my hands. Desertion in the Japanese army means death. If they caught him, they would cut his head off on the spot. If the Russians or the Chinese caught him, he would be tortured and killed.

I swallowed my spit and smirked. Who would have thought, a little prostitute like me, the scum of the earth, the lowest of the low, now holding a prisoner, now having power on someone else? Buddha turns the wheel in a crazy way sometimes.

When Liu-fang heard us coming, she jumped to her feet. Her mouth opened wide, and she scratched her head as if to make sure that she was not dreaming.
"Pil-nyo?" she asked in disbelief, taking two steps backwards.
I pushed the soldier forward and then made him kneel.

Liu-fang moved her eyes from him to me and back for a full minute, and then said, "*Ho Buddha, Ching ppang tzu wo!* (Ho Buddha please help me), where did you find him?"

I pointed to the woods, and threw her his backpack.

She sat now on the floor shaking her head. "There is no end to you, Pil-nyo!" She turned the backpack upside down and looked through his things. She folded the money and put it right in her pocket. The little hunting knife disappeared into her pocket too. Then she stepped up to him and kicked him right in his thigh. Liu-fang had enough hatred and bitterness in her to last her for centuries of reincarnations.

"Anatta! Onama ewa nan desikka?" (You! What is your name?)

"Haru, My name is Haru."

"Why are you in the woods?"

"I have deserted."

Liu-fang kicked him again, "I hate deserters; you are a dog!"

"Do-zo! Don't kill me!"

Liu-fang looked at me, and then at the gun. "What do we do with him?" She scratched her head.

I took one of the rice cakes and served one to her; we started chewing. We did not know if there were still Japanese forces on the roads. He might be of help on our way out of Manchuria.
"Sit up!" Liu-fang ordered him.
The man sat, and then looked at us curiously.

"Who are you?"

"We are the ones that ask the questions here!" Liu-fang got angry.
The soldier lowered his head.

"Why did you desert?" she asked.

"If the Russians would not kill me the Chinese would," he said shortly.

"Why did you run away; don't you have any dignity?"

"My will to live is greater than my dignity!"

Liu-fang scratched her head.   Strange Japanese he was, this young man.
"Are you private?"

"I am an officer!"

This was even stranger; a deserting officer would be very uncommon in the Japanese army.

"Your papers?"

He nodded toward his bag. Liu-fang emptied the outside pockets and examined his identification.

"He is not lying!" she concluded.

The man was fidgeting uncomfortably. He obviously did not understand Chinese. I kicked his hips. "*Suru no o yameru*, (Stop! Do not move!) Liu-fang raised her voice now.

"Were you planning to stay in the woods forever?"

"I wanted to figure out a way to go to Hong Kong," he said.

"Hong-Kong," Liu-fang echoed.
I could hear the wheels in her brain rolling, rolling fast. Hong-Kong was a destination she had never thought of. The British forces were in the process of coming back in. It was China but not mainland China. This was a very good idea. I could see her looking at the soldier with interest now.

"What are you going to do in Hong-Kong?"

Silent Marionette
침묵의꼭두각시

"I might be of service to the British forces, since I have been there for two years before I was shipped here." He said.

Liu-fang relaxed. The man looked sincere; he had no reason to lie. Hong-Kong was a brilliant idea for a destination now, and it would not hurt to have a man with us to protect us.

"Would you take us along to Hong-Kong if we let you live?" she asked. The man looked at us now. I was still holding the gun to his head. We both knew that we looked terribly weak,

"It's a tough trip; it would take a long time." He said quietly.
"We are tougher than you think," Liu–fang stated angrily.

I burst out laughing. My mute laugh was different from a regular laugh. It sounded more like an old loud engine breaking up; it was funny. Tough girls we were. Nobody would believe what we had gone through in the last two years, what we had seen and heard. It was unreal that Liu-fang and I were still alive.

The soldier, shaken by the sound of my laughter, shrunk into himself in panic.
"She is mute!" Liu-fang volunteered an explanation.

The soldier looked at me amazed. "But she can hear!"

"She hears better than any of us" Liu-fang agreed. "She also shoots very well!"

The soldier fixed his eyes on me.

"She also strips the skin off animals and humans in a second." Liu-fang was starting to enjoy herself.

I tapped on her mouth to quiet her. Liu-Fang never knew when to shut up.

I loosened his bonds in spite of Liu-fang's objection, and gave the soldier a rice cake and passed him his jug of water.

"*Arigato*," He nodded to me.

"Don't forget, her gun is still directed at your ugly Japanese head!" Liu-fang blurted.

He started biting into his rice cake, still gazing at me. There was no threat in the way he moved. This young man was quite comfortable with himself. I felt more at ease now and sat down on the ground to eat my rice cake.

"I will go with you to Hong-Kong," he then said.

The art of being a mute

Haru turned out to be a reliable fellow. He was resourceful and funny. We were used to him after few days in the woods, and learned to trust him. I had his gun and knife on me at all times, but I calmed down and gave him freedom. Apparently, he needed us as much as we needed him.

We would be his cover on the trip to Hong-Kong. He would disguise himself as my Korean brother, running away from the Japanese. In order not to be caught because of his Japanese accent, and not to have to explain and talk about himself, he would be a mute too. We were both born deaf and dumb; that would eliminate people's questions as to who we were.

He watched me very closely at all times; it looked to me like he was becoming fascinated with muteness. I was supposed to teach him how to become mute. It was strange for me, since I had gotten used to my muteness, to start digging out the details of how to become one.

I realized that muteness is a science by itself. I did my best to explain to Haru that it has nothing to do with the tongue, the throat, or the lips. I had to show him repeatedly that the throat is there to swallow and protect the breathing tools only. The tongue is to lick and the lips to be a doorway for food and speech. Muteness had to do only with the brain and the soul.

Speech is a common effort of breathing, voice and sound, but it is the brain, not the tongue, that unites all three to create speech. If you train the brain not to be willing to create the words, you become a perfect mute. It took some time to get to a silent understanding between Haru and me. He seemed to like being a mute and with time stopped talking all together.

Haru was creative; even Liu-fang had to admit that he was useful. He was a good hunter. He taught us how to catch deer and where to shoot them. He caught rabbits with his bare hands. We would strip their skin off and dry the meat preparing for the trip. Liu-fang and I went to the village and bought farmers' clothes and hats for all of us, and we got rid of Haru's uniforms.

The idea of Hong Kong served our purposes from all aspects. It was a window to the world. From there it would be easy to go anywhere we wanted. The more we thought about it, the more excited we became.

Haru was a good student; the muteness drew him in deeper and deeper. He would examine me 24 hours a day, as if studying me for a test. He followed each one of my movements; he would ask me questions and imitate my hand motions, my voice, the hums and whistling of my breathing, the way I tended to answer questions.

He copied how I carried my body, the stretching of the neck muscles, the lips shaking, the way I walked and stood, and how I ate and drank. He was after me constantly. I got used to him after awhile as one gets used to a shadow.

Liu-fang called him "Saru" (monkey). "Haru, saru, Haru saru," she used to sing to him, teasing him constantly. She drove him crazy, laughing at him for his imitations of me. However, Haru did not care. He seemed committed to being a mute. Haru took the issue of muteness from the point of view of pain. He imagined a big lump of pain clogging his throat, choking him so that he could not utter a word.

I agreed with that approach, but I wondered if Haru understood what pain was. There are many definitions for pain; there is the pain that is due to injury or illness, there is the pain of a distressing sensation in a particular part of the body like back pain or a headache, and there is mental or emotional suffering and torment. What was the pain that had shut me up forever? Which one of the above fit me? Was it all of them? I was sure there were other reasons.

Silent Marionette
침묵의꼭두각시

I would go back again in my mind to the day it had all begun, far away in my peaceful village with my Young-soo and my family. What was the most painful event of all the madness that occurred that day? Was it my mother being desecrated? My sister being robbed of her innocence and her life? The disgusting way General Toshihiro chose to introduce to me to the world of sex? My little innocent sisters, burning alive in the fire, holding on to each other desperately? Which one of these events had brought about my silence? What could a man like Haru possibly understand of pain, of reasons to tell the brain to stop communicating with the world?

Haru had been with us for an entire week. He was busy drawing a map and planning for the trip. I went into my sacred box and gave him papers and pencils. Haru too had some drawing talent and was a great mapmaker. He drew us a trail from Manchuria to go all the way by sea with fishing boats to Lushun, Tengchow, Tunghai, Liandong, Shanghai, Yahwan, Fuming, Amoy, and finally Hong Kong.

The journey would take us about four weeks, he estimated. His money would probably last for one week of boat fares and food for three people. I counted the money that I had gotten from the officers; it would last another week. We did not know whether Japanese money would still be acceptable in China, but assumed that it would be, simply because people would still need to engage in some level of commerce.

Liu-fang had no money at all. We calculated that after two weeks we would have to stop and work in some places in order to make money for the rest of the trip. We prepared as much dried meat as we could so that the money would not go wasted on food. Liu-fang collected berries and dried them in order to have something else to eat.

We would start our journey as soon as we had enough food and clothing, and as soon as Haru would be ready to be a perfect mute. We could not take chances on Haru being caught; if he were, we would all die as collaborators.

"Would you like to talk again?" he asked me one morning on our way to look for a hunt.

I shook my head "no."

"Why not?"

"I have nothing to say." I signaled him.

I knew that Haru had a problem with this issue. For him the general law of human nature would be to want to be like the rest of the pack. What blind person would not want to see? What deaf person would not want to hear? What dumb person would not want to talk?

It was my challenge to make sure he understood the mind of a mute. A mute from birth was different from a mute like me. Those like me stop talking because of a very serious, heavy emotional trauma. My brain had bestowed the muteness on me so that I could never assuage the burden of what had happened to me by confiding it verbally to the rest of the world. My muteness was an escape from having to testify to the events that had brought the silence upon me.

It was a crucial thing for Haru to understand. He had no idea what Liu-fang and I had gone through; he had no idea that we were used as sex slaves for the Japanese army. When he asked Liu-fang how we had come to Manchuria, she told him to mind his own business. As far as she was concerned, we had a partnership for one and only one goal, to get to Hong Kong. She would be on her guard with him constantly. Even though she had learned to trust his intentions, she trusted him only up to a point.

Silent Marionette
침묵의꼭두각시

She would check if I had the gun ready on me, and would always remind me that if I were to see anything suspicious about his behavior I should shoot him like a dog.

He tried to ask me several times what was I doing in Manchuria, being a Korean; but I would shake my head unhappily and angrily, and he would stop right away.

Haru did not suffer from my presence. Unlike other people that encounter mutes, he did not feel uncomfortable or annoyed with me. He did not have mercy on me or feel that he needed to help me. He was just curious about my muteness. He truly wanted to understand it and learn it.

I did not think that at that point he was interested in it any more because of the trip to Hong Kong; rather, he was interested in the muteness for itself, as an interesting phenomenon.

After twelve days, when we were almost ready to leave, he stopped talking altogether. When Liu-fang asked him a question one morning, he shook his head and did not answer. Liu-fang asked him again raising her voice, "Did you hear me, Haru saru?"

He shook his head again.

Liu-fang became upset; she got up, her hands on her hips. "I will ask you one more time, and you'd better answer if you know what's good for you!"
Haru gave me a quick glance and shook his head again, his lips closed tight.

Liu-fang grabbed the gun from me and pointed it at his head. "I will count to three. If you don't talk by then, you are a dead man!"
Haru's face was pale; his facial muscles started shaking. He obviously wanted to say something, but no sound came out of his

throat. I could see him stretching his body to its limit, standing on his toes, the veins in his neck popping out.

"One"
"Two"
"Three"

Haru closed his eyes. He did not move now.
Liu-fang put the gun down and said, "He is ready to go! He is a mute now!"

Silent Marionette
침묵의꼭두각시

Lushun

Coming out of the forest to a newly liberated Manchuria was astounding. For the first time in what seemed like an eternity, death's looming shadow had dispersed. Food was scarce and people would be happy with whatever little money they could get their hands on. It came as a surprise that boat fares were so low. Long lines of refugees waited to get on boats back home to their own countries.

The human streams of people waiting in endless lines everywhere was overwhelming. There were lines for food, for water, for medicines. Old people were fainting, little babies crying; it was a sad sight. We were mixing with the streams of people, terrified of losing each other. We were walking on both sides of Haru. He held our hands firmly. Sometimes it was hard for us to stay together as people were pushing from all sides, threatening to tear us from each other.

None of us had papers or anything to indentify us in any way. We had gotten rid of Haru's papers for our own protection. Liu-fang would tell anyone who asked that Haru and I were both Korean workers forced to work for the Japanese. Liu-fang had worked with us too, under the Japanese, in a factory. It was a convincing story. People would shake their heads mercifully when hearing that Haru and I were deaf and dumb.

With all the lines, it took about three days to get what we needed. The Russians were parading Japanese prisoners of war in long, steady streams. The Japanese looked like frightened children. The Chinese would break into the lines and attack the prisoners with stones and with their fists; some pulled their hair.

The noise and the stink, the heat and the humidity were sickening. Coming out of the silence of the deep woods into this horrendous mass of humanity was too much for me to take. Haru would hold my hand tightly. He was afraid of capture, and he felt my distress.

Liu-fang kept yelling at him not to bend his head in the ground all the time; the more he tried not to be seen, the more he would attract attention. However, he would pull his straw hat over his face and look down whenever he saw people; it was a natural reaction.

I would sit with him on my wooden box. Haru would watch his friends, the Japanese prisoners, being pushed around like dogs and sigh sadly. For us having been prisoners of the Japanese, treated like human garbage cans and sex toys for such a long time, it was a shocking sight. What Haru was going through, after growing up in Japan, serving the army for years, and being used to his country's absolute power, I could only guess.

Liu-fang was not as understanding and forgiving as I was; she never missed a chance to attack the Japanese soldiers together with the rest of the crowd. It was a different Liu-fang, no longer little skinny quiet girl who never answered back, never fought back. The only reason she had survived the brothel was her tendency to satisfy and the way she would obey orders without any argument.

This Liu-fang was bitter and loud, feisty and very angry. The horrors of what she had experienced in the last two years now sunk in. Many girls had committed suicide; many of them had lost their minds. It was a miracle that Liu-fang was still functioning. I understood her new attitude. She had nothing more to lose. She became a hard woman, and was determined to gain back the respect she deserved.

Haru suffered her anger the most, as if he was representing the entire Japanese nation. I would try to calm her down, but without success. She would attack him and insult him for no reason at all. When I tried to protest he would motion to me, "Leave her be, dozo, let her do it. I deserve every bit of it!"

Silent Marionette
침묵의꼭두각시

Nobody deserves abuse, I was thinking, not even the abusers themselves. I was angry at Liu-fang even though I understood her. I had had enough of the ugliness, the nastiness, and the insults. I was irritated with them. I would stamp my feet and growl at her when she would attack him, but Liu-fang would laugh bitterly and say that I was stupid and that I always had to look like the good person.

Haru was a decent man; he did not deserve her abuse, Japanese or not. When we had food, he always made sure to serve us first before he ate. He would constantly hold on to us, making sure we were safe. When a man would approach Liu-fang or me, Haru would clench his fists, ready to fight. He was a short man but very strong and muscular. I knew that the Japanese trained their officers in unarmed combat, and that they were proficient in martial arts

If we were to face any dangers, I knew I could rely on Haru to protect us. Liu-fang refused to understand that in spite of the sudden freedom that she was now experiencing, the danger was only beginning. My sixth sense was there for me again. People had become even more greedy and merciless than before. They would kill you for a slice of bread, for one coin. They would cut your finger off while you slept to get your ring.

My wooden chest drew a lot of attention. I saw people staring at it constantly. Haru told me that it would be better to transfer everything to a suitcase or a violin case, so I could carry it on my back and nobody would be suspicious of me hiding valuables in there. Eventually I realized that he was right. It was hard to run around with the big, heavy box. We kept getting into trouble with hoodlums trying to steal it.
Before we finally boarded the boat to Lushun, Liu-Fang managed to buy me an old, sturdy violin case. I transferred all my things into it.

She also sold my wooden box for a very good price. I was crying when I had to depart from my box. It had been the lifeline for me in the brothel. It was my first real present, my motivation to work and to survive. Liu-fang was disgusted with my display of emotion. She grabbed her bag and left the area.

"Pil-nyo" Haru said softly. I turned to him. He handed me a handkerchief. I wiped my face and buried it in his handkerchief; I could smell his sweat, his aftershave, his warm breath. "I will buy you lots of presents, when we get to Hong Kong!"

I looked at him in shock wiping my face with my sleeves. He had rarely spoken in the last week or two. I think it was the longest sentence I had ever heard from him. For the first time since my capture, I felt a warm feeling for a man. I smiled now, embarrassed, and handed him his handkerchief back.

The trip to Lushun was difficult. We had to squeeze onto the fishing boat with fifty other refugees like sardines. We were feeding on dried meat. We had enough to last us for two weeks, but we did not take into account the hungry people around us.

When a hungry child is pulling on your shirt, begging for some food, it is hard to refuse. Even Liu-fang softened up and handed some berries and meat to the beggars. Lushun port: 旅順口, the natural harbor, was now under the administration of the Soviets. Lushun port was a very significant port. It was known as Port Arthur.

The Soviets raised the USSR's naval flag over the city in 1945 when they reoccupied Liaodong and other parts of Manchuria. They established the communist Lushun City on November 25, 1945, to replace Ryojun.

The place was swamped with army vehicles and Russian soldiers. To our relief they did not check the passengers who came off the boat. It was still a very chaotic situation; they saw us as hungry, weary Chinese refugees, and left us alone.

Silent Marionette
침묵의꼭두각시

Reminders of the Japanese occupation were everywhere in Lushun. The street signs, the business names, were all in the language of the former conqueror, and the Japanese currency was still in use.

The entire city looked like it had just woken up from a bad dream. It was a city in transition. Nobody trusted anybody, and hungry people and children were roaming the streets looking for food in garbage cans, begging for something to eat from the Russian and the Chinese soldiers. I was sitting on a rock looking east toward the Korean bay. My heart was shattered. I missed home so badly, my eyes filled with tears.

Haru put his hand on my shoulder and that felt good. I needed comfort. Until then I had no idea how much I needed it. The last person on earth that I ever thought I would receive comfort from was a Japanese soldier. I put my hand on his, and we both shook our heads sadly, looking out at the bay.

Omani placed her hand on my weary head and whispered, "Be strong, Pil-nyo, I am watching you!" I leaned my head on Haru's shoulder and closed my eyes. Liu-fang forgot to be sarcastic. She landed her head on his other shoulder and we both fell asleep.

Qingdao

Our money supply was getting low. When we reached Qingdao in the middle of September, we could not believe how little money we had left. What we had would last perhaps another week. Liu-fang and Haru started talking about staying in town for a while, and possibly finding temporary work.

Qingdao bordered three major cities, Yantai, Weifang and Rizhao. It was still warm and moist in Qingdao. Because it was a monsoon area, there was rainfall constantly; but it was warm enough to swim. We went swimming as much as we could since the bathhouses were too expensive.

Haru was a very good swimmer and he taught us some basic swimming techniques. The water was refreshing and warm. It was good to stretch in the sea after a whole day wandering the streets.

After the war, the Chinese KMT (Kuo Min Tang) government allowed Qingdao to serve as the headquarters of the Western Pacific Fleet of the US Navy. Many American sailors were filling the harbors. They were different from the Russians and the Chinese. The Americans were good natured and relaxed young men. They were considerate and decent.

Just for taking their photos for them once or twice, they would give us American cigarettes and chocolates. None of us had ever come even close to a westerner in our lives. Haru had heard horror stories in the army about the Americans. The Japanese army had convinced the whole Japanese society that the Americans were merciless murderer-rapist cowboys. Haru was in absolute shock to discover them as kind and very pleasant young people.

Liu-fang was in seventh heaven. Her dream was to go to America one day. She would smile at the Americans and make conversation with them, asking them to tell her about America. She would communicate with them in sign language and sometimes find a translator who could speak Chinese and English.

She got small presents from the soldiers, American coins or postcards, and asked me to keep them for her in my bags. One day she disappeared with a blond American sailor and came back in the morning excited to tell us that she had made her decision to go from Hong Kong to America. She brought with her a pocket full of American crackers and candy, some dollars, and a bottle of beer for Haru.

I smiled to myself. Underneath it all Liu-fang was resourceful and fair. She had desires and dreams. She had even thought of Haru when she had come back with the presents. We did not ask her where she had spent the night with the American soldier; I would not expect a straight answer anyway.

Haru had not slept at all that night that Liu-fang had not returned. He was tossing and turning by my side. With every sound of footsteps, he would jump up to the window. I did not know if he was worried about Liu-fang, or worried that she would say something and the Americans would come to get him.

When Liu-fang came back in the morning, he let a sigh of relief and said nothing.

"What's the matter Haru saru, why don't you drink your beer"?

Haru tossed the bottle away from him and lowered his face.

"Drink your beer, Saru!"

"Do-zo! Arigato! No!"

"Suit yourself!" Liu-fang shrugged her shoulders. "I will exchange it for bread!" She left slamming the door.

I pushed my hand in my violin case and pulled a paper and a pencil impulsively, and drew him sitting there, his head down. Haru was lonely and sad in my sketch. It was the first time I had ever drawn him. I had never looked deeply into the details of his face. He did not notice me drawing him. It was the first time I had drawn since I left the brothel. I had no idea how hungry I was for the pencils; I attacked the paper and worked in a craze.

I realized that drawing gave me shelter; more than anything else, it gave me purpose. It was no longer a way to survive as it had been in the brothel. Now it was a need, and this time I complied with it and accepted it.

I woke Haru from his deep thoughts and handed him the sketch. He looked at the paper amazed; his jaw dropped, and then just like Nina he cried. Never had I seen Haru crying. I was wondering what it was in my drawings that made people so sad. I motioned to him, "Sorry!"

Haru stared at the picture and then said, "Arigato, Pil-nyo!"

Liu-fang kept disappearing for nights at a time. We never asked her any questions and she always came back, with money or food and sometimes jewelry. Once when I looked at her wondering, worrying, she blurted out at me angrily, "Once a whore, always a whore!"

Liu-fang was the reason I had kept myself alive ever since Miza's death. It was nobody's right or place to judge her. Whatever she had gone through in the last two years, she never ever mentioned again. She never talked about Lee-ping, and never mentioned her family. She would just look up at the sun and repeat her line, "The sun will never dry my tears!"

Silent Marionette
침묵의꼭두각시

Liu-fang, a ghost of a Chinese marionette, would never forget or forgive. I was praying to Buddha every day that she would not drown to death in her own self-hatred. Many times, she came back with bruises and black and blue marks on her neck and arms. She had never stripped in front of me since we got to Qingdao.

Because Qingdao was a major port city, there were people from all over the east there in spite of the war. It was an attractive spot for many, situated right on the southern tip of the Shandong Peninsula.

Many Koreans had settled over the years in Qingdao, which was also called Tsingtao or Pinyin, which means green and lush among the blue ocean. Germans settlers came in 1903 and founded the Tsingtao Brewery factory, but there were plenty of other sources of work there. Qingdao had a great variety of mineral resources and an ocean filled with fish and shrimp of kinds we had never seen before. All one had to do was to sit in the shallow water and catch the fish with one's bare hands.

There was no need for Liu-fang to do what she was doing. We could have managed on what nature gave us, the fish, the shellfish and the natural herbs and fruits. Something bigger than herself was driving her to hell. Liu-fang could not live with the self-disgust, the guilt, the pain, the absolute confusion and anger. She had to inflict pain and abuse on herself in order to find a reason to live. Liu-fang, like me, always needed a reason to justify her life. Now her reason was the need to punish herself.

When Haru would tell her that it was time to leave Qingdao, she would ask us to stay longer. "What's the rush, Haru saru? I bring you food and money, you and the mute are doing nothing but sleeping and eating all day. Why are you complaining? I need some more time here!"

Haru would look at me and keep quiet. We had been sitting far too long there. It was dangerous for him. People had started to ask questions. We were sleeping in a boarding house in a small room, telling people that Haru and I were brother and sister and that Liu-fang was his wife. However, people saw her running around at night, looking for the hunt, a very aggressive type of hunt, and they started doubting us.

Liu-fang was becoming more and more abusive toward herself and to us, day by day. She was flushed with the city Shigu (the worst downtown district). She was hopelessly drawn to the narrow streets, the lights, the drunken sailors, and the incredible taste of being able to choose her customers. Liu-fang at the age of eighteen was a destroyed human being. Her quiet, obedient attitude, her shyness, and her naive way of complying had all disappeared. She was associating with the dirtiest, the lowest life creatures in the Shigu, making the most dangerous alliances with the corner hookers, the violent predators, and the most wicked villains. She was playing Russian roulette with her life every night, as if she was craving the torture, and waiting for the most painful, horrible death.

Haru and I were waiting patiently, but the day came that Haru said that it was time to leave, with her or without her. I objected, shaking my head wildly, screeching my voice, growling. I could not leave her to die alone in the dirty streets of Qingdao. She did not deserve to be found dead like a dog in some gutter. Haru would never understand the sisterhood that forms out of torture, humiliation, and terrible pain and suffering. I was not about to leave without her, and Haru started losing his patience.

Lianyungang

After much begging and crying, we were able to convince Liu-fang to leave. The best way to convince her was to use some logic. Haru told her in a sudden wave of toughness and authority that she was destroying all of us. "If you want to indulge in your pathetic self-destruction you can stay here! We are leaving! You are dragging us to the month of November. Very soon it will be too cold to travel and we will never make it to Hong Kong."

Liu-fang looked at him surprised; she did not think that he was capable of taking a strong stand like this. She was shocked at his display of decisiveness. She was so used to him taking her abuse and insults quietly, that she saw him as her punching bag and her prisoner, and totally forgot that he was also a man.

Apparently, Liu-fang more than anything needed some discipline; she needed a strong hand, a guiding hand. Liu-fang was lost in a world of pain and guilt and chaos. Haru sensed that and decided to take the initiative and turn around his attitude 180 degrees. He would become the last word from now on.

When we got to Lianyungang, we were all very tired and hungry. The meat was long gone and our food supply was empty. Lianyungang sat on the crossing of eastern sea routes with western land routes.

This too was a beautiful spot on the ocean. Now when I finally had the chance to see it first hand, all the stories about China were true. My brother and Yong-soo were right; it was the most beautiful place on earth. One would love to live in a place like this, the ocean sights, the lush green trees and plants, the mountains in the background.

Of course, not all Chinese were small, smiling, kind people. Some were tall and nasty. There were rapists and thieves, murderers and liars; but overall Chinese were no different from Koreans or Japanese. I learned that a human is a human no matter where he comes from. I would sit and draw the locals and the refugees; sometimes I would be surprised to see a group of people gathering around me to watch me in action.

If I were lucky, a foreigner would even pose for money or food. Haru, who all of a sudden was behaving like an officer again, was guarding Liu-fang, driving her crazy with his warnings. If she managed to slip out he would follow her and stop her from approaching sailors. All I heard from her during those days was "I hate you, Japanese saru!, leave me alone, I hate you!"

However, he was not impressed with her bad language, screaming, and hitting. He was determined to set her straight. Haru told me that if she would not behave, she would expose us in no time and we would all be killed.

He was a rare talker, Haru, but Liu-fang made him talk all the time and he was not too happy about it. In fact, with all her anger she became more and more dependent on him. After a while, I noticed that whenever she talked or did something she would look at him for reaction. At night, she would always sleep by his side as if she felt safer near him.

Liu-fang started respecting Haru, and her attitude toward him was changing every day. She opened up to him now. I would see them sitting together. He was listening to her talking and crying. I assumed she told him everything we had gone through.

He would come back from those sessions exhausted, and it was obvious that he had been crying. He would not look me in the eye and would curl into himself silently. He became more protective of both of us. I was convinced that I should give him back his gun. The places he had to run around after Liu-fang were despicable places. I did not even want to know about them, but I knew she was attracted to the gutters, and over there you could find only human rats and snakes.

God only knew how many times Haru had to put the gun to some low creature's head in order to make him let go of Liu-fang. I kept the knife under my shirt. It was a good army hunting knife and I knew I could kill a man if he would try to harm me. Even though we always slept in a single room for the night, I never knew when some hungry man would barge in and try to rob us and kill us. That had happened a number of times since we had left Manchuria, and Haru then had shown his face-to-face combat skills.

Liu-fang did not argue when I gave him back his gun. I tapped her shoulder and she turned her distant look to me, and all she said was, "*Wo mi lù le!*" (I am lost). I was worried sick about her; I was afraid she had lost her mind. I would touch Haru's hand at night when I heard her crying out of sleep. Haru would hold my hand, patting it, trying to calm me down, to assure me that he was there for her.

Some good people would share rice with us since we were deaf and dumb. We found a proprietor who rented us a small room during our second week in Lianyungang. She took pity on us because she had a brother who was deaf and dumb. She liked Haru right away, and bought the story that he was my brother and that he was Korean. She would call him to give him portions of the food that she was cooking, and he helped her around the boarding house, doing all kinds of jobs for her.

The Japanese had shot her husband, as well as her two sons. She was a young woman in her late twenties and soon enough Haru would disappear into her bedroom for a few hours every night, after he made sure that Liu-fang was sound asleep. I did not mind. I felt that he deserved a break from the both of us. He had his needs too, and he would never dare touch us, knowing what we had gone through in the last two years.

The young woman was good to him and treated us with warmth and respect thanks to him. Liu-fang was not too happy about this romance; she would complain about it repeatedly. She herself did not know why she was irritated. Liu-fang had become used to the fact that Haru was always at her disposal and that he was somehow, in spite of the change of behavior and the display of independence, our private body guard, our shoulder to lean on, and Liu-fang's tail.

We both had come to take Haru for granted, but now things had changed. Haru was just another man with needs and dreams and a will of his own, and that scared us a bit. Back in the woods, the postwar feeling seemed sweet and wonderful, but after running around in China for more than a month, we realized that we needed a man to protect us.

There were too many predators everywhere, too much danger. Haru put our fears to rest one day by telling us to pack up. He had found a fishing boat that would take us to Shanghai for a reasonable price.

We were surprised. We had had no idea that Haru was planning to continue the trip so soon, but he apparently had stayed focused and torn himself from the warm bed of the owner of the rooming house. On a cool night at the end of October, we boarded a small fishing boat for Shanghai.

Silent Marionette
침묵의꼭두각시

Shanghai

On the boat to Shanghai, I got sick. First, I lost my appetite and could not eat a thing; I was vomiting everything that came to my mouth, including water. Then came the high fever. I was burning and the pain tore through my body. My head was bursting, my stomach killed me, I was crying and screaming for my mother, for Buddha, for Yong-soo.

From time to time when my mind had cleared, I felt Liu-fang and Haru from both my sides. They were massaging my body, calling me, patting me, washing me.

My mind was in a fog; several times Buddha called me to come. He would give me his warm assuring hand, but when I tried to hold on, it kept going farther and farther away. The pain was unbearable. I was dying; I knew I was. It was a slow, cruel death. The terrible chills were shaking my body wildly, and nausea threatened to blow up my mind.

The shadows of Haru and Liu-fang were hovering over me. They were both crying, one time Haru was begging, slapping me to wake up sobbing loudly. Liu-fang was on her knees praying to Buddha. In spite of my coma, I could hear her promising all the Buddha in the world that she would shave her head and become a nun if I would get better and live. There were shadows of people I did not know passing through my madness. The pain tortured me; I had lost my mind.

I cursed all the evil powers of the world. What did they want from me? Why me? Was I born with a sign on me saying, hurt me, abuse me? Did I bear some kind of an evil mark? Who wished me the torments of hell?

I wanted so to disappear, that I begged death to hold my hand and take me. After five days of sitting on the edge of life, I started feeling better. My throat hurt, and was dry. Haru and Liu-fang nursed me back to life with sips of water.

Shanghai sits on the Yangtze River Delta on the east coast of China. This is China's third largest island. The city is blessed with many rivers, canals, streams and lakes. Shanghai suffered badly under the Japanese. In 1932, the imperial Japanese Navy Air Service bombed the city in an effort to crush Chinese student protests of the Japanese occupation. Then in 1941, Japan took Shanghai under full control and stayed there until 1945.

Many Jewish refugees came to Shanghai in 1941. The Japanese created a ghetto for them where they all resided. Hitler asked the Japanese repeatedly to hand over the Jews to him, but the Japanese in spite of the restrictions they had put on the Jews decided not to give them over.

Shanghai was still licking its wounds when we arrived. The damage from the bombing had never been repaired; people were still traumatized and confused. There were 149 comfort houses in the city where little girls who had been kidnapped were forced to do what we had done.

The brutal regime's sins were everywhere. The horror stories that we heard from the anglers about rape, murder, humiliation and cruelty for cruelty's sake did not surprise Liu-fang and me, but Haru was clearly in shock. "I am ashamed to be a Japanese officer," he said to us in a tormented voice.

The anglers told Haru and Liu-fang that the best thing for me was to be carried to the Jewish ghetto, where I could find medical help and cheap room and board. Even though many people had left the Jewish ghetto as soon as the Japanese departed, many of them had decided to stay and settle in Shanghai.

Haru carried me on his back, all the way from the port to the ghetto, in addition to the bags and the violin case. By the time we arrived at the doctor's, I had already lost consciousness.

Silent Marionette
침묵의꼭두각시

I woke up in Haru's arms. I knew I was in a new place since his face above me looked serious and cautious. We had learned to read each other's expressions. I looked straight in his eyes. Haru was tired and tense.

He nodded his head to me for assurance and hugged me to his chest as if I were a broken doll. It was nice and warm in his strong arms, listening to his heartbeat like this, half-conscious as I was. I thought I heard him whisper in my ear, "Don't leave me, Pil-nyo, don't go!" but the fog impeded my vision and my hearing. I remember holding on to his neck, as if I was afraid I was going to fall, but then I fainted again.

People like us live only if there is a good reason to live. I had to remind myself of it, since I was a very assertive person and it was important to me always to justify what I was doing or saying.

Liu-fang continued her life in order to pay for the death of her family and for the death of Lee-ping; she would live for one aim, to inflict pain upon herself.

What Liu-fang and I went through was something only she and I would ever be able to understand. These memories would always stand as a wall between the rest of the world and us. I did not want to continue to live. The only reason I was still breathing was my violin case. What was in there had to be sent and buried. You cannot lie to the dead. I had made promises to Kumikko and Nina and I had to honor them.

When I woke up in the doctor's office, the first things I saw were pieces of my broken life sitting in front of me. My first thought was how I could ever put so many pieces together. Haru was sitting, holding me in his arms, looking at me frightened. He must have seen the broken pieces in my eyes, since he started crying.

"Poor Haru, you are a good man, a good Japanese man. Don't cry; don't be sad, none of it is your fault."

"Your pain is my pain Pil-nyo!"

"My pain is only my pain; nobody would ever understand it. You should leave us Haru, and you should go on your way!"

"I am not going anywhere without you!"

There is an irony in the fact that two mutes can speak louder than words. The nature around us is voiceless, but it cries out more loudly than any human scream.

Haru had definitely gotten good at being a mute; he could communicate with me without words. I knew he understood everything I was saying with my eyes. It was obvious to me at that point that all humans are in this world coincidentally. Nobody really ever chose to live, and once we are here, it is a chain of chores and obligations. Somebody out there is always dictating to you how to live your life and what to do with your life.

A kind-faced doctor is checking my pulse. His eyes are warm. "The poor thing has gotten dysentery," he says to Liu-fang in Chinese.

"She passed the worst stages of the disease. Whatever you did for her saved her life, but she is still very sick and needs care."

"What can we do doctor? Please help her!"

"She needs medicine; antibiotics cost a fortune!"

"We will pay" Liu-fang said.

I protested, I started growling, fighting to get out of Haru's hold, but I was too weak. He pinned me to his chest forcibly, "We will pay! Whatever it takes we will pay!" Liu-fang repeated.

That would wipe out all the money we had. We would never make it to Hong Kong. However, my voice was not heard. Liu-fang and Haru were determined to keep me alive. The doctor gave me a shot; he agreed to rent us a tiny back room that was used for storage for few days, so that he could watch my condition. My blanket lay between Haru's and Liu-fang's; I agreed to sip on some water and fell asleep again.

Silent Marionette
침묵의꼭두각시

"We all stand naked in front of the creator"

Pots are boiling on the stove in the kitchen; Hanna, the doctor's wife, likes company when she cooks. She talks and talks in a language I do not understand. Hanna does not care as long as she has a pair of ears to hear her. Friday morning is a busy morning. Hanna has to prepare the Sabbath meal. She has to clean the scales from the fish, pluck the feathers from the chicken, and peel the potatoes.

She is bustling around the kitchen giving orders to her daughters, shouting at he boys to move faster with their chores. When I try to get up and help, she pushes me away. "*Zuo!*" (Sit!) She orders. Too many hands in the kitchen would ruin the meal.

Hanna is far away from home, many continents away. She too is a refugee; she lives on foreign soil, she and her seven children, her husband and his father. Hanna wipes the sweat off her forehead and sighs deeply. She has no idea where Korea is, but she holds my hand and says, "It's an unfortunate story, the story of wars!"

She serves me the rice soup and says, "Eat child! You need your strength back!" She gives me a wise look and mumbles something I do not understand and then says in Chinese, "Don't judge yourself harshly, child. In the end we are all the same; we will all stand naked in front of the creator to be judged!"

I take the spoon into my mouth. The soup tastes good. Hanna is cutting the potatoes and her daughters are adding some water into the pots. The mother and daughters are working in harmony. My heart is breaking. Mother, my sisters, take me, I so miss you!

"Who loves little Pil-nyo most in the world?"

"Omani!"

"Who loves Omani most in the world?"

"Pil-nyo!"

"Eat child! Stop crying!" Hanna now wipes her hands in the towel and feeds me as if I were a baby.

"Open wide!" I open my mouth and she shoves the spoon in.

"You'll have a lifetime to cry; now you must eat!"

I wished I could put my tired head on Hanna's big chest. I wished I could curl in her warm arms and stay there forever. I wished I could understand what she was saying, her language, her prayers, her melodies, the yelling at the boys, and the lectures to the girls. The hot steam is coming out of the pots, the shadows of the girls become unclear, and Haru is there now to carry me to sleep.

The tragedy of human existence is tattooed all over Shanghai. The walls are sprayed with bullet holes. The city looks like it collapsed and died. The Japanese devils raped and killed everywhere. The stories of slaughter and torture are so intense; there are times that I have to block my ears not to hear anymore. Outside you can still hear crying and yelling at all hours of the night. The town is filled with wounded souls. Instead of the happiness, you would expect after the end of the war, there is deep darkness over Shanghai.

At night in the dim light of the oil lamp, the doctor and his sons would study their Bible and prayers around the table. We would sit quietly and listen to the strange sounds and to the beautiful chanting, and with time they became so familiar I could sing them in my head.

In those days, I drew almost two hundred sketches of the Jewish family and the city. Hanna was excited at my ability to draw, and asked me to teach her daughters. When her older daughter Miriam protested, she told her "Every other thing you learn to do is an asset. You never know when it will come in handy!"

I took the smaller girls to the woods, and taught them how to differentiate good herbs and mushrooms from bad ones. Hanna's soul became attached to mine, and the one-week stay extended to two. I finished all my medicine and became much better and stronger.

The money was finished and when Liu-fang got into one of her night adventures and came back bruised and scratched with a few Yuan in her hand, I decided to open Nina's envelope.

It took me time. I was staring at the big thick thing in my hand. I felt like I was opening Nina's unmarked grave. Nina had told me that the envelope was mine; she had asked me to bury her sketches only, but I could never make myself open it. Nina, the prettiest creature in the whole wide world, the pride and joy of her family, the swan in the lake of ugly ducklings, had killed herself and left behind a thick envelope. That was the only evidence that she had ever been on this earth.

I took a deep breath. The envelope still smelled of her perfume. I placed it on the floor and then bowed twice. "Here I am Nina, bowing to perfection. The bravest, the brightest, the most beautiful woman that ever lived, I am your memorial, I am your sister."

I tore open the envelope and held my breath; there was jewelry there, tons of it, along with gold and diamonds and thick packs of yen. There must have been thousands of yen there. It felt as though I had found a pirate treasure in the bottom of the ocean.

Nina had gotten her revenge; she was a rich lady, a very rich person, and now I was one. I collected the treasure and quickly put it back into the case.

I paced the floor. My head hurt. What I had in the envelope would let me live very comfortably for the rest of my life. The savings of a Philippine whore, dirty money that had come from dirty minds, belonged to me now.

Each diamond ring, each gold bracelet, must be valued at a fortune. Nina's General had settled only for the best. It was strange that she had that jewelry on her when she was arrested in

Manila. Clever girl was Nina, courageous and unique. People like Nina are born only once in every century.

I shoved the envelope deep into the violin case under the papers, and then went outside to look for Haru. I sat by him, looking at the bay quietly. He held my hand and smiled. When I handed him a pack of yen, his eyes almost popped out of their sockets. He did not ask me where I got the money, but he nodded his head, pleased. We had more than enough to get to Hong Kong.

There are few minutes between hunger and starvation; there is just a split second between life and death, between desperation and hope. I was sure Abazi would have added some sentences to insert here. I was sitting there on the edge of the Shanghai bay, Haru's arm around my thin shoulders. The sun was setting. I had never seen such a beautiful sunset. The autumn sky was clear and covered red. We both breathed the sea air deep into our lungs, and then Haru said his first sentence since we had in Shanghai, "I love you Pil-nyo!"

When he handed the money to Hanna, she hugged me for a long time and then said, "Don't forget child! We all stand naked in front of the creator!"

Wenzhou

In Wenzhou, I started drawing with colors for the first time in my life. During the war in 1937-1942 Wenzhou became an important port since it was under Chinese control. In the later years of the war, the port declined; and when we got there, it was starting on its way to recovery.

It must have been the most beautiful place I had ever seen; the exotic mountains, the beautiful water, the incredible sea made me cry every day. How could nature be so beautiful while all that evil was going on around us? What a cruel contrast is the beauty of the world and its wickedness.

That was the first time that I used Nina's money for my own pleasure. I asked Haru to buy me colored pencils. It was the first time I felt compelled to draw nature. I had always drawn people and sketched situations that involved people, but here in Wenzhou, I felt for the first time in my life that I had to draw scenery. My pencils would never be able to describe the beauty of the place; I had to have some colors.

Wenzhou was an intellectual city, the birthplace of the best and most famous artists, poets, writers, and artisans. This was a place for mathematicians, philosophers, engineers, architects and the most brilliant minds in China.

Haru built me a simple easel, and I would sit outside to draw the scenery. It would not take even seconds for a crowd to gather behind my back, watching me at work, stating their opinions. Before long, they were calling me the mute artist and some people would ask me to sketch them.

The people of Wenzhou were kind, lovely people. Those who could not pay me money for their sketches would bring me food or a pottery piece. Pottery was a big income source there, and with time, I made a deal with a young man. I was teaching him to sketch and he in turn was teaching me pottery. Haru was not very happy with my spending so much time with a young unmarried man. Between watching Liu-fang and me, he had his hands full. Liu-fang would snicker and say, "Haru-saru is paying the bill for the whole Japanese army!"

I took to pottery quickly. "It's all about focus," Chang said to me. "You need to work your stomach muscles in a harmony with your brain." There were wounded souls everywhere I went, Chang never talked about his life. He lived alone and did pottery for income. He cooked his own meals and was lonely. He was in his thirties. I had no idea if he had ever been married or ever had children. He never asked me questions and I just accepted him as he was.

Pottery artists are simple artisans; they make dishes and pots to be used for everyday life. That is why they have a very realistic view of life. Nevertheless, since it is a form of art, they are sensitive to philosophy, beauty and the afterlife.

Chang learned quickly the art of drawing the little nuances in catching small facial details, the techniques of light and shade, the tricks of using pencils and charcoals. Chang wanted to learn how to sketch so he could further perfect his ability to decorate his pots.

"No true artist or craftsman is good unless he knows how to draw!" he would say to me. Chang was a Buddhist. He too had many Buddhas like Omani. He built a bridge over a small stream on the way to his house and sculpted a Buddha there. That was the Buddha of the bridge. "A bridge is a positive thing; it is a connection. Connection is good, Pil-nyo. If bad people pass my bridge they'll fall right into the water!"

There was the Buddha of the wheels including the pottery wheel, and there was the Buddha of the fire; that Buddha was in charge of pottery pit fire, and cooking. The Buddha of the broom was in charge of cleaning. Chang never did a chore without praying first to his Buddha. "It's good for your sense of humility!" he said. There was a Buddha for every purpose in Chang's world, including one for speech, but Chang never pressed me to approach him. He just made sure to tell me that he existed.

Silent Marionette
침묵의꼭두각시

Those days in Wenzhou were a strangely relaxed time for me. My appetite was good; I was hungry all the time. Haru would cook rice for me, and Chang would cook me noodles. We would fish and fry our catch on the spot, and for a while, I forgot to feel guilty or dirty. The pain had almost vanished. Only when I stripped naked would the bruises and scars send me right back to the darkness.

Liu-fang would stretch her back on the sand and look at the stars after the meal, "Haru saru, make me tea!" and then since things were too peaceful for her she would sigh and say, "I wonder if Lee-ping sees us now indulging on good food with a Japanese idiot!"

It was the first time since being kidnapped that I slept well. No nightmares, no screaming or crying out of sleep, I would fall into a deep quiet sleep all night without waking up. This time it was I that needed nagging to go on with the trip. Haru was too concerned with the fact that I spent more and more time with Chang.

The pottery was an addictive business. Once I learned how to make a cup, I wanted to make a pot; and then it was how high I could go with my pot, how perfect the dish would be, the trimming, the glazing. I was so caught up with it that sometimes I would stay with Chang until early morning working and not even noticing it.

Haru would go out of his mind; I was getting too attached to the place, to Chang and to the coziness of the town. Liu-fang lost her patience. She would complain that it was the most boring place on earth and that she was going out of her mind from doing nothing. I could have stayed there forever. The place, the people, the energy of the city soothed me. In the end, I had to abide by my obligation to Haru and Liu-fang. I had to depart from Wenzhou.

Xiamen

Liu-fang disappeared in Xiamen. One morning we woke up and she was no longer there. Abazi used to say that a second divides life from death or hello from farewell. Abazi was always right.

Hanna the Jew thought that life was divided between day and night. "Eat today because tomorrow you die" or "God of Abraham have mercy! Today you live; tomorrow you are in a coffin!" or, "Today you're rich; tomorrow you're poor" and so on and so forth. One day Hanna and Abazi would meet in heaven and have a very heated discussion; it will be the ultimate east meets west.

We planned to stay in Xiamen for two days only. This would be our last station before we would travel to Hong Kong. The captain of a large merchant vessel closed a deal with Liu-fang on traveling all the way to Hong Kong with meals and a private sleeping corner for a reasonable price. Liu-fang had been very nervous. She was having a hard time with the fact that it was the end of the trip.

"Now it's your true moment," said Haru to her, "you are starting a new life!"

Liu-fang paled. She was silent and then rocked a little where she stood as if she were about to fall, and held his shoulder,

"Hold me, Haru-saru, I am dizzy!"

The evening before she disappeared, she broke the pattern of sleeping. Haru always slept between the two of us; naturally, we accepted it and got used to it. You never knew when some hoodlum would decide to attack us and to rob us. With Haru between the two of us, it felt much safer. He would fall asleep with one hand on my head and the other on Liu-fang's head. With time, if he took his hand off our heads, we would feel strange and wake up.

Silent Marionette
침묵의꼭두각시

The night before she took off, she wanted to sleep in the middle, and fell asleep holding both our hands in her hands. Liu-fang did not eat that day. Haru brought her a bowl of rice, but she rejected it. "Not hungry today!"

He did not insist; he had gotten used to her moods, but the warning bells rang in my ears. I was glad she went to sleep between the two of us. When she would start with her strange behavior, we had to keep a close eye on her.

However, in the morning when I opened my eyes, Haru was there close to me, his hand on my forehead and breathing peacefully, and she was gone. I got up and ran out to the owner's kitchen, I looked outside, I looked at the toilet facilities; she was nowhere to be found. My heart was beating fast; I was scared to death. I went back into the room and looked around. All her belongings were gone, her bag, her clothes, nothing left.

I shook Haru; my eyes widened from fear staring at his sleepy eyes. I started howling, my neck stretched, and I was coughing and choking. Haru recognized these symptoms with me and jumped up. His eyes were immediately alert; he knew that there was trouble. I pointed around me and showed him that her things were gone; I stamped my feet angrily and growled in rage.

"The bitch!" Haru spat, "That stupid bitch!" I had never heard him curse before. He was furious.

"I am going to look for her!" He pulled his pants up and left slamming the door.

"The gun!" I ran after him.

He shoved his gun in his belt and delayed his hand in my hand. "Don't worry Pil-nyo!" he said in sudden softness, and then went on his way.

Haru came back empty handed; Liu-fang had dissolved into thin air. He had checked in all the brothels in town, all the old comfort houses. In the port he had climbed onto every ship, entered all the bars, all the hotels, all the dark alleys downtown.

He looked for her for three days. We lost our passage to Hong Kong. Haru would come back after the night searches, drained from what he had seen, from what he had heard in the gutters of the city, in the most stinking swamps of town, desperate and dark. He would curl in my arms like a baby and cry, shaking from exhaustion.

When I stopped him after three days on his way out to try his luck again, he tried to pull away but I shook my head no! Stay! Haru then took me in his arms and cried. He would not go again to the dark world to look for her; he had to give up.

We made a sign saying Hong Kong and went to the marina to look for a boat. It was hard to bargain a price without Liu-fang. She used to love to bargain, but we were both supposed to be deaf and dumb, and people took advantage of that.

I had concluded a long time ago that people by their nature are either very good or very bad. I wished for those sailors the torture of hell, the most terrible diseases for their evil. I was very sad, wondering where Liu-fang had run away from her pain. Now when she understood clearly that the war was over, and her journey of self-torture had ended, she knew she would have to do the hardest thing of all, to start new life. Liu-fang could not deal with it.

Liu-fang was a broken marionette, shattered to pieces, humiliated, abused to her bones, angry, full of guilt, moving constantly between anger and madness. She knew that she would never be able to live a normal life among normal people. The guilt and madness had eaten her up from the inside out like predatory worms.

I put Haru's tired head on my chest and listen to him breathing. I cry, I whisper curses and obscenities, not knowing whether to be angry at Liu-fang or to feel self-pity for being left behind by her.

Silent Marionette
침묵의꼭두각시

"The Japanese will teach you a thing or two...." The Japanese left the scars of horror and lunacy on us insignificant marionettes forever and ever.

Little, broken, crushed, squashed, prostitutes are licking their open wounds. There are no medicines for their pain; the wounds will be open always.

The scars of the ugliness, the dirt, the abuse, will ever be stamped in the soul, in the guts, in the heart. Little marionettes, little broken sex toys, need a very good, specific reason to continue to live.

In the end, all the marionettes are gone; if someone does not kill them, they will kill themselves. Everybody leaves me behind. Haru will leave one day too. He will go back to Japan to his family and will think about our days together in the Chinese ports with a raised eyebrow.

I will be left alone with the ghosts of the past locked in my violin case, Omani, Abazi, my sisters, Kumikko, Nina, Mal-bong, Lee-ping, Liu-fang and thousands of others that came and went. I will stand in the train station, watching the trains come and go. I will dig a hole right there by the side of the railroad and bury my soul and my violin case to reach the final rest.

Hong Kong 香港

Hong Kong was a free port that served the British Empire. Many Europeans settled there, near Victoria Peak. The Chinese population did not have much to do with them, and the British authorities did not interfere with them.

The Japanese invaded Hong Kong on December 8, 1941. The Battle of Hong Kong ended with British and Canadian forces surrendering control of the colony to Japan on December 25. During the Japanese occupation, the locals suffered very badly from the merciless regime.

There were widespread food shortages, rationing, and terrible inflation because of the forced exchange of currency for military notes. Hong Kong lost half of its population in the years of the Japanese occupation. The stories of abuse, torture, murder and rape were told to us everywhere we went. Yet Hong Kong started recovering quickly as soon as the British took back control. When we got there, they had already begun clearing the ruins and rebuilding, and people were looking forward to putting their lives back together again.

I have no life to put together, nowhere to go. Haru and I are silent refugees in a home far away from home. He is a deserter and I am a prostitute. Two lost, wounded souls all alone in the world.

I would be the same anyway wherever I might go. I am nothing but a marionette, a piece of trash. I cannot but cry a river, thinking of my misfortune.

I am lying down on the soft sand by the ocean. The winter will come with all its might to Hong Kong very soon. The seasons are changing; nature is being nature. Across the bridge, above the tall trees, the moon is sailing slowly through the white clouds. My eyes are staring at heaven above. Omani is standing up there, and her long hair is blowing softly with the wind.

Silent Marionette
침묵의꼭두각시

There is no talking; Omani is leaning now in a white cloud on Yong-soo. I am happy to see them together now. I know she is safe if he is by her side.

On the wall of the house by the beach there is a big old handwritten sign in black charcoal, saying, "Kick the Japanese Imperialists out!" The old lady of the house is offering her stories about the Japanese devils, how they came and raped her little daughter. Twelve years old she was, shaking her body from side to side under a Japanese soldier. Like a slaughtering a duck, they bit into her little breasts. She was beaten to death after being raped by twelve of the devils.

The house is full of ghosts; the wickedness and fear of destruction has not left the colony yet.

I would listen to her stories and the blood would storm in my body. I would clench my fists and feel myself on the edge of madness again. The woman would go on and on with her stories about the Japanese slaughtering people like chickens. She would describe her pain in the cruelest terms, until her throat gave up from talking.

The anger would hit me again in big waves, threatening to drown me, boiling violent anger. I would stop eating then for days until the hunger would strike me like millions of snakes, crawling in my innards.

Haru would beg me to put something in my mouth; he would boil hot milk for me and feed me with a spoon. "For me, take it for me, if you have any mercy on my heart!" he would cry.

The lost souls of my marionette sisters are now floating in heaven with all the other broken souls of the Japanese victims. Tomorrow I will bury my violin case with all the drawings of Nina by the railroad, and send Kumikko's diary to her family. The winter will come to Hong Kong soon and the rain will wash my footsteps as if I were never there.

New generations of Chinese children will run over the bloody, sinful earth where the brothel once stood in Manchuria and fly their kites high up, toward the white, innocent clouds.

EPILOGUE BY NILY NAIMAN –USA

This horrific testimony is my demand from evil that it repent and ask for forgiveness. My purpose in writing this story is not to shock or sadden the reader. I am bringing the testimony of a comfort woman, one that survived among 200,000, under extreme circumstances. I deal with guilt, with evil and pain. Maikko's silence, as all post traumatic silences, freezes her relationship with the world and mostly with herself. Maikko's silence is louder than words, louder than screams; it is a way to earn time and solitude, a way to survive. This story is a demand for all human evil to stop.

Saeya saeya parang saeya,

(Bird, bird, a blue bird)

Nokdu batte anzi mara,

(Do not take a rest in the green gram field)

Nokdu kkochi ttoro zimyun,

(When the green gram flower leaf falls,)

Chongpo zangsu wulgo ganda

(Then, the bluish hemp cloth peddler goes crying)

EPILOGUE BY Brian SW KIM- SOUTH KOREA

In the long history of the world, there used to be many cases of human rights abuses, brutal actions and deeds done by the hands of foreign powers toward the weak countries and their peoples. We are well aware that Japan was not the only country guilty of those kinds of crimes.

It is true that many other countries, even so-called, countries known as the good, also would do similar sort of actions in inappropriate and brutal ways, and actually had a more or less tainted past throughout their history.

Still, nobody can deny the tragic history that there existed a countless number of sex slaves, miserable victims who were forced to pass through hardships during the period of the Pacific War caused by Japan.

My main purpose of this story is not anti-Japanese, but only to prevent in advance any possible occurrences of the same kinds of human rights violations and horrendous tragedies of the past, by recollecting some horrible memories and by sharing the bitter lessons from the past with all of the peace-loving people around the world.

Arirang

Arirang, arirang, arariyo,
Arirang gogaero noma ganda
(My love goes over the Arirang hill)
Narel borigo gasinen nimeun
(If you leave me behind you, my love)
Simrido motgaso balbyung nanda
(Your feet will hurt before long, my love)

Photos taken by Japanese soldiers during World War II

Silent Marionette
침묵의꼭두각시

Silent Marionette
침묵의꼭두각시

Silent Marionette
침묵의꼭두각시

Silent Marionette
침묵의꼭두각시

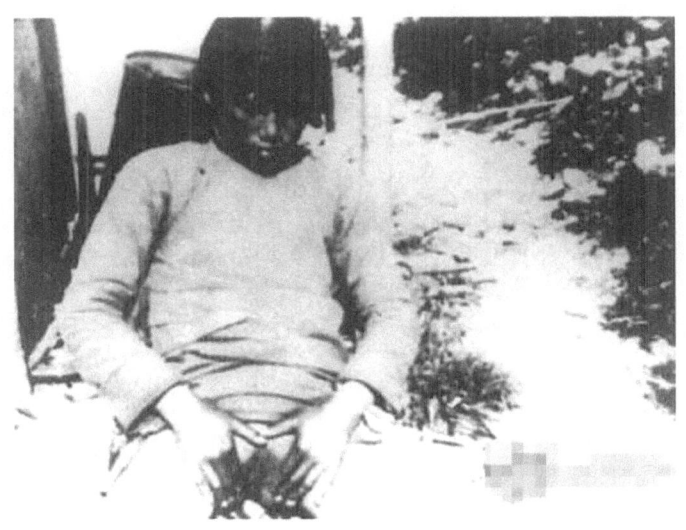

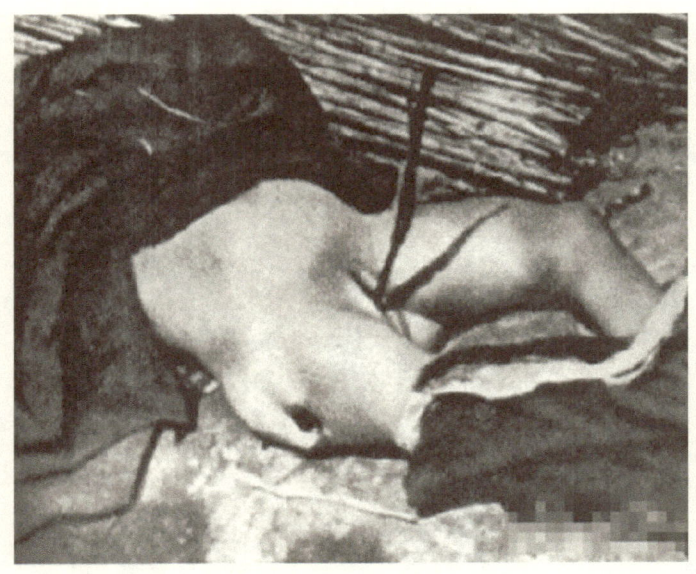

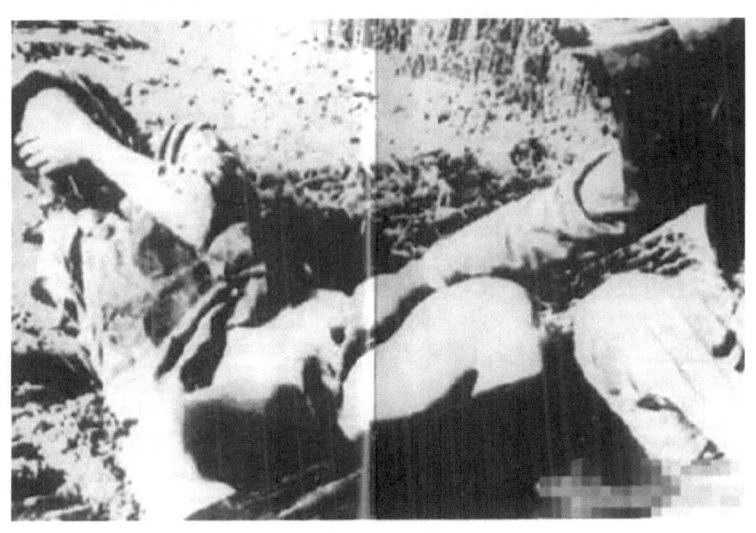

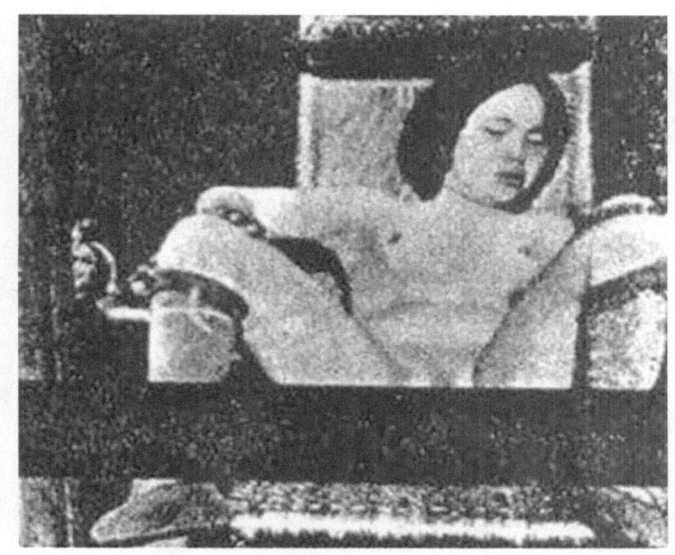

Silent Marionette
침묵의꼭두각시

Silent Marionette
침묵의꼭두각시

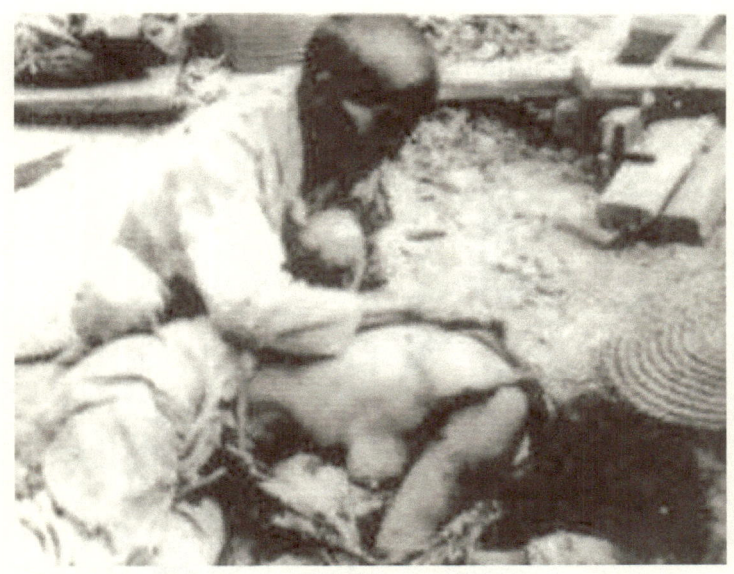

Silent Marionette
침묵의 꼭두각시

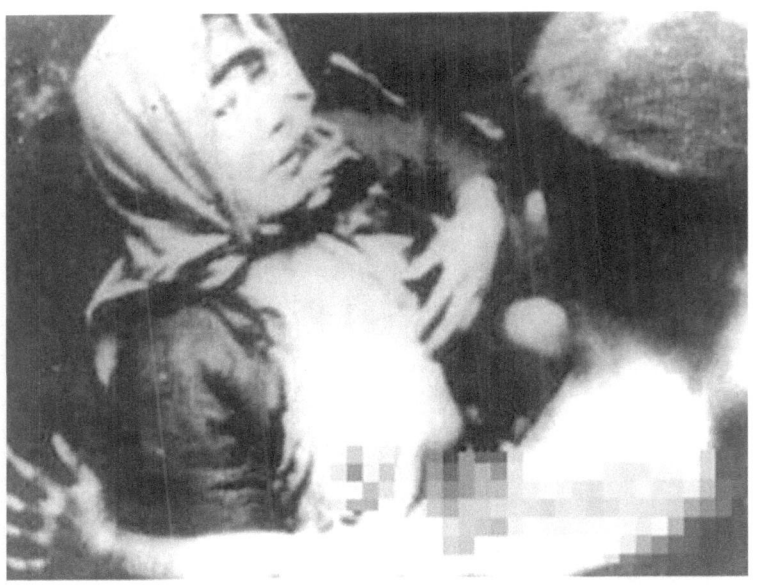

Silent Marionette
침묵의꼭두각시

칼로 목을 칠 때 몸이 넘어가지 않도록
발을 뒤로 묶어 목을 내리치는 순간을 포착한 사진이다

Silent Marionette
침묵의꼭두각시

일본군은 포로가 된 민간인들의 목을 베어
마치 상품을 진열해논 듯 전시하고 있다...

Nily Naiman

Silent Marionette
침묵의꼭두각시

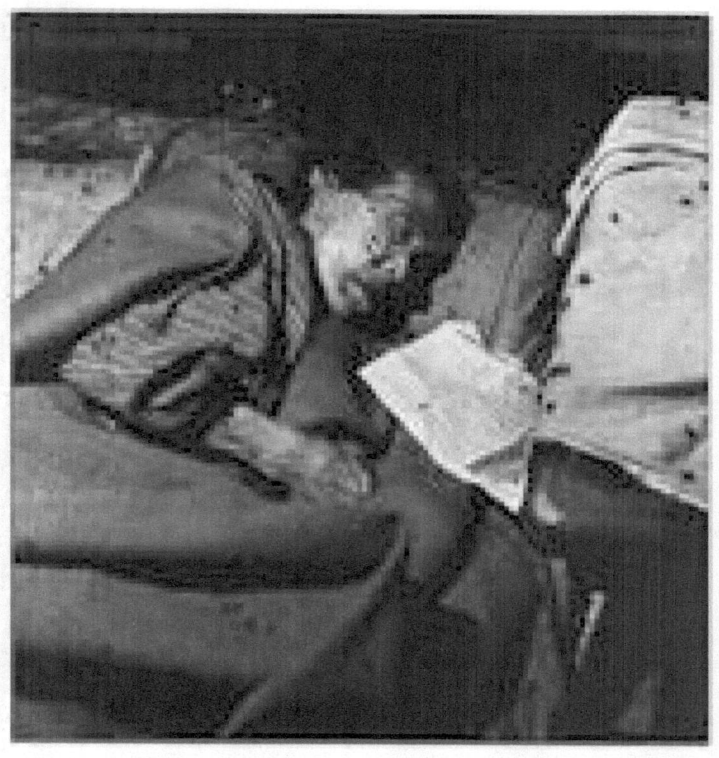

Silent Marionette
침묵의꼭두각시

Silent Marionette
침묵의꼭두각시

Silent Marionette
침묵의 꼭두각시